LAST RACE

A NOVEL

RICHARD MAY

I want to thank my beautiful wife and daughter for
their inspiration. This could never happen without their
souls. Like to thank all of those runners we joined in
the hundreds of miles of races in Austin, Texas, through
the years and would like to thank the spirit of Austin.
When you read the story, you'll know what I mean.

© 2021 Richard May | All rights reserved.
eISBN: 978-1-7363161-0-8
LCCN: 2021901547

Richard May Productions
Austin, Texas
www.LastRaceNovel.com
inquiries@LastRaceNovel.com

Cover illustration by Tawni Franzen

Prologue

I N THE EARLY 21ST CENTURY, mankind couldn't handle the perfect storm that unleashed the scimitar of our existence. Technology, greed, fanaticism and self-preservation combined to the tipping point of no-return.

To save the human race, governments sent dozens of manned missions to the moon, Mars and beyond to repopulate for a desperate chance to secure the future of mankind. Twelve of them were destroyed while twenty-five succeeded leaving the future of mankind in the hands of a few. For those billions of humans who weren't lucky to make the space exodus, they spent their last year on earth in mourning, decadence, violence or love.

One of the most inspiring stories is Griffin Johnson's last wish to run a marathon race with his friends and the love of his life, Sabrina. His wish came true that also inspired 100,000 others to join Griffin and friends for the annual and final Austin, TX Marathon held on the last day of earth.

Such intense inspiration doesn't come without a cost. Intense popularity and visibility attract the jackals of attention who seek to destroy and exploit.

Griffin Johnson never wanted this attention nor this burden. But now that it has been forced upon him, Griffin must choose what to do with mankind's Judgment Day and its fight in the battle between good vs evil for the last race.

CHAPTER I

Run for Your Life

G RIFFIN STARES IN THE MIRROR of a hotel bathroom inspecting the look of his recently grown beard and head full of dirty-blonde hair. His shirt is off revealing a musculature lean look of 24 years. He starts rolling his neck while holding each ankle stretching to his back one at a time readying for the race or, what has been dubbed, the last race.

He has his running group logo'd shorts on and looks as ready as one can be preparing for a 26.2 mile race. In the background, there are faint sounds of screams, loud pops and thumping music competing with each other. Sounds unusual in most circumstances.

He puts his racing shirt on and quietly walks into the hotel living room. Picks up the remote, points it at the TV and starts switching channels until he finds the only one airing. There he sees her at the news desk with a time clock in the background reading 8 hours 17 minutes with the seconds ticking by.

He picks up his sports watch and checks both are synchronized. He stares at the anchor woman who has come to typify the bizarre news of the past months. But he's really using the TV to stare blankly wondering where Sabrina is.

"So, Larry, have you seen him yet?" asks TV anchor Janine sitting at her news desk. Janine Miller typifies the TV news anchor. She sports a beautiful smile with perfectly concrete-set autumn brown hair. Dons intelligent eyes. Speaks with perfect enunciation and an aura that leaves you wondering if it all stops there.

"Not yet," responds Larry standing with a scotch-filled Waterford cocktail glass in his left hand while using his right hand to wave and shake hands as the on-site race ambassador.

He's fully broadcast remote ready with a tall tabletop holding his Apple laptop as his TV monitor and communications system. He's in front of the start/finish line with masses of people wearing running clothes and race numbers. Then others in outrageous costumes for the spectacle or part of the spectacle streaming in front and behind him.

Below him, there's a small patio table and a brown leather recliner. On the table sit a hotel bucket of ice next to a 25-year bottle of single malt Balvenie Scotch. Another four bottles hide underneath covered by a linen tablecloth out of sight from other hands and gullets.

He takes a sip, "But, it's quite a spectacle here."

The 20-foot tall and 30-foot wide scaffold grid start/finish line tower behind him. It was put together yesterday afternoon by the race organizers who have built and torn down that gate a hundred times before.

The horizontal grid locked on top has the large digital clock in the middle showing the beginning time on the front and finishing time on the back. At the moment, it's ticking down to the air pistol shot that ignites the thousands of runners to begin their journey.

At the top of the scaffold the announcer stands on a platform blaring out witty hype banter in between the standard pump-you-up rock songs. It's the textbook set-up helping racers prepare for their best time. Or, for many racers, to finish a marathon and cross it off their bucket list.

"So, Larry," Janine interjects trying to get back on point. "Can you describe the atmosphere there?"

Larry takes another sip, "Well, besides the fact that all life as we know will be extinct in about eight hours, it's a pretty hopping place. Show them."

Janine switches to Camera 3 posted on the top of the metal scaffolding 20 yards behind the start/finish line. She is determined to get the finale shot of Griffin and that's the camera to do it.

If anything, Janine is thorough especially being the center of attention. Janine prepared for her last broadcast setting up cameras at key spots for good cutaways when she needs them. She has full remote control of each camera so can pan from side to side and zoom in and out at her will.

There in full glory, the view shows the massive crowd that reflects the 'Keep Austin Weird' meets Bourbon Street meets the L.A. riots atmosphere. The swirl of emotions from inspiration to desperation captured in one shot and day.

Griffin peeks out the hotel room from the 8th floor window surveying the vast number of runners and on-lookers either partying up, getting ready for the race or both. From his vantage point, he can see up 1st street almost a mile south then to the north as it crosses Ladybird Lake into the newly transformed downtown Austin, TX.

Just before the bridge is where the racers wait for the start and will be when the race and world ends. At least if they stay around afterwards. Auditorium shores has plenty of parkland to supply land for thousands of people and is a pretty spot so perfect for ground one and zero.

The thick hotel windows help mute the cacophony of sounds but doesn't mute the machine gun fire that erupts in the background. The unexpected rapid fire of bullets makes him jump and remind him what day it is.

He hasn't heard that type of chaos in months. Now that the day is here, it should be expected. When news finally leaked a year ago, the level of panic, destruction and despair reached levels of more than one billion being killed in the first two months.

Five nukes in five different cities out of anger? Revenge? Bad luck? The one in Jerusalem made the most sense in a warped way. People have been fighting for that real estate since before Christ. It got to a point if the one righteous people didn't get it then nobody does. Every radical group claimed responsibility for that cloud bomb.

Washington D.C. was another given one. The U.S. has pissed off more nations than all so the chickens were coming back to roost atomically cooked or not.

Miami? Really? No one could figure that one out. Bikinis, bods and drug trafficking doesn't usually warrant a nuclear bomb set off. And no one took responsibility. Some people say the best explanation was a jealous NFL fan set it off to spite the '72 Dolphins for having the only undefeated season in NFL history.

Thank god for U.S. ingenuity in technological warfare to ward off the other dozen nuclear attacks on U.S. targets. Otherwise, the race nor any sort of order could have sustained. The final two nukes were Karachi and New Delhi and not too unexpected. Some even wondered why it took this long.

Chinese deaths are purported to be more than 200 million but experts think it is upwards to 400 million. The Chinese like their secrets. The deaths were a result in a three-way civil war between the "Princelings", Tuanpai and the newly organized

"Neo Liberalists" who finally had nothing to lose but revenge for decades of repression. Their civil war never ended. Chinese are committed to their jobs whether making puzzles for Americans or killing each other for philosophical dominance.

Then the onslaught of heightened wars, mass killings and suicides racked up the rest. It got to a point after two months that people forgot or quit caring what they were killing or dying for and mostly stopped.

Some took the anarchy as a sign to create their own post-apocalyptic gang of Mad Max rulers. Everyday Americans didn't stand for that and just grabbed their guns and killed them. Problem solved and order restored. Thank God for the second amendment.

Austin was no exception. It was actually a model for other cities to implement. Austin has a dedicated police force to implement the fairest possible law enforcement while being the judge, jury and executioner. It was out of character for the laid-back University town but Austinites didn't seem to mind.

Gangs were eliminated. Organized crime *removed* and the 'live music capital of the world' was able to sing along in as much of an orderly manner as possible. Don't mess with Texas. Don't mess with Austin.

The next eight months were basically peace and celebration in some sort of way. Some people even went back to work. Not back to the stock exchange but to local farming, hospitals and markets to help people have some sort of normalcy. The only thing expected was to contribute something of value in return. It became a barter society.

The big telcomm companies kept their lights on so to speak. Phone communication and internet were still accessible. Although many people never looked at the internet again out of protest or anger blaming those companies and the technology for this mess.

Each night feature concerts, theater, festivals or sports games. Opera hasn't been this popular in centuries. People gath-ered in unified fun and celebration in so many different ways.

It's amazing how quickly people can learn to grow their own food or, more important, the art of crafting their own beer or distilling their own vodka. It took the loss of civilization for people to become civilized.

In the past two weeks though the chaos, killings, suicides are back to the feverish pitch. Now on the last day, it's a match to see which philosophy will win over the last race of mankind. And then there's the last race of the Austin marathon that Griffin Johnson inspired.

Griffin puts on his black baseball cap with bright red letters spelling out his name. He wears the blue racing shirt with large font broadcasting the race name of "Last Race, Austin, TX" on the front and "Run For Your Life" on the back.

Some warped shirt designers printed a couple thousand with "Fuck Off & Die" on the back. That race shirt became so popular, the printers had to roll out another 5000 after the first batch of 500. They would have done another 10,000 if someone hadn't torched the building. Maybe that's how crafty entrepreneurs make things collector items. It's also the only racing shirt that doesn't have two dozen sponsors plastered on it. Doubt sponsors would get much return on this race but it is America and anyone who contributes must be recognized.

He grabs his numbered '1' racing number to safety pin to his shirt. Then puts on the mandatory crossing-guard, orange vest that makes him gag that he is forced to wear even if only for a short time. He looks down to those god-awful black shoes and socks. He shakes his head disgusted by his attire. *Just go with it. It's only for a little while.*

He walks to the door, opens it and heads to the elevator.

CHAPTER 2

The Interview

A MIDDLE-AGED JIMMY sits on the couch inside a dark living room of his upscale home watching Janine babble on about the stupid last race.

"If you're tuning in just now then you're joining in on a wild end-of-the-earth 26.2 mile race starting and finishing in downtown Austin, TX. We're estimating a group of 100,000 runners from all around the world with a cheering section of 25,000 all along the course."

Jimmy takes his rolled up $1000-dollar bill and snorts a long, thick line of cocaine on his glass table. He gags as the drug immediately jolts into his blood stream while screaming out loud.

"Ouch! Jesus!" he blurts out as he fully absorbs the cocaine infusion. He holds his nose shut as he slowly melts into the couch with a feeling of pure satisfaction. "Hunka, hunka burnin' love, baby."

As the cocaine seeps in, his facial expression shows an immediate sign of gratification and accelerated high. His foot is feverishly shaking up and down while he grabs a cigarette and quickly lights up. The coffee table is dirty with dusty white powder and a fancy ash tray full of crushed up cigarettes.

He throws down his plastic name card used to crush and line up the cocaine and takes a quick sip from his Jack Daniels bottle. Picks up his 33-magnum handgun and places it on his shaking knee.

Larry's face lights up. "Well Janine, I can hear some cheering through the crowds so it might be him coming up to say hello." Griffin is weaving his way through the hordes of runners as they pat him on the back, congratulate and thank him. "Well, well, well lookee who's here, the man himself. The inspiration for the race and, really, for our humanity at these last hours."

Griffin takes off the baseball cap. He has his head tilting down with an awkward grin not really knowing how to respond to that statement.

Janine interjects, "Before you begin Griffin, I'd like to give our viewers and you an update what's going on since yesterday. We've had 25 more satellite feeds to our broadcast since we last spoke bumping up our audience to more than 70 countries world-wide and a viewership of 65 million people. And all because of you. So, Griffin, how ya feeling?"

Griffin starts nodding his head showing his nervousness. Larry shoots a dirty look at the camera as Janine took his question.

"Fine, I guess." Griffin looks up at Larry with much more confidence. "Feeling really good, actually. I'm looking to break my personal record and run this marathon under two thirty-five."

"That's two hours and thirty-five minutes, correct? For, us non-runners," Janine continues.

Griffin nods while looking down and back to being uncomfortable with the interview and attention. Larry shoots another dirty look as Janine continues to control the interview.

Larry quickly jumps in, "For all of the new viewers out there, can you tell us how you and this event came to be on the last day of earth?"

Griffin nods again with an uncomfortable smile as he has to tell the story yet again, "Uh, well, this marathon was scheduled more than a year ago, you know, the annual Austin marathon. Way before we knew what was coming.

When the organizers found out, they obviously cancelled the event. Being in the running club, I knew the organizers so asked if they wouldn't mind if I could have their start and finish entryway with the clock and all so I could run the race. Was just planning to run it by myself."

Janine quickly jumps in that quickly irritates Larry, "Why running a marathon for your last hours on earth? Why that?"

"Well...um..." Griffin pauses then looks up. "When I'm running a race, it feels like the only time I'm running to something rather than away."

That statement left their microphones void of a response. Griffin nods his head then begins with more of an answer they would want. "Well, running is my passion. I was bummed out that they cancelled it but thought I would run it anyway. I love races and really wanted that official entryway and finish line.

I figured they're not gonna use it and it'll just be sitting there. If I asked, I thought they would say 'yes'. And they did. So now I knew how I would go out. The way I wanted. Finishing a race. Not just a race but a marathon."

Larry jumps in that irritates Janine in return. "Your plan to run it alone didn't end up happening, did it?"

"No, it didn't," Griffin responds shaking his head wondering how the hell it turned into this.

Now Janine's turn in their on-camera battle. "So, then what happened? How did it come to this?"

"Well, um, after a couple of days after I told my friends, surprisingly most of them said they're going to run it too. Even our coach. I thought 'wow', this is really great. Going out running and going out with my dear friends. Doesn't get any better than that.

Then I get a call from the organizers and they said they would like to run it with me. They're married and their two kids are avid runners and their passion is running. So, they thought it would be the perfect way for them too.

That's when they declared the race is still on. We thought it would be just handful of us running it, but evidently the word got out. Struck a chord with a lot of people and now here we are." Griffin looks around in astonishment shaking his head.

"But why a race? You could've just run 26.2 miles and timed yourself. And without all of this fanfare?"

"Uh, good question. I don't know. I guess there is something magical about an actual, organized race. There is an energy that can't be described until you run one with the crowds, the participants and the vibe. There is a singularity you can't experience anywhere else."

CHAPTER 3

Untied

SITTING ON HIS NICE LEATHER COUCH, Jimmy is staring intently at his big screen watching the interview with anger and disgust. He picks up the cocaine filled jelly jar and taps out a small rock, grabs his card and begins crushing the rock into a fine powder.

The card reveals a hospital identification card with his picture listing him as Dr. Jimmy Spangle, M.D, Breckenridge Medical Center, Psychiatric Dept. The doctor in his name is apparent as the house is filled with fine furnishings, large rooms and expensive paintings.

But all of that accumulation has a totally different meaning on this day. It's a tangible reflection of his life choices that either makes him depressed, angry or snorting grams of cocaine and drinking liters of whiskey. And now all of those emotions are being stirred up with this godforsaken interview.

His anger and disgust watching Griffin being so celebrated finally bursts out as he jumps up and lets out an angered war-like scream. He starts pacing back and forth clutching his shoulder length jet-black hair almost pulling it out cussing in a crying like manner.

"Godammit! You are such a skinny little faggot!" He starts breathing heavily trying to regain composure so sits back down, takes a small sip of Jack wincing at its bitterness then takes another longer sip now that Jack's bite has softened.

Griffin continues standing there listening to Larry talk wondering if there is a question in the near future.

"Hey, your shoes are untied," comes a female voice walking up to the interview. As it is a natural and universal reaction, Larry immediately looks down. Griffin, though, looks up as his eyes and smile go full wide.

He sees Sabrina staring at him with the same expression. Sabrina, Griffin's best friend and who he has been secretly in love with the day he met her, unexpectedly has shown up. Griffin is beyond elated. She smiles back with those hazel eyes.

Larry looks at both of them as the silence is deafening from the sensual and sexual energy emanating between the two. He continues, "You've become quite the hero."

Griffin gently slaps Larry's back without looking at him and leaves the interview straight to Sabrina who's in full running uniform showing her athletic body and natural beauty.

"You came back. What the hell are you doing here?"

"I wasn't gonna let you run a marathon without your partner, was I? And, besides, maybe you'll let me win this time." She's grinning wide as she looks deep into his eyes to see what she has always liked about him. A shy yet confident man with a big heart and the best part? He has a sarcastic and sharp wit that only rivals hers.

His smile finally breaks to ask the obvious, "Where are your parents? Why aren't you with them?"

"They are. They're doing the same thing every marathon. Waiting at mile 2 then mile 6 then, you know the drill. They're here to support us. They knew this is what I wanted to do so told me to go do it and they would support us like they do every race. Besides, I got tired of Katy and her friends. We have been there for nearly a month and I was close to strangling her and wanted my friends so I told her 'I love you' and we drove back."

"So, your parents chose you over your big sister?"

"They flipped a coin. And I won," Sabrina says with a sheepish grin.

"Did your Dad use the app?"

"Yeah. Why?"

"You know it has a cheater setting."

She smiles again, then quickly changes subjects. "Is the gang all here?" Sabrina turns around to see if she can see their running group.

"Yeah. They're over by the Thundercloud sign. I am so glad that you are here. It is now perfect. More than perfect."

"Whose tents are those?" She asks gazing at the line of ten-foot high tents with blue canvas tops that are seen at outdoor festivals and tailgating parties.

In between the many runners passing through her line of sight she can see her running group. They're stretching and talking in front of several large barrel grills underneath bellowing out smoke from the fires they've just lit for the cookout.

"J-Lo's family set those up. Instead of going to their house for fajitas afterwards, they brought them down here."

"Sweet," she smiles, turns back to Griffin. "Is the plan still in place?"

Griffin's looking down, inspecting her cap. She's 5"5' and he's 5"11' so definitely has the height advantage. She gives him the 'what?' look. "Just seeing what new hat you have on today?"

She's wearing her brownish red hair wrapped into her usual running ponytail inserted through the back of her pink baseball cap. This baseball cap dons the city of Port Aransas, TX with a glittering palm tree. The hat is brand new, of course. It always is with Sabrina.

"Oh, shut up," she playfully responds. "It's from Port Aransas, my favorite place in the whole world."

"Yes. I know it's your favorite place. We've only been there a dozen times together. And, yes, the plan is still the same but it just changed a bit."

"What's that?"

"You're now a part of it. Did you give your parents my route, or should I say, our route?"

"Yep."

"Clever girl."

Griffin puts his cap back on then turns to Larry and shouts out, "We'll finish the interview shortly. Be right back."

"So much for the interview," Larry grumbles. He turns back to the camera. "Griffin has his race shirt, number and vest on so he's looking ready. Why don't you let the viewers know all about that? I've got to pee and then pour me a cocktail of my choice."

"Why thank you Larry. I really appreciate that full disclosure," responds Janine in thick sardonic tone. She switches to Camera 1—herself. "Yes viewers, Griffin will be wearing a bright orange running vest and his race number has a timing chip in it. This way we'll be able to track his every step and see him easily throughout the race. And his whereabouts can only be seen right here on K-V-U-T Austin, TX. We have the world exclusive."

Griffin and Sabrina meet up with the running group. The group erupts to a big 'hello' to Sabrina and excited she has returned in full running attire. She has her deep purple sports top on with black running shorts outlined with a pink trim. All colors matching accordingly that makes it as much a fashion statement as a sports outfit.

They all high five, fist bump or hug each other. Lori's parents and brothers stop setting up their tables to give Sabrina their welcome hugs. Sabrina responds sheepishly, almost feeling guilty that she wasn't part of the committed group from the get-go. But that guilt quickly vanishes with everyone welcoming her with open arms and hearts. She feels at home now.

The group surrounds Sabrina with their continued welcomes then back to teasing of Griffin's worldwide fame.

"Through signing autographs?" says Gilbert with his thick Nigerian accent. Gilbert is walking in place in the middle of the four out the five-person running group acting like their running coach because he is.

"Fuck you," responds Griffin with a smile.

Raul pushes his way in to Griffin and whispers, "Dude, Sabrina showed up. Sweet. Your dream did come true."

Besides Sabrina, Raul is the next closest to Griffin. With both of their families abandoning them or the other way around they have that bond. Griffin smiles at that comment then Gilbert looks at him, "Let's do it."

They all surround Griffin to shield him from the crowd to head back to the hotel. The crowd cheers him on while he uncomfortably waves back. They quickly maneuver into the Hampton Inn and head to the elevators.

The five members of Griffin's entourage include Sabrina, Don, Raul, Lori and Gilbert. They have been running together for the past four years. They're close in running pace and ages except for Gilbert. Gilbert is older and faster.

They've run countless miles and drank countless beers together. All culminating in a deep friendship or, more like family, that running and especially races bring to its most heightened.

They enter the room just as Griffin left it earlier except this time Don is standing there dressed exactly as Griffin without the vest or cap. He is also built the same way as Griffin—his height, weight, hair color and even the beard.

Griffin looks at Don as they both smile. Don can't resist, "Your shoes are untied."

Griffin just shakes his head as he throws Don his cap and vest a little harder than Don expected. He unpins his number and while he wants to throw four opened safety pinned needles at him for that comment, he hands it to him with a smart-ass grin that Don happily returns.

Griffin rolls his eyes as he heads to the bathroom. Gilbert furrows his brow as he always does when he utters his ever-repeating question, "I don't understand the shoelace thing you say. His shoes are tied. They're always tied. Why do you all say that?"

Griffin smiles as he closes the door. He's not the one going to explain the shoelace taunt for the umpteenth time.

"You're the reason all of this happened, coach," Lori or J-Lo quickly answers as the others start groaning. Lori is affectionately dubbed J-Lo because she looks like Jennifer Lopez.

Lori is the most grounded of the group so many times becomes the self-appointed organizer or, with this group, matriarch. Every group has that one person who is the central coordinator for all events and Lori is theirs.

"You're the one who had him buy those really expensive ning shoes that had no laces but he had to have them on tending salary."

"So. Those are good shoes. Some things are worth the price." More groaning.

"Not for Griffin. They sucked. Anyway, Raul being Raul saw the fancy shoes that have no laces and tells Griffin his shoelaces are untied. So, what does Griffin do?"

"He looks down," the group responds in unison with smiles and laughter.

"So? Why not? It's a natural reaction. Make sense to me."

"I'm not finished. Later that night, we're all at Guero's after hours enjoying free beer that Guero's did not know about. But since Griffin closes the bar, we take full advantage of the fringe benefits Griffin gets by closing down."

"And boy did Griffin close it down that night," Don adds to the story as he pins on the number 1 racing number then putting on the traffic cone colored vest.

"Shut up, Don. I'm telling the story."

"Yeah, well you weren't the one who had to carry his lanky ass out to the car."

"Hello? With some help. Your drunk ass could barely walk let alone lift," Raul interjects.

Raul is the only one with meat on his bones so helping carry Griffin wasn't that difficult. He played running back and line-backer at a 3A school so is tough and strong. The odd thing about he dyes his marine cut hair bleach blonde is his 5' v that doesn't deter him keeping up with the his short legs and added bulk.

up and let me finish," Lori tells tapping

s.

ut something when Griffin starts star- just decides to put them on. Had them in the back and thought 'what the hell'. So, he's just staring at them intently then looks up and tells everyone that they forgot the shoelaces. That's when Raul looks straight at me then Don and grins big time."

"I told him to check the box. They must be in there," interrupts Raul taking back the story. "He looks in the box. Under the box. Over the box. Through the box. It's obvious he's shit-faced drunk at this time."

"Fuck you!" yells Griffin inside the bathroom. They all start laughing.

"So I point to the shoes and tell them not only did they forget the shoelaces, they forgot to put holes in the shoes where the laces go."

"We all say, 'they're defective," Lori says. "And since you opened 'em up and put the shoes on, you can't return them. You're fucked."

"And he starts moaning practically crying about how much he paid for them and he's busted and so on," Don adds.

"Fuck you!" Griffin repeats in the cavernous roar from the bathroom.

"He spent the next hour basically telling us his running days are over and he'll become homeless."

"Fuck you!!"

Everyone's laughing except Gilbert who is still not understanding the humor.

"So anyway," Lori grabs the story back. "It's not until the next morning when he puts the pieces together that he realizes what fool he made himself out to be."

"Fuck you!!!"

Gilbert just stares. Lori tilts her head to the ceilin exhaustive look, "Guess you had to be there. It was and we rub it in every chance we get to tell him his shoes are untied. The only difference now is he never looks down."

"I don't understand you Americans. Very confusing you are to me," Gilbert confesses.

"We're not confusing," Raul answers. "We're confused."

"If we're so confusing," Don jumps in looking to Gilbert. "Then why are you here?"

"You know why I here. I'm here running with you because you are my family. My real family died in the war. When they awarded me a full running scholarship to the University of Texas, I never left."

It's now Gilbert's turn to repeat his story. His story though is more of a vehicle for a valued sermon and a great motivational tool. "Running was what saved my life. I was only survivor because I ran faster than the attackers who came to the school to kill me and my schoolmates. So, running became my life. Now I coach. And you are always my favorite so when Griffin started the race again, it saved my life again."

"Do you know Gilbert was invited to be on Nigeria's Olympic running team but declined," Sabrina says turning to Lori and Don.

A loud 'what?' from the two goes stereo. Gilbert revealed that ~~ret to very few people. Griffin, Sabrina and Raul were one of

'~cline?" astonished Lori looking to Gilbert.

·n to pieces by fighting tribes. I ran from

kill me because I have a different tribe

? to represent a country that kills each

. I told them until they can live under

ter what tribe then I cannot represent

"What did they do?"

"Nothing."

Don turns to Sabrina, "How did you know all of this and we didn't?"

"If you are sincerely interested in somebody, you ask questions and listen. You'd be amazed what happens with those simple steps."

The room is silent absorbing the wisdom. Raul looks to Sabrina, "I wish you would have used your own advice." Sabrina is taken back by that comment wondering what the hell he means.

Griffin emerges from the bathroom a changed man—literally and figuratively. He is clean shaven from the beard and the head of hair.

He's now wearing worned, white running shorts with a small burnt orange Longhorn logo on the bottom front right.

He has an old white Austin marathon race shirt from a race several years ago. It's the race shirt from the marathon he trained Sabrina for her best time so it carries memories of special importance. The shirt proudly displays their running group's logo promoting their elite status.

He looks down at his watch and shakes his head. *Time, of all things.* He takes the watch off and happily tosses it into the trash.

He has a brand-new pair of running socks and dons his new Nike ZoomX Vaporfly specialty marathon shoes. They have laces, of course. He spared no expense *borrowing* these shoes from the local RunTex store.

The shoes are the oddest part of his ensemble as they are brand new and the only color these shoes come in are neon green. The shoes grossly stand out as glowing radioactive swamp shoes that do not coincide at all with the rest of his running outfit.

For the most part, Griffin's marathon attire looks like they were gathered from the garage sale on the way to the race. Every part of him from the clothes to the hair or lack thereof is the exact opposite of what he was wearing 15 minutes ago.

The gang starts clapping and cheering the new, cleaned-up Griffin. Actually, the Griffin they're used to seeing as a laid-back neo-hippy Austinite. The hair growth was pre-planned for this moment.

Raul proudly announces, "Okay, Our Griffin is back!"

"I didn't really care for the beard. Made you look like some 'Just For Men' commercial," Lori proclaims.

"I didn't either," Griffin admits.

Gilbert looks at everyone. Being 6' 1", he has to look down on everyone. His wire framed body shows nothing but bone and muscle except for the paper-thin afro. There is nothing about him that doesn't scream runner. At twice the age of all the others, his presence and the wisdom in his eyes command respect and admiration.

"I want to say what honor it has been being your running coach for all these years. I am truly blessed." They all nod relaying their appreciation.

Griffin chimes in, "All of you know I just wanted us to do it together like we have done every race but I can't handle this circus. That was the last thing I wanted. I don't know how it got so out of control. So, I want to thank you for doing all of this so I can have my race back. But I never wanted it to be without all of you. So, thank you. Besides, I only slow you guys down."

Lori blurts out sarcastically, "Yeah, right." The others join in knowing Griffin is one of the elite runners.

"Remember my parents will have fajitas, water and beer waiting for us at the tents so stay there until all of us are there."

"Yes. Sabrina, Raul and I will be there," answers Griffin.

Raul subtly waves his hand shaking his head, "No, dude. I'll run with the gang and meet you two there. Sabrina will take care of you. Way better than I could."

They turn to Raul with a surprised look especially Griffin. Griffin looks deep into his eyes and knows he's being real. No one knows better than Raul how much it means to him that Sabrina showed up.

Sabrina's looking at Griffin. It's slowly sinking in on what Raul said to her earlier. Griffin turns to Sabrina and smiles nodding his head. She returns the smile but adds a wink.

He turns back to Raul, "Did you take care of us?"

"Damn straight, homey," Raul responds.

"Took care of what?" Don asks. Raul smiles big.

"You know that Mercedes we were hanging out next to down at the Thundercloud spot?"

"Yeah. So."

"It's mine. Well, it became mine. Was my asshole boss's so I stole it yesterday. As a last middle finger to her."

The whole group is either laughing or too shocked to start laughing yet.

"Good. She was a bitch," adds Don then holds his head in a pondering position. "Well, hold on. How does that take care of us?"

"In the trunk, her body is in there."

"What?! You're kidding, right?"

"Of course I'm kidding, you stupid fuck. I have two big ass ice chests full of cold beer waiting there for our usual celebration. And yes, Gilbert, there's also a bunch of water to properly cool down."

"Good," Gilbert nods in approval that Don is following strict running protocol. Gilbert doesn't understand the beer thing.

"All right guys," Griffin says, fist bumping the gang. "See ya on the other side."

"You still going the southern route? The one that goes through the U.T. area?" Raul asks coinciding his fist bump.

"He better be," Sabrina says with a demanding tone. "That's the route I gave my parents."

There they all stand in silence as a moment of tribute to their memories, the journey, mission and ruse that is about to follow. Lori gives Griffin then Sabrina a hug. The rest of the group follow with an added "love you" or "see ya on the other side".

"It's time. Let's do it." Gilbert concludes.

Raul looks at Griffin and Sabrina, "OK, you two lovers. Don't get any ideas when we leave you two alone in this hotel room. Never know. Sabrina, you could make Griffin's dreams come true."

Griffin looks at him with an exasperating stare while Sabrina turns to Griffin and smiles. Don smiles, winks at Griffin then puts on his polarized, wrap around sports sunglasses and leads the group out the door.

On the ground floor, the elevator door opens and the entourage appear surrounding Don posing as Griffin. They walk out as if Griffin aka Don was the President of the United States and the rest are his secret service.

The crowd cheers as they go out the doors. The Griffin stand-in is smiling, looking mostly down waving his clenched fist high. Don has become Griffin. And he loves it.

In the room, Sabrina is still looking at him with a smile. Griffin turns to her, "You ready?"

"For what?"

Griffin rolls his eyes. He grabs her hand and walks to the bedroom.

Unlocks the door, goes into the corresponding room to the front door. Slowly opens it. Peeks out. Seeing no one, they exit.

CHAPTER 4

His Own Terms

L ARRY'S ON CAMERA TALKING to the viewing audience. He's wearing one those barely green buttoned-down, short sleeved Mexican shirts with perfectly starched khaki shorts and topsiders. He's in his 60s but doesn't look like it. He's had that salt and pepper head full of hair for twenty years so his age is elusive to anyone who doesn't know him.

"I've been a successful lawyer for the past 30 years and a damn good one if I may add. But I always wanted to be a broadcaster, a sports broadcaster in fact.

That's why it's such a great pleasure to be here with you—all of you, throughout the world, to carry the story of Griffin and this last race while we all wave our merry hands to end of the world."

Janine walks back to her news desk after going to the bathroom to watch Larry rambling to the audience. "Whoa there, Larry. A little focus here. What's going on down there? Let's talk about that."

Larry nonchalantly turns around, takes a sip of scotch then back to the camera. "Looks like it's about to start."

Jimmy is still keenly focused on the TV shaking his head, "I've never seen such a bunch of idiots in my time. If the world wasn't gonna end, I could'a made a shit pot of money off these bozos. Oh! Oh! Oh!"

He picks up his gun, points it at the TV and BANG. The TV explodes toppling over to the floor.

"There. Diagnosis done. Glad my policy is to pay full in advance." He takes a sip of his Jack then looks around. "Well, shit. Now what am I going to do? Brilliant."

Jimmy gets up goes into the kitchen and comes back with a smaller flat screen. He takes an expensive vase placed on top of a tall three-tiered glass table and throws it across the room shattering to pieces. He plugs the TV in and changes the channels until he finds Janine. He goes back to roll out another line cringing at the sound of Janine's voice.

"Ok, everyone at the race. You should have downloaded the race app by now. I want you to take photos throughout the race and post them on my Facebook, Instagram or twitter accounts.

If they're good, I'll show them on screen and help keep track on Griffin's progress and highlights of what's going on. You can see each of those accounts at the bottom of the screen.

I can see they're about to sing the national anthem so we'll remain quiet and the race will begin. Griffin, thank you for being such an inspiration for all us and to all of the world."

Jimmy's eyes begin to scowl as rage beams through his eyes. He picks up his iPhone and starts swiping and typing.

Gilbert and the three co-conspirators huddle at the starting line protecting Don in the middle. The hive of nearby runners buzz around them to be next to the star. The heightened attention has Don and group constantly placate the doting racers with 'thank you's' and nods of appreciation.

"Remember," Gilbert turns around, lowers his head and voice. "The world is looking to Griffin, Don, to inspire them so let's not disappoint. Don, you must play the role. All of us do. Wave. Raise fists of glory letting people see that Don is Griffin. Not Don. We'll surround him. Shield eyes from getting too close."

"Don, you are so loving this, aren't you?" Raul says looking at him with his own mischievous grin.

"Hell Yeah! I get the spotlight while carrying Griffin's inspiration. AND allowing Griffin to run it on his own terms. It's a win-win. Maybe I can get laid somewhere on the way and take full advantage."

He looks to Lori, "Interested?"

"Good try," responds Lori.

"We need to make sure we don't get busted," Raul interjects. "They have us monitored like a felon and they'll quickly be able to see us once we separate ourselves from the herd. Don, keep your face down as much as possible. Keep your sunglasses on and always have us surround you."

Gilbert looks to the group, "Don't let any come take self-me's with him."

"Selfies," says Lori.

"Huh?"

"Nothing."

CHAPTER 5

Orgy Baby

U P AT THE TOP OF THE RACE PLATFORM, a beautiful young African American girl sings the national anthem while the entourage lay below her about 10 yards in front of the platform.

Being at the front of the line is more difficult than Don and the rest imagined. Gilbert knows it all too well. When in competition, position is all that matters. Don, Raul and Lori are getting anxious. Runners are surrounding them not only for position but to be close to greatness.

Most of those who approach them with slaps on their backs and wanting to take selfies is fine for a while but now it's beginning to feel like annoying flies buzzing around. Don begins to think this may not have been such a good idea after all. *Don't these people need to focus on the race and their own life?*

Gilbert senses their nervousness. "We need to start a fast pace. We're faster than 95% of these people especially those that distract us. We'll set ourselves from the herd to run by ourselves. We maintain fast pace until mile two then back to plan. Agreed?"

"Aye, aye coach," Raul responds. Don and Lori nod in agreement.

A young girl in her early 20s weaves her way through the smothering crowd. Being pregnant, she gets somewhat of an advantage. She's wearing a long flowing skirt with a nylon cut off tank top exposing her pregnant belly of six months. She approaches Don with a blinding beam in her eyes.

"Would you bless my baby for us?"

Don is as uncomfortable as one can get. This is definitely a situation he never dreamed he would be in. His voice void of any confidence, "Excuse me?"

"Touch my child," she says looking down at her protruding belly smiling in a Stepford way.

Lori can't stand it anymore, "Get out of here. Now."

The other three look at her in surprise as that is not typical Lori fashion.

"You knew the end of the world was coming and you went and got pregnant. Why? Unbelievable, get out of here now. You disgust me."

The girl who has short, brightly dyed pink hair is caught off guard but unphased. She slowly turns to Lori and pierces her brightly lit green eyes to her and calmly responds, "My child is beautiful and will guide me through the next life."

Lori is even more disgusted, "You brought another life to be killed is what you did."

Don and Gilbert are not drivers in conversations so are waiting for the next move from somebody else. Raul intervenes, "Yes, your child is beautiful."

The immediate crowd is silent watching the surreal scene unfold. Lori looks to Gilbert and shakes her head. She's about to explode.

Raul continues, "What do you want? Griffin will dedicate this race to your child. Would you like that?"

She looks to Raul and smiles, "Yes. Please. That will help in our journey."

Raul turns to Don and nods his head, "Tell her, Griffin. It'll mean a lot."

Don is dumbfounded not really knowing what to do. He should have never volunteered this role if it meant playing out these scenarios. He looks at Raul then back at the girl and tries to utter the right dedication. "Yes. This race…is dedicated to you. Or, I mean, to you and your…child."

"Kiss my stomach, please. That will mean so much."

When I see Griffin again, I will wring his neck. Don knows he's caught in a bind as he really has no choice but to kiss this stranger's stomach for god knows what reason. He looks to Lori who is fuming then looks to Gilbert who gives him the 'suck it up' look.

Raul is the only one that feels his discomfort but knows if he just does it, hopefully she'll go away. Don turns to her, looks her in the eyes and smiles the best as he can. He lowers his head and kisses the top of her belly gently then remarkably tells her, "Your child is safe and in the hands of the creator."

Don didn't know where the hell that came from but sounded good. She smiles large while looking down at her unborn child rubbing her belly gently. She looks up at Don, "God Bless You." Then walks off.

Did that really just happen? Don looks around while his gang and all those around them are just as bewildered. This is when Don is most appreciative of his wrap-around, mirrored sunglasses so everyone can't see that he is more freaked out than they are.

The crowd around them start going off on the scene from Stranger Things. Yes, it's one of those days. The end of the world brings out the most bizarre people and the most bizarre out of people. Lori is looking at them pissed they played along.

Raul looks back at Gilbert and Lori. He pauses then presents his analysis, "Orgy baby."

"What?" Gilbert says puzzled.

The end of the world accelerates the primal emotions of mankind that killed millions of people in war, suicide and senseless killings. It also brought about the acceleration of daily Greek-lored orgies that sprung up nightly in every community thus coining the term 'orgy baby'.

Either no one had contraceptives nor cared but went to the opposite extremes of mass murders to their sexual desires of mass group hedonism. One of the most significant repercussions was the pregnancy rate jumped 500%. If, for some miracle, today could be prevented, a large generation was guaranteed by the excesses the pending last months of existence will bring out in humans.

Lori looks at Gilbert with an exhaustive demeanor knowing she has to explain yet another term, "Groups of strangers get together and have group sex with no care with whom it is or the consequences. Those are called orgies and thus those irresponsible people who let themselves become pregnant are now carrying what is called 'orgy babies'."

Gilbert is trying to process this information as his African heritage didn't have such an event.

Lori looks back at Don and Raul, "You create life to make a human being not as an afterthought. That's what got us in the mess in the first place."

Don and Raul remain silent. Don looks at Raul, "Did you recognize her?"

Raul smiles, "No. So I know it's not mine."

Lori explodes, "You have got to be kidding me! You went to those?!"

Both of them start stretching exercises trying not to look Lori in the eyes. Lori shakes her head in further disgust. She tries to detach herself to retain some sort of control. It's not as easy as she thinks. Her patience has evaporated.

"I will not stand for this. This is our race too," she says turning to Don and standing as close as possible, eye to eye. Don has his mirrored glasses so his fear-freeze expression cannot be seen but his stillness shows it. If it were not that Lori was so attractive he would be in complete fear.

Lori takes the safety pin on the top right of his race number as she tells him, "Stay still and don't move." He obliges her feeling better that she is undressing him so to speak. He's doing the same thing to her but in his mind. She quickly unhooks the four safety pins, pulls off his race number. She takes one of the unhooked pins and slowly, gently pokes Don right in the chest.

"Ow! What did you do that for?" Don says rubbing his pin pricked chest wound.

"Just because," Lori says with a smirk.

She drops the number on the ground. The timing chip and GPS are embedded in the number. Now that Don is no longer wearing it, their tracking just became much more difficult.

Raul and Gilbert smile now knowing her intentions. Lori winks at Don and quickly turns around. Don breathes a sigh of relief then offers up his observation, "I didn't know if you were going to choke me or kiss me. I was hoping for the latter."

Lori just sighs with more exasperation. She turns around, grabs his head right behind his cheeks and plants a long, hard kiss right on the lips then turns around again with a playful smile that no one can see. Don's happy, Gilbert smiles while Raul feels a little slighted.

She turns around, "I kissed and poked you so will you shut up and focus on the race?"

CHAPTER 6

Are You Ready?

G RIFFIN AND SABRINA STAND 200 yards back on the same side as the platform. They want to be far away from the group so as not to be noticed but not too far to make sure they finish close in time. They also need to be in position to easily split off and run their own course.

The anthem finishes in which the young African American girl performs flawlessly. The crowd roars in applause. She looks to be in her early 20s and probably on her way to stardom with those pipes and looks if the circumstances were different.

She hands the microphone to Grandma then gracefully walks down the metal stairs waving to the crowd with a smile from heaven. Grandma winks to the girl then calls out to the audience, "OK you motherfuckers, are you ready?!" She pauses as the crowd goes wild, "Betcha never heard those kind of words coming from Granny, eh?"

The crowd starts laughing, cheering her on. She's wearing a long, light pink dress with layers of fake pearl necklaces draped around her neck holding the starting gun down at her side. Her gray hair is wrapped tightly in a bun to avoid any entanglement to the pistol.

"I'll see ya at the pearly gates if they let you in!" She points the gun to the air and starts the countdown, "Three, two, one." She quickly drops the gun to her temple, pulls the trigger and blows her brains out. Looks like the starting gun is a real gun after all.

The crowd is stunned then starts shrieking throughout. The race has begun in the dark spirit that permeates today which is why Griffin has been so embraced. Sabrina and Griffin witness the horrific moment causing Sabrina to break down and cry.

Don and the group start running not knowing what happened behind them but doesn't sound good. There are some things in life that are best not knowing.

Griffin looks to her, "Let's go. Just don't think about it. It'll all be over shortly. Let's go."

She is shaking as they start to walk. Other racers saw the suicide, others didn't so it is a mixture of shock and excitement. Thousands of runners begin to move forward as a blob to the tune of ACDC's "Highway to Hell" blaring over the loudspeaker.

"Jesus Christ!" Larry shouts. "Janine, switch to you until we can get ourselves together. Jesus! I can't believe that. Janine. Janine?"

Janine sits at her desk watching the mayhem grinning. Jimmy is staring at the screen watching the panic unfold. He smiles, looks at his phone and hits enter.

Janine finally switches back to her as her grin instantly turns to grave concern. "The suicide of the starting lady has everyone in shock. But the race must go on as people keep pouring through the starting line. Many of the runners may not even know what has happened."

Don, Raul, Lori and Gilbert have run enough races to know that gun sounded different. Then the screams behind them reinforced their suspicions.

Gilbert's brow furrows as his team stands still. "Focus!" He growls. "Move!"

Don and his team now represent humanity's unity on this last race although the beginning doesn't seem like it. Even though they didn't see Grandma blow her brains out, they feel it.

Several hundred yards back, Griffin grabs Sabrina's hand as they start moving with the crowd, "Just follow me and look straight ahead. Don't look at her."

Sabrina is trembling, "I can't do this! Not if it's gonna be like this. I can't do it!"

"It'll all be over shortly. Just come with me. Trust me. Let's get away from this spot."

They start moving with the group. When thousands of runners are packed tightly, no one can start on a run. Everyone starts with baby steps for much longer than their adrenaline can handle especially after witnessing a suicide. The baby steps finally turn into a walk. Several minutes later a fast walk. Then another several minutes to give them enough room to start a slow running pace. Sabrina is still crying, staring at the ground.

She looks to her left to see the gun on the ground with blood dripping high above it. Runners stream by it next to the black curtain covering the vertical scaffold. Some know it's there, others don't or don't care.

Griffin and Sabrina silently run with the group for a while then split at the designated intersection. While they split from the main group, there are still plenty of runners copying them avoiding the endless human stream. Griffin and Sabrina just hope their route doesn't follow theirs for the entire race.

The carnival atmosphere is alive and the 26.2 mile last race has begun.

CHAPTER 7

Game Over...

T ANK IS WATCHING LARRY AND JANINE on the big screen in a crowded bar filled with his genetic-less family of twenty years from the Austin police force.

While each have their own motif, the group is mostly dressed in biker, military and police attire. It's smoke filled and all have cocktails, wine or beers of their choice. Most have firearms at their side or stacked on the table.

Tank is in his late 40's, wears his police uniform and drinks a tall beer in a frosted mug. While he's the Austin Police Chief, he chose his beat cop uniform rather than his formal attire. In his heart, he protects the good guys in the streets with a gun rather than in an office with a computer.

He's a large man that reflect someone who works out regularly and one you wouldn't want on your bad side. Despite his intimidation, he has a calm and approachable manner to him. He's half watching the race and the other half watching his fellow police officer show off.

Darren is looking through his scope focusing on his first target—
a lone star beer bottle underneath one of those old wooden

milk crates. Darren's sort of lanky for a cop but still has meat on his bones. He keeps his blonde hair short so hair never creates trouble when eyeing a human target or beer bottle to shoot down.

He's been the APD designated sharpshooter for the past ten of his twenty years on the force right out of the army from Granbury, TX. There's a reason he's been the Texas' Police State Association's sharpshooter of the year for five out of the past six years. The year he came in second, he attributes to two too many Trudy's margaritas the night before. Never affected him before but still makes a good excuse.

He has a steadiness and a low pulse rate that would make a funeral director want to poke him with a surgical knife to be sure he was alive. Add steel concentration with a 20/15 vision, the bullet from his gun is hard to escape. Just ask the Lone Star beer bottle in his sights now.

The crate housing the bottle has four wooden slats on each side leaving but a couple of inches for the bullet to penetrate. Makes for a tough shot. The problem is that's not enough challenge for Darren so his onlookers and fans have stacked wooden chairs and bar stools in front of all three lone star targets that sit 20 yards away.

And, last but not least, they didn't open the windows. He has to shoot through the window half-way into the beer garden where his friends have methodically set up a weird but entertaining challenge for him.

Behind him is Johnny, a mid-20s African American cop and his blondish-red headed wife, Dana, of the same age. They met as recruits and stayed together ever since and compete on who's a better partner under the sheets or on the streets chasing down criminals.

Add the other fellow police officers, some family members and friends huddling behind to see if Darren can pull off knocking down three beer bottles through the malaise of objects in less than 15 seconds. And a lot is riding on this—forced tequila shots for those who lost the bet saying he couldn't or those who bet he could.

For the record, the only reason those bet against him was because of Darren's inebriation level and they were the ones that set up the challenge. To lose would face their own defeat not setting up a proper challenge for the awarded marksman.

"OK. Everyone shut up!" shouts Dana. "Give him his concentration so I can watch you losers drink up."

"Fuck 'em," Darren says eyeing into position. "Won't mess with my concentration."

The whole gang lets out their own expletives reacting to Darren raising the challenge another level. Darren lowers his head parallel to his rifle and whispers, "Three, two…"

Bottle one smashes. Darren turns 20 degrees to the center. "Three, two…" Bottle two smashes. It's dead quiet in the bar now. Darren turns another 20 degrees to the right. "Three, two… game over."

Bottle three smashes and so do some other beer bottles thrown against the walls by those who just lost the bet. The whole bar is in an uproar cheering on Darren's born, army trained then police honed sniper abilities.

Tank, his wife and Ernie are at the bar laughing at the spectacle of Darren being Darren—the center of attention. Each are enjoying their libations with the last race on the TV behind the bar. Tank likes his locally craft beer. Marian, her red wine. Ernie's using this last day as a good excuse to finally open his Macallan single malt Scotch. The last day of existence brings out the best.

Ernie views the expansive room of Players Patio Bar and Grill where his Austin police family decided to spend the last hours together. Some are shooting pool. Others throwing darts then Melia and her mother strategically pushing the heavy metal pucks down the long shuffleboard table to score the first hanger.

Then there's Joe tending to his famous briskets, chicken, ribs and sausage for the continued feast for the day. He and Ernie have been slow cooking eight briskets, 10 whole chickens, 20 racks of ribs and 40 links of sausage for 16 hours in the Players famous smokehouse.

Why cook for the 20 people there when you could cook for the 40 people who could show unannounced? That's barbecuing the Texas way. Joe closes the rusted, steel prison door that traps the heat and smoke and starts sauntering over to the bar.

"This was a good idea," Ernie says to Tank and Marian.

Both of them smile back while Tank toasts the air and tugs down a swig of Austin's Dillo Tail Pale Ale. Joe walks up to gently lay down four pieces of the brisket just sliced off. Joe's a burly man, six feet tall with dark curly hair that can squat 300 pounds 20 times in a row so watching him gingerly handle the food is a bit amusing.

Ernie grabs his piece immediately knowing the reward while Marian waits until Ernie's orange gorilla paw hurls to his mouth. Ernie is sometimes referred to as the orangutan as everything thing about him is orange. His hair, ruddy complexion, orange freckles and even his eyes seem orange. Orangutans are dangerously strong for their size so the name fits his 5' 10" brick frame.

Tank and Ernie served as Navy Seals in Afghanistan while Marian was a Navy combat doctor. It's no coincidence that they all happen to be serving on the same police force and together for their last day. When serving in Afghanistan, that's how they had to treat every day.

"Tank! Have a bite," Joe says chewing at the same time.

Tank ignores him at the moment while he surveys the room counting the many deep connections he created through his years of service. Being the chief of police, these APD officers are his most loyal. The sheer numbers, laughter and camaraderie show the family they've formed defending the streets of Austin. All under Tank who is a decorated veteran turned police officer turned elected chief of police.

While Tank is a veteran spokesman for the APD and knows how to skillfully weave through city politics and flowing red tape, deep down he's a cop and a soldier. Standing at 6' 4", 220 with wavy black hair, he has a linebacker's body and an actor's face. He looks more like a character from an Avengers movie than a public servant.

Marian is a petite woman of 5' 6 who has a look of a gorgeous Midwestern plains woman with eyes of subtle blue steel. She has a blonde, striped short comb over that would put Miley Cyrus to shame. Her elegant look reflects a reason she's with Tank then another that is unknown. She has an alt to her that doesn't fully align to the boy scout but maybe that's it. Tank needs an alt side.

She hops off her bar stool next to Tank. She looks at him scanning the camaraderie and emanates a smile. She gently tip toes up to his cheek and kisses him that pops out a deep smile from him without looking at her. She knows. She goes around the bar to refill her wine and any other drinks that may need some refreshing.

Tank, Ernie and Joe who have served together the longest turn back to the TV where they've been keeping up with the crazy race of the human race that could only be concocted in the 'Hippie Hollowed' town of Austin, TX. Watching TV would be the last thing they would ever do on the last day of earth but they admit to each other this last race is a bit interesting.

CHAPTER 8

Who Are You?

JIMMY DROPS HIS BACKPACK onto the glass table. Picks up the tall jelly glass jar full of pinball sized cocaine rocks. Looks at them, smiles then puts it in one of the many side compartments. He starts tossing magazines of ammunition into the bag plus two more desert eagle handguns.

Goes into the kitchen where you can hear him washing out a plastic sports bottle and returns with it empty. On an accelerated cocaine high there is a different perspective to life. Every action is carefully executed, deliberate with the most efficiency that has ever been done in the history of mankind.

He carefully but intensely places the sports bottle down on the glass table. He grabs the 750 ml bottle of Jack Daniels, pours the whiskey into the bottle until it spills over full. He carefully but firmly tightens the cap then turns it upside down to make sure nothing spills or leaks. Seeing none, he smiles. He places the now full whiskey thermos into a side compartment.

He looks around through the clutter of vices on the table and grabs two packs of Marlboro reds. Puts one in his front Hawaiian shirt pocket and the other in the backpack. He sits down to snort a quick line before leaving but starts to gaze blankly into the table. He can't tell if he's looking at the carpet through the glass is what's distorting the image or the several grams of cocaine in his system. He reaches for the coffee table to maintain balance but misses falling into the coffee table onto the floor.

After 20 seconds in a dislocated fog, he forces composure crawling himself back on the couch trying to sit up. For all he knows, he could have been there for hours. As he fumbles into the pillows, he slowly turns around to sit in an upright position. He's breathing heavily holding his head in his hands. *How did it come to this?*

He starts crying into his hands that quickly become clenched fists of rage. He grabs the coffee table from underneath and jumps up flipping it upside down to the floor smashing the glass top and everything else onto the floor. His living room is now fully decorated to match the day's theme and the sum of his life—shattered.

As he stands the best he can, he pulls a cigarette out, lights it and analyzes the room as a psychiatrist would do a patient. He puffs out a large bellow of smoke followed by a loud sigh wondering where the line is drawn from a euphoric cocaine high or a heart attack. *I guess I'll find out.*

He grabs the backpack and walks towards the front door. He passes a family portrait hanging on the wall with him in a nice dark suit, his wife in a light blue dress and their teenage son all posing perfectly for the camera.

He looks at the photo with a cold, dark stare then opens the closet door adjacent to the portrait. He grabs his white, medical coat and puts it on. He walks back several feet to look in the mirror to see what he has become.

With knee length Greater Northern black linen shorts, a wildly obnoxious Hawaiian shirt, bright new white Nike tennis shoes and now with a doctor's coat, he is in his own full uniform to carry out his most important and last mission of his life. As he passes by the kitchen, a large blood splatter is sprayed on the stainless steel refrigerator door with a body on the floor covered by the kitchen island. Only two lifeless legs with women's shoes stretch out beyond the island.

He keeps walking and on the other side of the kitchen, his teenage son lie dead on the floor with a bullet hole in his forehead. Looking straight ahead, he opens the door and leaves the house forever.

Janine is quickly scrolling through her Facebook posts while Larry chatters in the background, "You know when I started college years ago, the RTF program was just starting. I adopted that major until my mother found out and basically forced me to pre-law and law school..."

Janine reaches over and pushes a button and talks to her mic while continuing to pay attention to her computer screen, "Larry, will you shut up and interview someone."

She sees something that makes her stop.

NEWS EXCLUSIVE: I AM GOING TO HUNT
YOUR PRECIOUS GRIFFIN DOWN AND KILL HIM.
XXXOOO CANDY MAN

She quickly types back: Who are you? Here's my number, 512-555-1517. Call me.

CHAPTER 9

Game On

J ANINE IS STARING AT HER IPAD with an irritated look. Griffin hasn't moved in 10 minutes. She keeps it on Camera 2 so Larry can ramble on to the viewers and she can concentrate on Camera 3. At least he's got some good bullshit.

She zooms in as close as she can to the starting line looking for him according to the GPS chip. *Hopefully he wasn't trampled to death or killed.* She pans from far left to far right and stops smack dab in the middle. There it is.

She sees his race number on the ground crumpled up but clear enough to know it's his. *Is he fucking with me?* She looks up from the monitor to stare blankly trying to think of the reason why it's there. *You've fucked with the wrong woman. Game on.*

Griffin stops Sabrina now that they are at mile one. He looks her eye to eye. "Are you okay? We can stop if you want. Go down to the lake and just sit there and talk or something. The spot we always like to people watch."

"No, no, no. I'll regroup. I want to run this. With you. I want to see my parents. Let's keep going. I'm fine. With all that's been going on in the past months, I should have expected that." She's wiping her tears, shaking her head and manages a smile. "Okay. Let's move on. We'll be at the mile two marker quickly."

They resume their pace. Runners are still abundant but not crowding. After some silence, Griffin resumes the conversation. "So, any plans today?" Sabrina starts laughing and pushes Griffin lightly as he smiles back. "This will be our 27th race we've run together."

She turns to him, "27, exactly?"

"Exactly. This is our fifth marathon. We've done 10 halfs, two 30Ks, two 25s, a ten miler and seven 10 Ks."

"And you're certain of this?"

"Spot on."

"Wow," she pauses to soak it in.

"I think the toughest one was that 25K in the hill country when it was like 25 degrees with a wind chill of zero."

"I agree. Where the six of us climbed in my old beat up Corolla waiting for the race to start."

"Yeah and Gilbert got mad and started bitching at us for not being outside doing our stretching exercises."

"And he gets so mad that he starts speaking so quickly, you can't understand a thing he says."

"He got so mad at us that time, he went Nigerian on us and then we really couldn't understand him."

"It didn't help that we all started laughing."

"No. That didn't help one bit."

"I no longer your coach."

"That's right. I no longer your coach."

They start laughing at the memory.

"Remember, I don't know the route. I know of all the mile stops that I showed my parents but I'm counting on you for the actual route," Sabrina reminds him.

"I know and I will never let you out of my sight. Up here, we're taking a left that should get us even further from the main crowd."

The left they take puts them in what is called "apartment row" or the locals call "apartment throw". The series of apartment buildings are sixty years old and look like not one repair has been done in those sixty years.

They would not have taken this course as it can be a bit dangerous. But on the last day of earth, the lines of dangerous and safe places are completely blurred. Oddly enough, 'apartment throw' is eerily empty. They run down the street feel-ing like they're in slow motion. Nobody is around.

They run past a large, abandoned Red Bull delivery truck to see an African American girl sitting on the steps of her porch. The girl is surveying the neighborhood with eyes of deep wisdom from what looks like a six or seven-year old.

Sabrina stops and pauses as she and the little girl's eyes lock onto each other. Sabrina holds a running breath then exhales to calm her down as much as can be in long distance races. She walks up to her and squats down to eye level.

The girl looks up with her full ebony eyes creating a sun's reflection from her long glossy hair pulled back in a ponytail. Her spot clean blue floral dress shows today is special. Makes Sabrina wonder if she knows what's going to happen in several hours.

"Watcha doin' lil one?"

"Just watchin'. Hey, do you know where everyone is?"

"I don't know. Is it different than usual?"

Sabrina is trying to talk in a calm voice but is difficult at the beginning of a marathon. The rhythmic ease of breathing actually comes miles into the race and not in the beginning when fresh. Griffin is pacing back and forth behind them admiring how comfortable Sabrina is with children.

"Yeah. There's usually a lot of yelling and people being mad at each other. Now it's all quiet. I like it."

Oh the irony, Griffin thinks. Back when it was normal, this place would be designated as crazy and dangerous. Now with the world at its craziest and most dangerous, this is a place of peace and calmness.

"Where's your family? Your mom and dad?"

"Mom's in the living room watching that weird race and I don't know my daddy is. He's been gone for a long time."

"Why isn't your mom out here with you?" Interjects Griffin. Sabrina turns her head around not appreciating his comment. *Men.* They have a hard enough time understanding woman let alone girls. Her look tells him to shut up and that she has it under control. He, at least, understands enough about woman to shut up for the moment.

"She can't really walk when she's on her medicine. She just stares at the TV with a weird smile. She'll be asleep fast anyway. Are you running the race?"

"Yes we are. We decided to go this route so we could stop and say hi to you."

That gives Griffin a big smile.

"Really?" The girl says with an even bigger smile.

"Yes. Really. That's why Griffin chose this route," she looks back to Griffin. "He knew you would be here and that we need to stop by and let you know everything is going to be fine. Wanna come with us?"

That makes Griffin's eyes bulge and smile go away.

"No thanks. I need to take care of Mommy. She needs me. Besides I like it here now that no one is around that scares me. I'm going now to check on her. Bye. Have fun on your race. Maybe I'll see you on the TV."

If she only knew. She jumps up from the steps with a bigger grin on her face and a chore that she looks like she's done many times before. Checking up on mommy after she's taken her *medicine*.

The girl turns around with a quizzical and confident stare, "Are you going to win?"

Sabrina smiles and simply answers, "Yes."

The little girl returns the smile, "Good." She opens the screen door and walks in with a commanding control rarely seen in a little girl let alone adults.

Sabrina turns to Griffin with a look of amazement, "I don't even know what to say to that. That was good planning on your part that's for sure."

"Ha ha. That was just luck. Good luck."

"You sure about that?"

"No."

"It's like today. Did today happen from bad luck? Or bad planning?"

"Come on. Let's go."

"I swear you're taking us farther from where I told Mom and Dad mile two will be," Sabrina says getting worried.

"Don't worry. There's some cross country on our route. Follow me."

They resume their pace through the eerily vacant scene from an Omega Man movie. After several blocks, they pass the last apartment building into the large parking lot full of abandoned cars and potholes.

The parking lot is enclosed by an 8-foot chain link fence with barbed wire looped on top. Sabrina wonders if they took a wrong turn. Griffin just keeps running straight towards the fence at the farthest back. Sabrina's look turns to a worry hoping he's not expecting her to climb over that.

At the metal pole, he grabs the wire mesh and pulls it back revealing an opening. They crawl through the fence from a line where the chain link fence was cut. Strategic planning on Griffin's part. The parking lot borders up to a railroad yard on the southern end of the 20 mile hike and bike trail.

They run through the railroad yard, down the grass hill leading into the hike and bike trail split by a river canal. By 'river', it's more like a big creek. The 'river' word must have come from the convention visitors and tourists' department. Today's creek level is pretty low so hopping over rocks to get on the other side without getting their shoes wet is easy. They run up to the other side and turn to head west.

Griffin leads them straight into the cedar tree'd forest bordering the running trail. It's the beginning of the Texas Hill Country with cedar trees galore, an occasional Texas Live Oak set upon an uneven bed of limestone rocks as far as the eye can see.

"Get ready as we're running up hill and the path is not smooth at all," Griffin shouts out.

"Yeah. I know. It's not like I've never hiked this before," she shouts back.

CHAPTER 10

Tears in Heaven

THE TEXAS HILL COUNTRY shouldn't be called neither a hill nor country. It's more like cavernous gullies of jagged rocks with crooked Christmas tree rejects to give the illusion of forest green living and makes for difficult maneuvering when off trail.

When they're at the top, the hill country terrain leads right back down to the next gulley where part of the Barton creek tributary wanders. Below there is a low water concrete crossing which leads them up another hill into a surrounding neighborhood and city streets.

Strangely enough, though, they hear music faintly in the background. This music has a different vibration to it. It's alive. They look at each other with acute curiosity. *What more can unveil itself on this day?* They turn towards the music and start scooting down the hill with a calculated process trying not to slip on the many loose rocks.

As they scoot and slide further down to the creek bed, the music slowly gets louder and deeper with a full sound and feeling you wouldn't expect in the middle of the woods. There are the standard instruments of a rock band—drums, guitar, bass and keyboards—along with several singers. One lead and maybe three or four backups. There are percussion instruments, strings and horns that give it a concert feel. The song starts sounding familiar but they're not close enough to know yet.

As they slide to a stop, they stand up and brush the rock dust off their back side and immediately head for the music. They're now on one of the main trails of Barton Creek so have full motion towards the sound. Now it's more of a mission than curiosity.

As they approach, the music is loud enough to ascertain what style, how good the musicians are and if the song is one of those that fit in their collection. Griffin stops their pace and turns his ear, "It's a ballad. That much I can tell."

"How appropriate."

"Shhh. I can also hear many more voices in the background."

"Is it a choir?" Sabrina stops breathing for a second to give her ears less intrusion.

"It's the audience. They're singing along. Come on."

He starts jogging then stops again. "Oh Jesus," Griffin says as he quickly drops his head not believing the song they're playing.

"What?"

"It's 'Tears in Heaven' by Eric Clapton. Really? That song? Rub it in, why don't you."

"Hey! That's a good song. And they're doing it really well."

"Yeah, yeah, yeah. It is a good song but…"

He stops as they turn a small corner around the cliff wall with a large boulder jutting out. That's when they see what they hear. Sabrina looks over his shoulder. At a loss of words, she utters just one, "Wow."

The Barton Creek greenbelt is an aquifer fed creek that flows in and out of limestone passages, boulders and grass islands.

Sometimes there are parts of sprawling open water that's six feet deep, twenty yards long then most of the times trickling lines webbing its way to the next pool.

The creek runs in and out of carved out rock passages leaving many areas where swimmers can sit, stand, sunbathe or, in this most unusual of circumstances set up a large, intricate set of musicians with an electric sound system. Worrying about electrocuting themselves is obviously not a high priority today. They smartly had wireless instruments and microphones to be as cautious as they could.

There had to be at least 15 musicians along with eight singers being orchestrated through a 64-channel mixing board. It's a musical production that would only be seen at a Pink concert or the Grammy awards. On this day, no expense is too much.

Some of the musicians are on metal stands shooting out from the water. Others balance on the boulders or rocks then the rest roam through the forest amongst the crowd. It's as much Broadway as a live concert.

Audience members are in the water or on rafts. Most are sitting on the rocks or nestled in the trees with their drinks and food toasting a band of musicians that obviously represent Austin being the 'live music capital of the world'. Griffin and Sabrina stand silent listening and watching a moment that a day like this must create.

Griffin whispers enough to be heard but not to upset the music. "Mankind is so capable of creating such beauty and harmony together."

"Like the race?"

Griffin turns to her with a surprised look. He stares at her stoically then looks back at the musicians and the audience as a whole. At this moment Griffin is part of the music where he is one of a united group experiencing humanity together.

That's when it really sinks in—the singularity of an audience in a concert or a group of runners. Or one runner uniting thousands of runners to experience humanity together.

Griffin and Sabrina stand silently until the song finishes and the audience roar in applause. The sound of applause reflects singularity as much of appreciation.

Griffin turns to Sabrina, "Yes. Like the race. Come on. While I'd love to stay here. I think the race needs us. Or, I need the race. Let's go." He looks towards the band and audience with a gracious pose. "Thank you."

They turn back down the trail to get back to the race. In the background, the band begins another song. This one is much more upbeat.

"Wow. Good. I thought they might play 'Knocking on Heaven's Door,'" Sabrina comments in a jogging pace now.

"No. This song is pure Austin and perfect for us today."

"Why? What is it?"

"First, it's Willie Nelson. Second, it's 'On the Road Again'."

CHAPTER II

This is Candy Man

JIMMY LOOKS AT HIS PHONE. Presses the highlighted number on the message and lets the ring begin. Janine answers, "Whatcha got?"

"This is Candy Man. You need proof I'm real?"

"Have it?"

"You have FaceTime on your phone?"

"I'm a network anchor. What do you think?"

"I'll call you right back. On FaceTime."

"I might answer. I might not," she hangs up immediately.

"Network anchor, my ass," Jimmy mutters to himself. "You're the morning traffic girl who is only prime time now because everyone else has a life."

Jimmy grabs into his bag and pulls out one of the handguns. He puts it in his right front pocket of his shorts. Looks around with a grin then heads directly across the street.

He walks up to a red brick, New England styled house. It's always confounded Jimmy that someone would actually live in a brick box with some broken off pool stick columns. Yet someone, somewhere specifically designed this house to be made. And someone bought it for a lot of money. He rolls his eyes at the eye sore but shakes it off knowing his neighbor is a gentle old lady.

He walks up the short brick steps to stop at the immaculate white-painted door. He pulls out his iPhone and as promised, he's calling Janine back on FaceTime.

On first ring, Janine answers, "What?"

"Here's the proof." He's talking as he rings the doorbell. An elderly lady, Mrs. Woodburn, answers the door in her long, light pink nightgown. She is leery as all are when a surprise doorbell rings.

But she happily recognizes her most favored neighbor. Jimmy is consistent in helping take in and out her trash, recyclables and compost each week. With a wide smile she appreciatively proclaims, "Well hi Jimmy. What's going on?"

"Hello Mrs. Woodburn. Would you mind holding this and chatting with this lady?"

"Okay. Hello," she says with a puzzled response.

He gently hands her the phone with the screen facing her. She stares at the screen looking at Janine who has a more than obvious skeptical look. The old lady stares stretching her memories knowing there is something about this woman that is strangely familiar.

Then it hits her. "Oh my, it's the news lady." She smiles with excitement. "I'm watching you right now."

Jimmy pulls the handgun out and BANG, shoots Mrs. Woodburn in the forehead. She immediately falls dropping the phone.

"Oh, shit. I hope I didn't break the phone. I should have asked her to step out on the grass," Jimmy says talking to himself. He picks up the phone and looks at Janine, "Is that proof enough?"

Janine un-phased, answers, "I'm announcing it now. Or, how far away are you from the race?"

"Ten minutes. Just as long as I can get through."

"Okay. Call me when you get there then I'll announce it."

"Why the wait?"

"Makes it more dramatic. Keeps them watching and wanting more."

"Wow. You're one sick bitch. I could have made some serious money on you too. Oh, I'm going to be at the north end of the Capitol if anyone wants to join me. Tell them to bring their own firearms."

"Well, that changes things. I'm reporting it now."

CHAPTER 12

Watching Our Race

G RIFFIN AND SABRINA RUN-CRAWL up a steep slope to stop at a wooden privacy fence butted up to the greenbelt. Sabrina is adhering to her previous statement, following and trusting Griffin's lead. At this point, Griffin looks like he knows what he's doing.

Griffin bends down and grabs one picket from underneath with one hand then his middle finger into a drilled hole in the middle of a board several feet above. He carefully pulls it. Surprisingly, a whole section of the fence comes out.

Sabrina looks at Griffin with an odd expression. Griffin looks back, "What?"

"Plan that did you?"

Griffin with victorious satisfaction replies, "Yep."

He sets the separated section to the side and pokes his head through to view the backyard and surrounding properties. Property so close to the greenbelt is prime thus expensive and each house shows it.

The house in front of them looks like it has been empty for months. Griffin looks around at the back of the other houses just to be sure. Never know on this day, whatever neighborhood it is.

That's when he hears a sliding glass door open in the neighbor's house to their right. Griffin waves down Sabrina to hold on to see what's going on. With the neighbor's door open, he can hear the TV. It's Janine covering the race. Then a zip and a stream of liquid are the next two sounds.

"Is that man just peeing in the yard?" Sabrina whispers with an irritated tone.

"Yeah. Welcome to a man's world. Can you hear what Janine is saying? I want to know what they know."

"Well, I would if he would quit tinkling."

Griffin turns to her, "Tinkling? Really? Isn't that the word you quit using after 2nd grade?"

She pinches his side hard. "Ouch!"

"Shh."

Griffin shushes her back while he returns to spying. The man finishes his business then turns back and the glass door shuts and so does Janine's voice.

Griffin waves Sabrina in as they run over to neighbor's fence to see and hear what's going on but they're too far. They find the biggest gap in the fence to peer through to get the best view.

Even with the limited vision, they can see him in the cavernous, luxurious living room. He dons a thick white hotel bathrobe, beige Outfitter shorts and somewhat of a beer belly in one hell of a house.

He's in his jammy mode so to speak but it's obvious he just took a shower. And returned from his hair stylist. He's perfectly coiffed and has a swagger of a man going to the catellion tonight. *The things we do on the last day of earth.*

He walks into the sprawling kitchen that, from the looks of it, isn't used that much but makes him look and feel rich. He opens the door to the microwave to grab a bag of scalding puffed up Orville Reddenbocker popcorn bag to quickly toss on the counter.

Orville man shakes his hand from the heat and smiles at his Gordon Ramsey skills. He carefully pulls the top of the bag as the steam shoots out. He quickly pours it into those crystal bowls only served for Thanksgiving and Christmas dinners.

He picks up the bowl and heads to the real meaning of the last day of earth—the TV. As he stands motionless with an analytical stare, he grabs the remote and starts turning the volume up. He smiles and nods his head repeatedly at Janine's broadcast. He looks down to the remote to jolt up the volume more.

Griffin hears an odd echo coming from the speakers. His TV and sound system are definitely up there in the thousands of dollars if not tens of thousands.

"Really?" Sabrina says in a talking voice. That gives her the eye from Griffin. He doesn't want to get busted. "He's eating popcorn, watching our race, ALONE on the last hours of earth. You have got to be kidding me. That's the reason right there that we're in this mess in the first place. I'm going over there and just thank him for being rich, fat and lazy. It really helped."

"Chill. You don't know if that's even his house. He could have lost his family and this is all he has left. Or he…"

"Or he killed his family and he's hungry after chain sawing for an hour but probably not. He's a rich divorced asshole with two kids that are with their mother right now while he's eating Orville Reddenbocker."

"Shh. I want to get closer so I can hear. And what's wrong with Orville Reddenbocker?"

She pinches him hard again.

"Ow! Would you quit that!"

He lightly runs to the front gate and opens it as quietly as can be.

Sabrina follows. They peer out to the posh neighborhood and looks clear. He turns to the neighbor's house and can see in through the side window. He looks at Sabrina, nods and smiles. They both creep up next to the window leaning on the brick wall. They can hear Janine reporting.

"Hey Larry, do you mind putting down your 17th drink and turn the camera around to show some of the characters waiting for Griffin? Or would that be too much time off your glass?"

"Too much time off the glass. And too much time off of my pretty face," Larry responds.

Janine responds even quicker, "Okay, viewers. To spare you the time of his face, I am switching to some photos and video coming in of the Griffin posse. They've now passed mile two."

When Janine changes camera views, Orville tilts his head in exasperation to yell out, "Oh come on! Keep Larry on. At least he's interesting. He's the star of the show!"

Sabrina is even more irritated now, "Tell him to go get a gun and do us all a favor."

Griffin turns to Sabrina holding his finger to his lips for the 'be quiet' sign. He pokes his head again and sees varying shots on the TV of Don and the posse. He got what he needed. They still don't know that Don is not Griffin. Their plan is working.

He looks again and sees Orville gone. Hopefully went upstairs. They turn around to a shotgun pointing at them from the Orville man.

Griffin turns to Sabrina, "I guess he heard you."

CHAPTER 13

You Can't Kill Me

"TRESPASSING AGAINST THE LAW in these parts." Orville man stands there in his robe glaring intensely. He's an older, white gentleman in his 50's with thick white hair parted to the right. He's not happy and has a twitchiness that unnerves them. *Is he hopped up on something? Or just aching to do something bold on this day?*

Griffin and Sabrina just stare speechless. This wasn't in their itinerary. Griffin starts, "Hello sir, we're running the race so wanted to get an update from the TV. That's all."

"Doesn't look like you're running. Looks like you're sneaking up to steal my property."

"No. We want to join the race so needed an update."

"Why here? You could have turned on any TV in any house in this neighborhood yet you're at my house. Looking through my window. Specifically for the broadcast of the race."

Sabrina had enough, "You sure are paranoid. You had it on while we're passing by so it was convenient. That's it. Can't you see we're in running clothes. We're breathing hard and sweating. We could give a shit about your house. Just let us go."

She starts walking up to him. He cocks the gun and points it at her. Griffin starts walking up with her. He's rotating his aim between the two.

"It's probably not even loaded," Sabrina says with full command.

"You want to find out the hard way?"

The conversation is beginning to confirm her expectations. He has a bitterness to him. His eyes look hardened and has that mouth with the subtle but cemented scowl that happens after years of holding the face that way. Griffin keeps inching up closer while Sabrina moves closer but further to the side to split them up better.

"Sure. But the honorable way. Shoot a round up in the sky and prove it."

Sabrina knows challenging the ego of a man, especially rich men can be the best bait of them all. And most of all, a challenge from a young, good looking woman. Orville turns the gun up to the sky then blows a round. That's her cue. She runs straight at him pushing him backwards to trip over the brick runway to his house.

Griffin follows and leaps over the bricks. Orville finally gets the next round loaded when all he sees is two feet falling on his face. That gives Sabrina enough time to kick the shotgun out of his hands while he's still reeling from the slam to the head from the full weight of Griffin's body. Griffin scoops up the shotgun and points it straight at Orville.

"Look at me, prick," Sabrina triumphantly says with her new-found confidence. Griffin remains silent.

"You can't kill me," Orville says rolling around trying to get his bearing straight enough to sit up.

"Um, actually I can," Griffin retorts. That gives Sabrina a surprised look.

"I'm the reason you're running. I'm the reason the race exists."

Griffin and Sabrina look at each other not knowing what to say. This serendipity crap is getting even weirder. *Does he know who he is talking to?*

"Okay. Why is this race yours?"

Orville wobbles to sit up. He looks at Griffin, "I own the station that's covering the race. Without the recognition and broadcast from a major network channel, the race wouldn't exist."

Again, Sabrina and Griffin look at each other. They thought the encounter with the little girl was mind boggling then the band in the middle of the forest but this pushes it to a level they would have never thought existed.

Griffin pulls the trigger. The ground next to Orville's leg blows a new hole in the perfect yard as several BBs from the shotgun shell penetrate his lower leg. He begins to scream loudly holding his ankle and calf. Griffin wants to injure the foot enough that it's too painful to charge or chase them.

Griffin cocks again and pulls the trigger. This time aiming further from his now injured leg. Another hole in the ground and a scream from Orville. While the newly blown out hole is further from his leg, it still has the same fear effect.

Griffin cocks again and shoots at the ground further from his leg and nothing. No more shells. Just what Griffin wanted. He nonchalantly nods towards Orville, "Thank you for the race."

Griffin swings the shotgun as hard as he can across the street behind him. At the same time, a gently-used white sedan slowly glides to a stop. Through the glass, the shaded form of a nerdy looking man in his 40s approaches the house. He's looking at them with trepidation but the commotion doesn't divert him.

He sees Griffin and Sabrina staring him down while Orville rolls around in pain. He turns his car off a nd w aits s everal seconds staring back in an uncomfortable manner. He has the book-smart, unkempt look and judging from his car doesn't live in this neighborhood. There is a s taring c ontest g oing o n w ith Griffin and the new guest. The gentleman is more than happy to concede defeat.

He scoots back to get in alignment to the rear door and slowly opens it. All while he's looking at Griffin and Sabrina. Orville's vocal whining is annoying but Griffin and Sabrina tu ne it ou t with the new engagement. Sabrina grabs Griffin's arm as both get tense wondering what he's going to do. *Is he grabbing a gun?*

For a brief moment, they lose eye contact as he grabs an old, brown leather briefcase and a bottle of champagne. He remains behind the car door waiting to see what Griffin and Sabrina do.

"You okay?" he shouts to Orville. Orville's wincing has gone down a notch but still lies there holding his ankle in biting pain.

"Does it look like I'm okay? Jesus, will you do something? Get my gun and bring it to me."

Griffin with a commanding look tu rns to Sa brina, no ds to- wards the direction of the Austin skyline. Sabrina knows the sign and gladly returns her body language of agreement. Griffin starts his running pace but a little quicker. Sabrina glares at Orville and joins Griffin. Griffin stares at the stranger as they pass. The man just keeps his distance until they're far enough away.

Griffin turns to Sabrina, "We need your parents."
Sabrina in controlled shock responds, "Yes we do."

They run a block down to take a right at the closest street. They look to see the stranger running to Orville in a deferent but pathetic type of rescue. They pass out of sight giving a sigh of relief to a greatly unexpected and bizarre encounter.

In the yard, Orville is hobbling up, holding his leg in wincing pain. He takes one hand off his bleeding leg to a one-legged hop back into the house. In his painful defeat, he stares to Griffin and Sabrina run past the corner house to leave his view forever.

"That's such bullshit and what a little prick," Griffin blurts out. Sabrina turns her head to him a bit surprised on Griffin's anger. Griffin tends to be even keeled. "He's not the reason the race exists. He's the reason it got so fucked up and turned into a warped commercial. It was supposed to be a race with runners who love running. Not some circus his station created."

Griffin is really venting now. Sabrina stays quiet listening. She enjoys when Griffin emotes with a fire. It's rare but good to hear. After silent running trying to absorb the encounter, Griffin calmly announces, "There is something going on."

"Oh gee. You think?"

That comment didn't help Griffin offer up his philosophical musings. The out of left field existential observation wakes Sabrina up from her shock. "Okay. I know what you're saying. But I don't know what you're saying. What are you saying?"

"What the fuck is going on? Some sort of universal clash? You squeeze lives together for a last seven hours and all of sudden it happens?"

"What happens?"

"Coincidence doesn't exist. Coincidence...is an illusion. A word to give us an 'out'. To pardon us from taking responsibility that we are all interconnected. That's why today has happened."

"A pardon for what?"

"The choices we made."

Up ahead, the neighborhood turns into a placeless-ness scene from anywhere, America. On the main road, there's a Starbuck's on one corner, McDonald's across the street, Walgreen's across on the other corner and, yet for some reason, a CVS on the fourth corner.

While the short cut sent them through Alice's wonderland, it worked. Once they approach the corner Sabrina looks where she should and points with exhilaration, "Look, there they are."

CHAPTER 14

Together as a Family

MOM AND DAD STAND BEHIND the Starbucks with portable ice chests full of necessities marathoners need to maintain a grueling run. Dad's pacing. Mom stands frozen staring at the street corner where Griffin and Sabrina are supposed to appear. She's on the phone half-listening to Janet. Janet likes to talk.

Behind them, herds of runners continue down Burnet Road. It runs parallel to the main road so acts as a secondary path to accommodate the overflow. Their meeting spot is just far enough away from the runners to be hidden enough.

Mom and Dad are in their late 50's. Dad has grayish dark hair. Mom's the same age but no gray. Whether from dying it or not, you couldn't to tell. Her hair is brown with highlight streaks and perfectly placed as always.

Dad is comfortable with tennis shoes, shorts and a white polo shirt untucked. Mom is in her summer dress looking ready for lunch with her bridge club. At the first sight of Sabrina, Mom quickly interrupts Janet, "I see your sister. Gotta go. Call you later."

Mom exhales for the first time in minutes. Dad holds up two water bottles waiting for them. Leave it to the father to show emotion with gifts. Sabrina runs straight into them instantly crying in their arms as they "circle hug" her tightly.

Griffin grabs one of the waters then pats Dad on his shoulder for a 'thank you'. He would refuse as it's too early for water for his regimen. But after a polite refusal in the third race, Dad told him if he ever refused again he wouldn't get a drop. *Ever.* Don't mess with Texas hospitality.

"Hi honey. How's it going? Are you okay," Mom starts crying with her.

"I don't know. I don't know," she says, tears rolling down her face.

Griffin interjects, "Well. We started off with a bang. Then met a little girl alone in the street. She explained us the meaning of life. We saw a concert then were nearly killed then nearly killed a friendly neighbor. Other than that, it's been pretty uneventful."

"Excuse me?" Dad says. He looks to Griffin with that 'better be sarcasm' look. Griffin just holds his hand up, tugging a small sip of water.

Sabrina starts wiping her tears and lifts her head and even starts a small laugh, "I think this is the only time in my life where my avoidance personality will come in handy. It was totally bizarre. I'll have to explain at the end of the race. Right now, I just need to run. Run away from this pain and run to a life where we can just live like happy people."

Mom and Dad don't know what to say while Griffin stays in the same shock condition as Sabrina. *Did they really just take the gun away from a stranger who owns the TV station stalking them then shoot him?* Time has a funny way of revealing itself and the parts you thought you never had.

"How's Janet?"

"Well, you know. She's Janet. She and the family are having a party with some friends. Hopefully they are watching the race. We just got off the phone with her when we saw you. We know how you two are so we'll call her back when you leave," Mom says sheepishly.

"Oh Mom. I love Janet. You know that. It's just that she is the most annoying person I know and I'm in a better mood when she's not around or talking. Which, I don't know if that ever happens, the not talking part."

"Oh Honey, I'm sorry."

"I'm just kidding, Mom," Sabrina says shaking her head with an added eye roll and grin. "Kind of. What about Carolyn? Did you find her?"

"No. We keep trying. I thought at this point, she would break her religious rules and just talk to us. Just to say goodbye."

"I've tried again too. Even contacted her friends. They don't know where she is or have her phone number. They don't get it. I don't get it. They're kind've mad and I don't blame them. Drop everyone and everything you've worked for, for a man and a religion."

"A cult," Dad adds. "And her boyfriend is a convict and a conniving son of a bitch that used religion to take Carolyn away from us."

Mom throws a quick look at him. "He was arrested. That's all. It could be all a mistake."

"He was arrested with 50 pounds of illegal substance with the intent to distribute. He's a piece a shit convict."

Griffin smiles full in clandestine. He knows the reference oh so well but not the full story. He joins the conversation, "None of you like talking about this, do you?"

Sabrina looks at him shaking her head knowing he's fishing for more backstory.

Mom answers, "You know it's not something I like to talk about nor am very proud of. She's a good kid and I can't believe would fall for such mind control."

"You always make that reference. What is it?"

Dad grabs the conversation, "She's not allowed to interact or have any relationship with anyone who is not part of their religion. Not even family."

"What's the religion?"

"Pick one."

Now Mom is getting flustered. "OK. OK. Enough with Janet and Carolyn. We're here together as a family and that's all that matters. You want some water or energy bars? Anything?"

"No thanks, Mom. It's just mile two. We won't need anything for a while. You know our routine. You're the best," Sabrina says drying her tears breaking a smile.

She turns to Griffin, "Ready?"

He closes the cap tightly and hands it back to Dad, "Thank you as always." He turns to Sabrina, "Let's do it. Maybe it'll be just a calm and peaceful race from now on."

Sabrina turns to her parents with the most grateful look a daughter could express. The parents return the look from a deep emotion that only parents know. She hugs and kisses them both. Griffin stays in pacing mode as he smiles and waves. They hit the pavement running.

CHAPTER 15

You May Kiss the Bride

GRIFFIN AND SABRINA are basically running alone now. Things are a bit calmer. There are still runners that come in and out of their path but not many so they can run at a pace more their liking.

They're running south on Mesa Road which is about a quarter mile parallel from the actual race route on MoPac highway. Mesa is part office complex, upscale homes and condominiums. It's in the middle of an 80-year old neighborhood so the Sycamores, Live Oaks and Spanish Oaks give it good shade and a pretty route to run.

"Why didn't you ever ask me out?" Sabrina asks. That adds yet another surprise to the run. He immediately responds as if he's waited for this question for years, which he has.

"Cuz you always had a boyfriend."

"I haven't had a boyfriend for two years. Those were just dates. I may have gone on several dates with a few of them but nothing ever serious. You knew that."

"You always had dates and you always talked about them. I didn't want to be one of the many. I wanted to be able to have your undivided attention and not be distracted with all the others. You know how shy I am. You really think I would have just pushed my way in?"

"Well, I wish you had. I always was hoping you would. I almost came to the conclusion you were gay."

"What changes it now?"

"Well, that comment in the hotel room and the way you've been acting lately kind of gave it away, don't you think?"

"Will you marry me?"

"What?"

Griffin grabs her arm, stops her then lowers himself down on one knee. Trying to propose breathing hard is not as easy he thought. But Griffin's sincerity and this moment he has always wanted, he is able to speak as calmly as possible, "Will you marry me?"

Sabrina looks at him a bit startled at THE question then with a big smile says, "Yes, yes. I will."

"We have to make it official, though."

"Uh, well Justices of the Peace or ordained priests may have other plans at this moment."

Griffin jumps up, stops a runner and asks, "Do you mind if you marry us real quick?"

The runner stops, "Um, I'm not a minister."

Griffin looks at him then does the sign of the cross and pops him lightly in the forehead while speaking, "On the name of the father, mother, holy ghost and prime minister, I now pronounce you as a certify priesthoodedness with the power to marry."

The runner is a bit surprised by the quick ordainment.

"OK. You're certified now. You may proceed."

The runner is still confused but gladly obliges. He turns to Griffin, "Um, will you..."

"Griffin," Griffin interjects.

"…Griffin. Take this woman…"

"Sabrina," Sabrina interjects.

"…Sabrina to be your lawful wedded wife?"

"I do," says Griffin with a wide smile and full conviction.

"Will you, Sabrina, take Griffin to be your lawful wedded husband?"

"I do," says Sabrina with an equal, wide smile.

"I guess I now pronounce you husband and wife. Right?"

Griffin and Sabrina stand there staring at each other in silence. They finally look at the runner nodding their head waiting.

"Oh! Sorry. You may kiss the bride."

Sabrina takes full initiative and gives Griffin a long, passionate kiss. The runner starts in, "Uh can I go?" Sabrina waves her hand shooing him off while still embraced in the kiss.

"Congratulations," he says smiling as he resumes his race. They unlock and with true happiness.

Griffin looks into her soul through her eyes and lets the three word sentence go, "I love you."

"And I love you," says Sabrina back. This time Griffin takes the initiative and gives Sabrina a long, passionate kiss. Another runner runs by, "Get a room."

In their kissed embrace, Griffin lifts his hand to present his middle finger to the passer by. She then looks at Griffin, "Hey, you wanna run a marathon for our honeymoon?"

"Good idea. Let's do it."

Off they go.

CHAPTER 16

Good Journalism

J ANINE BEGINS, "We have breaking news, ladies and gentleman. We have confirmation that a man who calls himself 'The Candy Man' is going to hunt Griffin down and murder him before he finishes the race.

The man is in his early 40s, black hair wearing a doctor's coat and Hawaiian shirt. He also made the statement asking anyone to join him on this deadly hunt to meet him on the north side of the Capitol with firearms and a painted X on your body."

Larry responds with complete exasperation, "What the hell did you just say? Why did you report about this crazy man wanting others to join? Do you know what you just did?"

"I'm just reporting the news. That was his official statement thus reporting it. That's called good journalism."

"You're not reporting the news, you're inciting it. That goes against all ethical standards of journalistic reporting. I can't..."

Janine hits the monitor 3 button then the comm 2 button and cuts Larry off. Janine knows the playful, clashing banter they engage is good for viewership. News is entertainment after all. But when Larry starts pushing the boundaries of her power, she has to put him in his place.

She talks into the direct comm, "Larry, don't ever question my journalistic integrity. If you do it again, I will cut you off for the remainder of the race. Do you understand?"

"Yeah." Larry waits so comm 2 can be turned off. "Bitch."

"The comm link is still on."

"Good."

Janine pushes Monitor 1 button back to her. "So, Larry, any reaction from the crowd about these latest developments?" Janine pauses looking at monitor 2. "Larry, what are you doing?"

"I'm gonna sit in my comfy chair I brought. My feet are hurting. My back is hurting and I'm getting shit-faced so gonna keep reporting in comfort."

"Do you think that's a good idea being our on-site reporter?"

"Yeah. I can still reach my drink sitting down."

Larry lowers the tripod down to a sitting, shit-face face height then lifts the entire tripod with the camera affixed to set it in front of him. Larry falls into the chair. Sits up to look in the monitor and adjusts the height and angle perfectly to his liking.

"Now, much better. And made sure to re-fill the ole' scotch and ice. So, yeah, people are very worried now that Griffin is a marked man. Have a lot looking at me wondering how they can help. And, I say, Griffin sure could use some help so hopefully there's some out there who can rise to the occasion."

Janine cuts him off. "Sounds like you're inciting news by throwing out that not so subtle cry for help."

"Learned from the best, didn't I? Just trying to even the odds for ole Griffin."

"Yes, you have learned. Good job. And, by the way, our worldwide viewership has increased 10 million people since I announced the call for murder. And keeps going up every second.

We're going to be two of the most famous people for the last hours on earth."

CHAPTER 17

The Look

S OMETHING STOPS TANK'S SMILE as he focuses on Janine and Larry's update. What Janine is reporting is not to Tank's liking, not at all to his liking.

As he sits there stone-faced still, he lifts his fingers t o h is mouth to bellow out one of those Texas high-shrieked whistles that only a handful know how to do. Or actually spent the time practicing.

The bar becomes eerily quiet. Everyone looks at Tank, Ernie, Joe and Marian staring at the TV with their backs to them. That's an obvious cue that the TV is now controlling the mo-ment. *How appropriate.*

They all start watching the TV that's closest to them. Dana walks over to the remote and hits the volume to a level they all can hear. Janine is repeating the update again and again as TV anchors like to do. Martinez walks up to the bar standing behind Tank to fully absorb the newscast.

"Can't we just die in peace?" He says talking to himself but enough of a volume for all to hear.

Tank puts his beer down looks at Ernie, Joe, his wife and glances over his shoulder for a look at Martinez. He has that determined mission-force look. Joe and Ernie do a quick glance knowing what's going to come out of Tank's mouth next.

Ernie starts, "I know that look, chief. What are you thinking?"

"Uh-oh," Martinez adds. "The look."

"This is wrong. The kid just wanted to run a marathon with his friends. Then it becomes a circus and now an assassination chase. I can't let this happen."

Joe slumps his shoulders as he responds, "Cap, this is out of our control. We're here. Having a good time. Spending it with our family. It's time to let it go."

Tank swivels his bar stool to face Joe, "Let what go?"

"Being the guardian of good. It's over. We lost."

"We haven't lost yet. At least lost the best part which is the part we control."

Marian responds immediately, "Go get him, hon. I know how and why you tick."

Tank looks at Ernie then nods his 'you ready' head. Ernie dutifully nods back. Tank looks at Joe hoping for the answer he wants and needs. Joe stares at him silently for several very long seconds, "I'm in captain,"

Joe really has no choice. Without his comrades, he's alone. He married his job and stayed that way for two decades so ending his last day on duty makes the most sense.

"Me too," Martinez immediately chimes in.

"Looks like plans have changed, gentlemen," Tank proclaims.

"And ladies," Marian politely adds.

Tank points at the TV and with his booming voice, "The runner, Griffin. The news lady is telling us that some crazy man and probably many others are gonna hunt him down to be killed so he doesn't finish the race. For what reason? I don't know. She didn't say. But we're cops, we know what it is.

It's just bad people out there doing bad things to good people. Not in my town. I'm loading up. Anyone else interested in protecting him then I welcome your help. I signed up to serve and protect and if there was any time that we need to do that. It's now."

"Yo, Captain!" Dana yells out. All eyes turn to her. "It's obvious we all wanted to spend the last hours together. Doing what we do best," she looks around strategically using the comedic pause. "Drink!"

The gang starts laughing, toasting or chugging down.

"But I don't know about all of y'all but the only thing better would be chasing down a bunch of criminals wanting to murder innocent people together as a group. Our motorcycle APD gang together on the streets doing what we love. So Johnny and I are in."

"I'm in," Escobar raises his fist. Escobar, or Scoba as he is more commonly called, has been in the force for less than a year so is killing for action. Now he'll literally get the chance. His 6-foot body frame of pure muscle along with his Apache and Hispanic features give him the advantage of a look that can arrest you without the cuffs.

"Cap, put me on the rooftops and I'll make sure every racer finishes," Darren adds.

Tank looks around seeing the same mission in their eyes and it makes him happy. He turns around sees Ernie smiling at the camaraderie Tank so inspires and his wife smiling as always in her unwavering support.

"Thank you all," Tank says nodding in deep appreciation. "If you're joining our protective detail, make sure we all have each other's cell phones plus our comms ready. Martinez, Scoba, you brought your police motorcycles, right?"

Martinez and Escobar both respond, "Yes sir."

"Martinez," Tank says turning to him. "Stay here with your family and do what you do best. You're in central command of communications. Monitor the news lady and keep us updated at all times. Looks like that's where we get the best information."

"Yes sir."

"Need your laptop?" Melia asks looking at her father with eyes of excitement being part of something cool with the adults. She's eleven years old and knows the computer better than her old man. He's more than happy with the help.

"Please, sweetie. Thank you."

Melia is taller than most eleven years old at 5'3". She has long, sleek black hair and a face of a 35 year old sage. She has always been mature for her age and now it's her time to shine.

"Oh! And grab my pistols."

Martinez' wife, Maria, pipes in, "I'll run down and get them. Should be easy. Traffic's light today."

Maria is a spitting image of Melia or the other way around. They are lean with a cherub face that when they smile their eyes squint so much that the only thing seen is the light in their eyes.

"Wait!" Melia blurts out. "I'm coming with you."

Martinez isn't finished, "And grab all the ammo I have left. You know where those are. And bring yours!"

"We know," Maria answers.

"That's my girls!"

Maria and Melia start running towards the door as she passes Tank, she looks at him, "Don't leave until I get back. I won't be long."

"Hurry up," Tank responds. "If you get a speeding ticket, don't worry, I'll take care of it."

"Ha ha. We'll be back," she says in her best Terminator voice.

Tank turns to the group, "Okay. Listen up, people. While we're waiting on Maria, let's do an inventory check on all weapons, ammo and comm systems."

Tank goes up to the bar lays his arm fully down on the bar covering the entire width. He walks down the bar with his arm locked in place sliding all bottles, glasses and cans collecting his arm to the end. With one full swing, he thrusts all the items smashing to the floor. Now the bar top is clear and clean.

"Lay down whatever equipment we have so we can distribute to the best of the group and strategy." Tank wipes his arm clean and dry as Marian walks up to give him the 'OK' sign that his comm is still in his motorcycle bag. Tank smiles and gives her a wink. She's always one step ahead of him. He turns to Joe and Ernie, "Bring your comms?"

They quickly nod. They rode over in their police motorcycles where a backup set is always stored. Part of the perks of being best friends with the chief of Police is they get to keep their police bikes on the last day of earth.

"We are the only ones with the comms so you will be relaying information from Martinez to the group. So stay close. Looks like we may be the only ones on a direct line to Martinez so we're it as far as coordination goes."

"All of us have our cell phones so we can use those," Ernie adds.

"Have everyone plug in their phones now. It'll only be for a few minutes but bumping up the charge is important even if it's only a percentage or two. Scoba, pull up the marathon map and start calculating distances for Griffin, Candy Man and map out the best route to intercept."

"On it, Captain," Escobar responds.

"I'll be back. Need to change."

CHAPTER 18

Dying to Kill

J IMMY DRIVES HIS CADILLAC SUV through the Capitol grounds without any real care for people or items in the way while singing the 'Candy Man Can' song. He smashes into a Hyundai Sonata which jostles him but had his seatbelt on. The airbag never released which irritates him especially for the money he paid for its conspicuous consumption.

He leans over to the passenger seat and grabs the jelly jar and taps out a small rock of cocaine on the arm rest. Takes out his name badge to crush down the rock just enough to make an acceptable line of powdered pebbles. Lines it up and snorts a fast one.

He gets out with his face wincing. Takes a sip of Jack and looks around at a small militia of around 60 people in the lawn. Each have their own firearms and a white X painted or drawn somewhere on their clothes.

He takes another sip then pulls out his water bottle as a follow-up. He pulls out a cigarette, lights it and smilingly inspects his newfound troops. He climbs on the hood of his car and waves his hand, "Who's here for the hunting down and killing of our lil' hero Griffin?"

A large shout and waving of firearms erupt in unison.

"OK then. All gather around." Jimmy starts to look around at everyone and their random X's painted or drawn on themselves. "What's with the Xs?"

A young, fit man with a crazy look in his eyes yells out, "That's what the lady on TV told us to do. That's what she said you wanted us to do."

Jimmy looks at him closely. He has an imposing look that could work to Jimmy's advantage or the other way around. He must have just shaved his head prior to arriving as it's reflecting sunlight like a car's headlamp.

"Why are you here?" Jimmy asks.

Bone is wearing an army jacket without a shirt underneath, army green pants and black combat boots. The jacket has swastikas stitched on each arm and a painted white X on the front pocket. He's holding an AR-15 and two handguns shoulder holstered and a bag of ammo.

"I'm here to kill the star."

"What's your beef with Griffin?"

"People like him."

Jimmy stares at him silently. He can't tell if he's serious or not. He's wearing wrap around mirrored sunglasses so his eyes can't reveal anything and his poker face is good, almost too good.

Jimmy starts inspecting each of Xs displayed, "Unbelievable," he says talking to himself. "She is one twisted bitch. She needs to be able to better identify us killers. She is manipulating my crusade."

He addresses his newfound army. "OK. Let's get this mission straight. We are going to be honorable killers. We are not killing innocent runners, bystanders, anyone. We are specifically hunting down one person and that's it. Now if someone gets in our way or you accidentally hit others then so be it but no mass murdering. We've got standards here."

"We'll see about that," Bone mutters under his breath.

"Griffin is a puppet for the media and the establishment to manipulate us good people. They're the ones that brought this world to where we are today. And now this Griffin is yet another one of their false gods and their diversion so they can avoid blame. And, for that, he needs to die. For what he represents and the fools who follow him."

He looks around wondering if they are understanding the power of their mission or just a bunch of twits wanting to play army. *A bunch of twits*, he thinks.

"Trust me, we're doing him a favor. He will thank us all for killing him. After Griffin then we're going to hunt down the news lady and eliminate the media once and for all."

An older, balder and fatter self-proclaimed vigilante, Rob, wears a faded white 'Make America Great' tee shirt too small for public viewing shouts out to Jimmy, "What about the old man?"

"I don't know yet. I kinda like him. He's so honest that's it's refreshing, almost anti-media establishment. But, for now, let's go get us our precious winged lion."

"Huh?"

"Nothing," Jimmy says shaking his head then under his breath. "Moron."

"So, what's the game plan," Cheryl asks.

Cheryl weaved her way up to the front. She's with Jay, a younger, tent pole of a boy/man wearing blue jeans that can only stay on because of the tightened belt. He has piercing blue eyes with short comb-over blond hair interlaced with brown streaks and a look straight from GQ. His faded tee shirt was strategically chosen as it has an American flag X'd out to show loyalty to the hunt.

Cheryl is a young, good looking woman in her late 20s with a buzz haircut wearing army fatigues, a backpack with a shotgun in her hand. She has a tattoo on her neck of a red heart with a deer rifle poking through it.

"I'd like to lay out some strategic plan for you but don't have to. Chill for a moment and I'll get it for you." He pulls out his cell phone looking around at his newfound army. Cheryl sets her shotgun on her shoulder, shifts on her left leg and tilts her head inspecting Jimmy to see if he's real then looks at Jay.

Jay looks back at her then takes a long sip of his Monster drink and shrugs back with that 'I'm just here for the ride' look. Jimmy looks at both of them then winks at Cheryl as he puts the cell to his ear. Cheryl just rolls her eyes.

"Yeah," Janine answers.

"OK. Where is he? We're ready."

"I'm not telling you. That violates every code of journalistic ethics."

"Um, did I dial the wrong number? This is Janine, correct?"

"Yes, it is. Do you have news to report?"

"Well, looks like we have 80 or so strong. All with Xs on their bodies which I never ordered, by the way. Do you know who did? An ethical reporter perhaps?"

Silence.

"We are hunting Griffin and Griffin only. Please tell runners to not interfere or get in our way. As long as they do that, they will be fine. We're at the Capitol so let the hunt begin," Jimmy hangs up.

"You know that's bullshit, don't you," Cheryl says to Jimmy.

"No, I don't. What?"

"You've got 60 or so here with twitchy fingers that are here to kill people. You better keep that in mind or you'll be the first one they kill."

"They're dying to kill," Jay interjects. They both look to Jay not knowing how to respond to such wise, yet grim-like, prophesy from the boy.

Jimmy looks back to Cheryl, "What's your name?"

"Cheryl."

"Don't worry, Cheryl. I inflated the numbers of our army to instill fear in other runners to leave us alone. And, Janine's not the only one who knows how to use the media. As far as all of these twitchy fingered fucks, I have their command."

Jimmy looks behind Cheryl to see a 30-something man wearing a blue long sleeved outfitter shirt. He motions the brown haired man over. Jimmy smiles at him then bends down to whisper, "Do you mind doing me a favor?"

"Yeah, sure." The man happily returns.

"Excellent. Thank you very much. When I ask the crowd if they have my command, I want you to tell me that you'll do whatever you want, okay?"

"Okay. I guess."

"Excellent. Thank you again. Much appreciated." Jimmy smiles appreciatively then stands back up. He shouts out, "OK X army! The only way we can succeed is through a disciplined army so I need your confirmation that I have your loyalty and I am in full command. So, I want to hear it from you."

A murmur of 'yea's" permeates the crowd. The brown haired man looks at him and stalls. Jimmy smiles at him sincerely nodding his head. The brown-haired man looks back feeling better about his words, "I'll do whatever I want."

"What did you say? I'm not sure everyone heard?"

"I'll do whatever I want!"

"Fair enough," Jimmy responds as he turns his pistol to shoot brown haired man in the head dropping him instantly. The crowd turns silent. Jimmy pauses then repeats his question. "Okay X army, am I in full command?"

A 'yes sir' is loudly returned from everyone except for Bone that Jimmy didn't notice. Jimmy looks down to Cheryl, "Looks like I have their command."

CHAPTER 19

This is Austin

L ARRY IS SITTING DOWN pouring a cocktail for Leslie, a pencil thin, older man with a long brown beard standing wearing nothing but a thong, pink tutu and a tight shirt with the famous graffiti'd wall alien donning the "HI HOW ARE YOU" on it.

"So, how do you think I'm doing as the on-site talent? Pretty damn good, huh? Hey, say 'hi' to the world," Larry boasts.

Leslie looks into the camera and blows a kiss, "Hi world!"

Larry interrupts, "Do you mind stepping back just a bit. I want the world to see you in your daily dress or lack thereof." Larry says with a smile.

"Of course!"

Leslie steps back to get in full view of his regular uniform of thong, tutu and shirt. His choices of shirts change regularly. Sometimes he'll wear a wedding dress and the color of tutus changes otherwise that's Austin's Leslie.

"Larry!" Janine cuts in.

"Hey, Janine. Where've you been? Leslie and I have been entertaining the viewers."

"We've got an official news break regarding Candy Man. Official sources say he has amassed an army of nearly 100 assassins, all with Xs marked on them on the hunt to kill Griffin.

We are warning all viewers and racers to avoid Candy Man's army at all costs. He has stated that those who do not interfere will be spared and those who do will be killed. Again, avoid Candy Man and his army at all costs. You will be able to identify them by the Xs on their bodies.

Looking at the time and the course, we estimate that Griffin should be in the middle of mile 7 and 8 which would put him on Lavaca Street heading towards 15th street."

Larry shoos Leslie off then turns to the camera, "Would you shut up! Quit telling them where to go. You're demented."

"I report the news. As is. What others do with it, I can't control."

"Jesus Christ. We want Griffin to finish the race!"

"I am a reporter through and through and have to report the news accurately and fairly," Janine responds. She looks down at her monitor. "Your interview with Leslie generated 3 million more viewers and my announcement bumped us another 10. Thank you viewers for what is turning into one hell of a last race. Stay tuned as we will stay on top of this dramatic turn of events. We need more eyes on the ground so please keep tweeting me at #JanineSays. So, Larry how's it going down there?"

Larry shakes his head, takes a sip, "Well, guess I need to find another weird Austinite to interview while you help Candy Man kill our beloved hero. I don't know. I doubt if I can find anyone weirder than Leslie." Larry pauses, looks around then back to the camera. "Never mind. This is Austin. I can."

CHAPTER 20

The Queen Bee

TANK WALKS OUT OF THE BATHROOM wearing a pink, floral printed prairie dress. Looks just like those vintage, sleeveless dresses that at least one woman is mandated to wear in a TV western. And Tank is wearing one with a stone cold face that only reflects the mission he has committed to undertake.

Over the dress, he's wearing a gun belt with two handguns and a sash carrying eight magazines full of bullets. Underneath, he is still in full police uniform.

Most of the cops start cheering and clapping. Others are looking at Tank with a confused stare. Dana walks up to Ernie to whisper, "What the hell?"

Ernie turns to Dana, "What?"

"Look at Tank! He's wearing a dress for Christ sake. Does anyone notice?"

"Yeah. And your point is?"

"Tank is gay?"

"He's a cross dresser. Not gay. Big difference."

"And you've known about this?"

"Yep. I think it's common knowledge with all of the veterans in the force."

"And nobody has said anything?"

"He's a UFC world finalist, an ex Navy Seal and was awarded the Navy Cross. Are you going to say something?"

"I see your point. Does his wife know?"

"Who do you think made the dress?"

"I wonder what would happen if the public found out?"

"It's Austin. He'd probably win by a bigger landslide."

"Wow."

Tank walks up to the bar where inventory has been laid out. "OK, officers. Status report."

"We have 10 9 mms, 8 M&Ps, 4 sigs, two .30/06, one AR-15, one AK 47 and, of course Darren has his Mk 12. There's plenty of ammunition and interestingly enough Johnny had a couple of hand grenades. I didn't ask why," Ernie reports.

Tank looks at Johnny who's now in full police attire. He's dressed to serve and protect then die.

Maria and Melia return with their weapons. Melia starts emptying out her full array of a pre-teen's ammunition—laptop, Ipad, Iphone and all the cords that correspond. She smiles as she holds up a smoke grenade, "I also brought those smoke grenades lying in the back of the closet."

"Oh yeah. Forgot about those," Martinez responds focusing on his station. Melia returns a sly grin. Martinez puts the two dots together.

How did she know and what was she doing snooping around in the back of my closet? At this point, who cares. He smiles back with a quick look to her. "Good find."

Tank continues, "OK, Joe. Distribute accordingly. You know who's best with what. I've got my sigs and ammo so I'm taken care of."

Joe immediately gets to work. That's when Tank goes over to his wife and gently touches her cheek with his hand, "You're coming with us, right?"

Marian's already there. She has her brown leather coat over her Sugarland concert tee shirt holding her navy issued, nylon backpack that's seen some serious combat.

"Yes. I'm a Navy doctor, soldier and a sure shot. Really, I'm more valuable than you."

"I know. I don't feel safe without you," Tank says with a wink and a smile. "All we have to do is kill the Candy Man and the rest will scatter."

"Kill the queen bee and the hive scatters," Ernie adds.

Tank stops and looks at Ernie, "What'd you say?"

"Kill the queen bee and the hive scatters. Why?"

Tank stands there staring at him. "You just made me realize something. Candy man's not the queen bee. He's the head worker bee but not the queen." Tank grabs everyone's attention with that comment.

"Who's the queen then?"

"The news lady. As long as she can broadcast then that Crazy man knows where Griffin is. She gets the information from the viewers. Broadcasts it as if it were news. Candy man gets the *news* and goes exactly where the news lady instructs him. We need to shut her down as soon as possible. It may not stop crazy-man from hunting him but sure will make it damn near impossible to find him. Honey…"

Marian knows where this is going. "I'll go to the station and shut it down," she boldly states. "But what exactly do I do? Kill her? Not really comfortable with that option. Sort of defeats the whole spirit of the mission."

"No. Don't have to nor want to. Destroy the broadcast device. It could be a camera or hell, a laptop. Who knows these days. But you'll be able to tell. If it's a camera then you need to destroy the broadcasting studio inside the KVUT studio that's technically broadcasting the signal. Here, take this."

He hands her one of his pistols. She shakes her head 'no'. "Keep it. I brought mine. What about the other guy, Larry?"

"He's in our corner. Hell, he's the spark to this whole mission. He's doing the same thing as Janine except on the good side. We need him so Martinez, make sure you listen to him as much as Janine. "

"Got it, boss," Martinez shouts back.

"Johnny!"

"Yeah boss," Johnny says across the bar.

"Bring me one of those bad boys, would ya please."

Johnny walks over and begins to toss one of the grenades to Tank. Tank's eyes bulge as he tries to catch it but Johnny never lets go. Tank sneers at him as Johnny saunters up grinning to hand him the grenade. "Thank you." Johnny couldn't resist. There are some perks underlings get on the last day of earth.

Tank smirks back. Marian is not amused. Tank turns to his wife, "Use the gun to control her. Shoot whatever broadcast device she is using. Find the studio where all of the controls are and take this grenade." Tank holds it up to make his instructions very clear. "Take this pin out then lift this lever. Throw it in the studio then run like hell. You'll get six seconds."

"I know how to use a grenade. I served in the same two combat missions as you did," she says with that 'wife' look.

"Just making sure. That's all."

"So let me repeat your plan to get it straight. I just walk into the station, open the door, point the pistol at news lady. Shoot whatever she's looking at. Find the broadcast studio. Throw the grenade in there. Close the door as I'm running like hell. I added closing the door if you didn't notice.

Then say 'sorry' to news lady but your show has been cancelled due to bad ratings. Blow her a kiss then call you to find out what trouble you're in so I can come save you too. And during this whole time, the news lady just sits there patiently waiting on me to ruin the one thing she chose to do for her last hours of her life without a fight. That's what you want me to do?"

"It could be that simple."

"So, you don't think she'll have a gun? Or a friend there with a gun? Or several friends with AK 47s? I'm going to need more firepower."

"It very well could be which is why I'm giving you level two. Johnny!"

"Yeah, boss."

"Give her the second and bring those smoke grenades."

Johnny walks up and gently hands Marian the second grenade and lays the two smoke grenades on the table.

"If she is armed or has a small group then these will do you fine. You can smoke them out with the grenades then use the others to destroy the broadcast. If she has a small army, then call me. We'll send reinforcements. Let's find out first so we can stay as strong as possible protecting Griffin. And, she could be all by herself. You never know."

"That sounds as reasonable as can be expected in these circumstances."

"Kill the media bee and the hive will scatter. Good call," Johnny says. "Never would've thought of it that way."

"You don't fuck around do you?" Ernie says as the others start smiling. "I guess that's why you got the big bucks."

Marian looks at Tank, "I know where the station is. It's not too far so I should be there fairly soon. I'll coordinate with Maria on cell phones so Martinez can coordinate communication. This way you can stay focused. I'll call you though if I need help. Maria," Marian says turning to her. "I have your phone number programmed in mine. My phone is fully charged. Is yours?"

"It's plugged in so I'm good and I have yours programmed in mine."

Marian turns to Tank. "Stay in close contact with Maria. I'll coordinate through her."

Tank nods. "Have your gun on you? You need it close and not in your backpack."

She pulls opens up her jacket showing her 9 mm. "I guess all of that god forsaken target practice you forced me to go is going to pay off." She walks up to Tank and they embrace in a long kiss. She pats his cheek and gives him a big smile and looks to Maria. "OK, girlfriend. Let's do it."

Tank and Marian walk out the bar. She jumps onto her ruby red Sportster and puts her helmet on. "You know, I always wear a helmet when I'm on this damn thing. Protect myself from cars, pavement. Never thought I would want it for bullets."

Tank smiles as he watches her go then turns around knowing his mission begins.

Joe comes out, "Hey, we're short two guns. Otherwise they can use knives, pipes, bats, fists and whatever they can find."

Tank studies him analyzing the situation.

"Some of them didn't know they were going on active duty."

"No worries," Tank says as he pulls his two guns out and hands them to Joe. He takes off his sashes of bullets and ropes it over Joe's neck.

"What about you?"

"Don't worry. I'll be fine."

Maria rushes out the door and shouts, "Hey, news lady says Griffin should be at Lavaca heading towards Congress. If we know, that means they know. Y'all need to leave. Now!"

They all start exiting the bar, putting their helmets on and jumping on their motorcycles. Maria runs up to Tank and whispers, "She says Candy Man has a gang of nearly 100 on the hunt."

Tank looks at the twenty of them and turns to Maria, "I guess it'll be an even fight then."

CHAPTER 21

Forgiveness

G RIFFIN AND SABRINA JUST PASS mile marker five. It's
not the standard mile marker in competitive races but a
large black three-dimensional numbered '5' alongside a pictured
frame Christian angel. The '5' and angel are prominently set together on the side of a Chick Filet.

Runners need markers. Especially in races that are more than
10 miles long. It gives them time checks, context and most of all
small goals to achieve to help carry the ultimate goal of finishing
long races especially a marathon.

Griffin mapped out his alternate route and made sure it ad-
hered perfectly to the 26.2 mile of a marathon a month ago. Last
week he biked his way through the route marking the miles in
many creative and symbolic spots. He emotes a smile when they
pass his works of art especially this one.

"What's with the angel?" Sabrina asks.

"It's Angel Number 5 that according to psychics is a sign of
major changes soon to come."

"And you know this how?"

"Turns out my next door neighbor is a psychic so gave me a
free reading. She was having a 'going out of business' sale. When

she pulled out that number, I thought it would make an appropriate mile marker, don't you?"

"Remind me if tomorrow happens that we don't give you too much free time on your hands."

When Sabrina and Griffin hit the 10K range, they're entering their running zone. That's when the internal machine kicks in. The body has its focus, breathing and pace in full rhythm to conquer the 20 more grueling miles to go.

With long distance races, runners have two worlds to conquer—the physical and the mental. The physical is the easier as it can be achieved with training and practice. The mental is a different beast especially for 26 miles. Many runners count numbers in their head. Some wear earplugs full of music or motivational chants. Others just let their minds wander to whatever world they choose or the work project they need to solve.

Then there's Griffin and Sabrina who like to talk during the race. Talking for 26.2 miles or for just five minutes during a race is impossible for many runners but for others it's natural, almost mandatory. That's why Griffin and Sabrina made such good running partners.

"What ever happened with you and your parents?" Sabrina asks.

Griffin stays silent for a moment, "I called them eight months ago and talked to them, mostly to Mom and a little to Dad. It was a good conversation. I asked them to come down and spend the rest of time here in Austin. They were nice and said they would consider.

Never heard back so I called them again two weeks ago to tell them I love them and was sorry we couldn't figure it out. They didn't answer. For all I know they killed themselves."

Sabrina's being cautious. "What didn't happen?"

"Forgiveness."

"Why? What happened?"

"Nothing and everything. It's hard to explain. Dad was a surgeon. Mom was a country club wife. We lived in a big house, swanky neighborhood. I had all the trinkets a boy could ever want but never had them. Dad was bitter and Mom was cold. She would participate in my life if it looked good otherwise she'd hire it out. She wasn't mean just kept her distance.

Dad was nice but in a formal way and when it looked good otherwise my sole purpose was to represent him and the family name. And in my family, representing the family name meant being a doctor. That's what he had to do so I had to as well. He resented Grandpa all his life for making him be a doctor so I bore the brunt of it.

He made sure I would be a disappointment no matter what. Dad needed me there to punish me for being him and if I wasn't him then punish me for not being him. That's where the running came in."

Jesus, thinks Sabrina. There was always a gap in Griffin's story but she could never put it all together. *Why does it take the end of the world to reveal ourselves?*

"What do you mean, the running part?"

"Running was mine. Neither of them liked it nor were runners. Mom didn't understand the attraction. Dad just thought it was a waste of time. Dad didn't like I was good at it which made me want to be even better and made Dad even angrier. He said running wouldn't make me a doctor."

Griffin's passion for running and this last race are becoming even more understandable to Sabrina. This last race and how it got so big and out of hand wasn't a coincidence. *Coincidence doesn't exist.*

"I was 17 and we were in Provo, Utah at an American Medical Association conference. It was a big deal. Dad was a big shot in the association. On the board of directors and wanted to be President for the next year. He was in line. On the executive committee. Raised a lot of money for their charity and PAC. Did everything necessary but lost in the election.

Someone undermined him and was elected instead of him. They gave him "Benefactor of the Year" award hoping that would placate him but all it did was make him angrier. And I have never seen him so angry in my lifetime. I didn't know what a big deal it meant to him so I was oblivious to the whole thing. After the banquet, we were in the hotel room and at this point Dad was pretty drunk. And he's one of those angry drunks.

He would always start on Mom with his berating and belittling then get to me. Mom was his warm-up act so to speak. I told him to not let it get him down and go for it next year. And this is where I fucked up. I used track to try to calm him down. Maybe I did it on purpose. I don't know. Anyway, I told him it took me two meets before I won the 5000 so don't get discouraged. There's always next year.

He picked up his award and turned it upside down so the heavy part was on top like a heavy hammer. He lit into me being a pussy runner who would amount to nothing but running stupid races that got me nowhere. He threatened to bash in my knee with the award to remind him who's in charge and to end this running thing once and for all and start studying to be a doctor like him and Grandpa.

He walked up to me and asked if I want to be a pussy or a man. In other words, if I wanted to be a man then he would bash me in the knee and take it like a man, leave running and start focusing on med school. And if I want to be a pussy he would leave me alone to run alone. I couldn't afford a broken knee with a track meet one week away. I didn't know what to do. I was scared. In another no-win situation he loved to put me in. He screamed at me to look him straight in the eyes like a man and answer his question.

I kept staring at the ground hoping he would stop. Just let me go to my room. He waited and when I wouldn't look up, he said 'that's what I thought, you are a pussy, get out of my sight'. I left to go to my room and didn't look him in the eye for several months. And even after that, it never was the same. Even worse than before. I hated him and I hated myself.

When I received my track scholarship to the University of Oregon, I left it on their bed and headed to Austin. Got a job at Guero's then met you."

Griffin pauses searching inwards for redemption. "I should have said something to him long ago. I should have said something that night. I should have looked at him eye to eye daring him to go ahead and hit me. At least I would have stood up for myself but I didn't and it has haunted me ever since."

"I'm so sorry Griffin. I had no idea." Sabrina feels awful for not knowing the full story. *Like Raul said, I should have listened to my own advice.*

"You definitely couldn't have related. Your parents are perfect."

"They're not perfect but pretty damn close."

"Which is why you're perfect."

"I'm far from perfect but thank you."

Griffin and Sabrina run together in reflective silence then Sabrina blurts out, "How many kids would we have?"

"Um. I don't know. How many would you like?"

"Two."

"Well, you said that quickly. Been planning that number for a while?"

"Yep."

"And the reason is?"

"With two, you have a perfect foursome for Just Dance, Monopoly, card games and doubles tennis. And almost all cars and dinner tables fit four perfectly. And, you don't have the woe-is-me, pathetic middle child."

"Aren't you a middle child?"

"Exactly. Where are my parents? I'm thirsty now and we're coming up to mile 6."

"Listen to you. You know you can always count on your parents. Cuz, there they are."

CHAPTER 22

Run Away

C HERYL WALKS UP TO JIMMY holding her Iphone, "Griffin is at mile 9 on Lavaca Street heading towards 6th Street. What's odd is that he's not on the course. They took a different route. That's why it's taken so long to find him."

"Hmm. Wonder why he's running a different route and how do you know that?"

"The news lady just announced it."

"That's my gal. That's like 10 blocks away. This'll be easy." Jimmy starts barking to the group. "Need 10 of you get on 16th and head towards Lavaca. Need 10 of you get on 15th head for Lavaca. Rest of ya, come with me."

"Is Lavaca a street or a restaurant?" says Rob scratching his belly.

"Jesus," Jimmy looks to Rob staring at him. *I should kill him right now.*

Don and the group have finally given some separation to the crowd. Add the fact that Lori dumped the GPS at the beginning of the race they are in better positioning than originally planned. Gilbert looks around to see they have some room to spare. "Slow down to a 7. We're not here to win. We're here to give Griffin the distraction to run his race."

They all match Gilbert's pace as he slows down 30 seconds per mile. Thirty seconds slower per mile feels like slowing down 10 minutes per mile at that pace and length.

Lori wanted to make it more difficult for the news lady so she and Gilbert mapped out their alternate route. Good idea J-Lo, they all relayed. With Don's outrageous costume, though, photos are still being posted, twittered and Facebooked enough for the crowds to find them and catch up.

"I should just punch them out," Raul says referring to the continued stream of strangers approaching them for some 'close to greatness' blessing.

"You're part of a running team not American football team," Gilbert says.

"I'm not usually a supporter of Raul's approaches," Lori inserts. "But I've seen points in our run where I wanted to punch them out too. I think it's time for step two of the plan."

"I'm all for it," Don responds. "I like we're expediting our steps to get lost in the crowd. I'm not sure how to explain it but the attention isn't real. It's like a commercial."

"Okay," Coach Gilbert says. "Up here at Brazos, we take left. Then off to a sprint to MLK. That should help throw off parasites."

"Thank you," Raul interjects looking at Lori who nods in return.

An 'amen' comes from Don when he is abruptly interrupted by a middle-aged woman riding up behind them on her bicycle. *Not another crazy.*

She gets in alignment to their pace, looks to Don and tells him in a frantic voice, "You need to get out of here. Hide. Run away. Something. There's a whole mob coming to kill you." She looks back. "Now!"

"What?" Gilbert says.

"What are you talking about?" Raul says in a protective voice. Raul spent most of his childhood fending for himself so part of his path to manhood was unfortunately with fists and guile. He senses this is a moment for both.

She looks at Raul, "It's just been reported on the news that some crazy man and his gang are coming to kill you. She said the street number and everything. That's how they know. So they're right there behind the corner."

All of them look back knowing she's real. Lori absorbs the information watching the woman being hysterical but genuine. "Let's go!"

At that moment, they start hearing shots fired and the crowds across the street screaming and running. Don looks across the street, "Come on, we need to hide."

Jimmy and his gang arrive to the scene where Janine calculated Griffin would. Jimmy scans the area. He can't get a good assessment with it being so crowded with runners and onlookers.

Bone sees Jimmy's frustration and decides to make the clutter easier and takes out his AR-15 and starts mowing down dozens of runners with an ease the weapon allows. Jimmy looks at him in dismay as he directly disobeys his first order. Once Bone finishes enough of the runners, he turns to Jimmy with a glare of defiance and victory murdering a dozen or so runners who happen to be at the wrong place at the wrong time. Or as Bone made it so.

"What?" Bone says looking at Jimmy with steel defiance. "You made it clear to leave everyone alone that didn't get in our way or pose a threat. Correct?" Bone looks around then turns back to Jimmy. "They were in the way. I took care of it."

"Unbelievable," Jimmy responds locking eyes with Bone.

He turns around and happens on Cheryl's gaze with that 'I told you so' look. He turns to Bone.

"OK. Thank you. I guess. Now that you've given us clear vision. Where are they?" Bone just looks at him coldly, no answer. "That's what I thought."

Bone's anger just jumped a couple of notches.

Don and group jump through a smashed window into Dan's Hamburger restaurant. The inside looks trashed. The booths and tables are locked into the cement floor so only chairs are strewn throughout. They head towards the back hoping no one saw them.

CHAPTER 23

Griffin's Mine

JIMMY STARTS LOOKING AROUND to get some sort of fix on the situation. The area is now clear of runners. He looks across the street at an old man sitting on a barber chair outside an old-time barber shop. It's almost as if he's waiting for his haircut. Or in this instance, a haircut and shave. He definitely could use it. Add a bath. And some clothes that have been washed in the past year.

But the old man just sits there, staring him down trying to hypnotize Jimmy into the same trance. Then with pure conviction, he points to Dan's Hamburger behind Jimmy across the corner. Jimmy pauses but his light pops on. He smiles and looks behind him.

He starts waving to the group pointing at Dan's, "Ten of you, go to the back, stand guard and make sure no one escapes. The rest of you, break up to stand on each side of the doors as back up."

Jimmy salutes the old man who smiles back. He looks to the remaining, "Griffin's mine." Jimmy turns around and enters through the smashed glass. Bone follows him closely.

"Warriors, come out and play-ee-ay," Jimmy chants. Jimmy turns around to see Bone on his tail and gives an irritated face. Cheryl, Rob and Jay carefully enter but several yards back.

Jimmy walks quietly behind the counter heading through the kitchen looking around with gun ready. Jimmy sees a closet with the door slightly open. He smiles and approaches the door and casually opens it. It's empty.

He heads towards the very back and one side is a bathroom and the other is the walk-in freezer. Both doors barely open. He looks at each and picks the freezer. He slowly opens it and there they are. They have their hands up staring straight at Jimmy with frightened looks. Jimmy inches out a devilish grin, "The me a t locker. How appropriate."

Don blurts out, "I'm not Griffin! I'm no t Gr iffin! We'r e the decoys. Please don't shoot us."

Jimmy's grin turns to a perplexed look then anger, "Come out of there. What are you saying? Come out!"

The group quickly exits. They look at Bone's chilling eyes on their left then pause to Jimmy's angry eyes on their right. Being cornered, they huddle against the checkered tile wall.

Jimmy goes to Don, grabs his cap then glasses and slings them across the kitchen to look at him close up. Don's eyes reveal the fear grip-ping him frozen. Jimmy tilts his head back and forth inspecting him closely.

"You're not Griffin. Wh at th e fu ck. Wh y ar en't yo u? Wh at the fuck kind of game are you playing?"

They all stay silent not knowing what to do.

"Tell me!" Jimmy points his gun at Don's face.

Lori takes charge as usual, "Griffin couldn't handle all of the attention. He never wanted it so we came up with a plan that Don act and look like him so he could run it by himself. That's it."

"Well, where the hell is he?!"

"We not know. Could be anywhere?" Gilbert answers. Jimmy turns his gun straight to Gilbert's forehead. Gilbert is unfazed.

Lori, "We don't know! Really. There are so many courses out there and he never told us which one he chose in the end."

Bone inserts himself irritating Jimmy further, "Is he even running the race?"

"We think."

"Then tell me where he is!"

Lori keeps trying to cool the situation down. "Look, the race got so big so quickly that new, alternate routes were springing up daily. That's why you see streams of runners everywhere on different routes. They could be on any of them. Or they could've made their own. We don't know."

Jimmy starts blinking and becoming unbalanced. He reaches for the tall, metal shelf next to him but misses. He crashes his body into the shelf throwing the few pots and pans left clanging to the wall and floor.

It's a confusing scene now. There's a duality of the maniacal killer to the bumbling idiot. Jimmy crawls himself on to the side of the toppled shelf, breathing heavily trying to maintain consciousness. He sits up on the side of the shelf to stare at the floor wiping the pouring sweat from his forehead. He stays silent for what seems forever then starts crying mumbling to himself, "How did it come to this? Where did it go so wrong?"

Bone is looking at him in disgust while the others are surprised and don't know what to do. Jimmy waves his gun looking down and crying, "Just go. Leave me. Get outta here."

The group looks at Bone with his AR-15 in a twitching hand not knowing what the next move will be. As they start to cautiously leave, Gilbert looks down at Jimmy, "Why Griffin? Why murder?"

That makes them all stop. Jimmy's head is still drooping to the ground. He's slowly regaining his composure as the crying stops to answer his question in a weak, quivering voice, "Why not?"

Lori turns around all the while Don can't believe they're having this conversation when Jimmy's letting them leave alive. "No. Seriously. Why? He didn't do anything to you. You don't even know him."

"How do you know I don't know him?" Jimmy responds looking up at her.

"Do you?"

"No."

Lori just shakes her head and looks to the guys especially Don who is about to jump out of his skin. She nods her head to the direction of the door. She understands they need to go before one of them changes their mind. Bone is giving her the look of death, literally.

"Then why?" Raul presses the question. Jimmy's head is still weaving back and forth staring blankly to the floor.

"I want to kill him because I don't like him."

Gilbert and Don see that Raul is pushing his limits. They open their eyes wide to get his attention. Bone enters the conversation. The tone turns dangerously dark, "Yeah. I don't like him either. And I don't like any of you either so let's finish this conversation with a bullet in your heads."

"No." Jimmy blurts out as best as he can. "Leave them alone."

"Yeah," Don adds feeling really scared now. "Listen to the Dentist."

"Psychiatrist," Jimmy corrects him. "Let them go. They have nothing to do with this."

Bone's teeth begin to clench, "No. They're his friends. They tried to fool us. They need to die."

"Don't do it!" Jimmy is still trying to regain composure but can't so is at a clear disadvantage. "They're just followers. The idiot followers that don't know any better. Let them go."

Raul and Lori are trying very hard to let the 'idiot followers' comment go. Don could give a shit as long as 'alive' is part of their names. Gilbert remains stoic.

"Bone, let's regroup," Cheryl says walking into the kitchen with Jay. Rob stayed behind. Cheryl's doing the classic redirect to get Bone focusing on another subject. "Griffin's still out there so we need to formulate a new plan."

Jay is standing behind Cheryl, her confidence and her weapon realizing this death mission is too real for his comfort. Cheryl looks at the group, "Come on guys. Get outta here. We have business to conduct and you're in the way."

Lori looks sternly at her gang, "Come on. Let's go. They don't want us here."

This time their pace quickens as they exit the restaurant. Cheryl and Jay follow them. Bone can't believe what he is seeing, looks down at Jimmy still staring at the floor. Disgusted, he follows the group outside.

They all walk out to the gang looking at them intensely, guns aimed at them not knowing what to do. When they see Cheryl and Jay waving them off, they relax their weapons looking for answers.

Gilbert and the group move quickly through them with their heads down praying they walk away alive. Each of the X men look to Cheryl wondering what's going on.

Bone walks out, "That's not Griffin. They're decoys. Griffin's still out there so we need to track him down. Candy Man is crying like a baby in there so it's up to us to find him. Griffin could be anywhere. Apparently, there are all sorts of routes so someone google something to find these alternate routes. Call in the other groups and call that news lady bitch."

"What about them?" Rob says pointing to Gilbert and the group.

"Kill them. I'm in charge now."

Each of the runners can't believe what they just heard. They squeak out to be an inch away from safety to then be killed. Even on the last day of earth, this is still way too unfair.

"Wait," says a voice. Bone turns around to Jimmy's pistol pointed at his head. BANG. Bone falls to the ground with a bullet dead in the forehead.

"You've been relieved of duty," He looks to the gang. "Call in the other groups and tell them we're formulating a new attack plan. Oh, what else did he say? Oh yeah. I'm in charge. Any questions?"

Jimmy looks at the Griffin decoys and nods his head to leave. Gilbert and gang leave immediately. The hunters stay at full attention to Jimmy whose now schizophrenic personality has returned to the murdering cokehead.

Jay politely raises his hand. Jimmy turns to him, "Yeah?"

"Uh, not to state the obvious, but why don't we just wait at the finish line and kill him when he arrives?"

"You obviously don't have a girlfriend. What in the fuck is the fun in that? We have, what, four hours left and you want to sit at a finish line waiting? No. I'm spending these last hours on the hunt and making it a hunt and kill that will last onto the next incarnation. Still, good point. Need a group to head to the finish line as a last resort if you want. Any volunteers?"

A group of ten raise their hand. Noticeably, Jay doesn't.

"OK. I don't want you at the finish line as that defeats the whole point. Camp out at mile 24 or so and keep a close watch. You're our last line of defense. Who has cell phones?"

They all raise their hands.

"Good. Pull them out and dial my number. Ready? 512-567-5970. You three in the front leave these names I now give you." He points to each one as he christens them.

"You, Larry. You, Moe and you Curly. You three in the back. You're Lock, Stock and Barrell," he points to his right to the group of four together. "You're the Avengers. This way I'll know you're the four."

The crowd enjoyed that name calling with chuckles throughout. The three stooges and their compatriots weren't as amused.

"Why don't you just use our real names?" Curly yells out.

"Shut up and just go with it. Makes you special so I remember your importance."

That was enough of a flattering response to placate them.

"And make sure each of your groups are not together. Spread yourself in three groups through miles 23, 24 and 25 so we have three patrols to make sure they don't finish."

Moe waves his hand to the newly anointed gate keepers, "Come on. I know the perfect spots."

CHAPTER 24

We Did Our Job

G ILBERT AND TEAM RUN pass the corner out of sight from the X soldiers to slow down to a pacing walk and controlled breathing. They are trying to detangle the web of emotions jolting through their body. That's when Raul sees the old grizzly, bearded man sitting on a barber's chair.

Raul finds it unusual on this day that his attention has not for one second landed on the four runners. Grizzly man is purposely avoiding them. Raul also notices there is no one around. All runners have diverted their route to avoid the corpses and crying injured. Raul turns around to see where he is sitting, the line of sight views Dan's perfectly. Raul stares at the motionless buzzard of a man who gazes at nothing especially Raul. That's all Raul needs.

Raul walks up to Grizzly man and without hesitation lands a straight right to his jaw that knocks him over the chair. He lifts the old man who looks to be 120 pounds and slams him into the glass. The crack in the 1950s window and the old man's face show the force Raul used.

Lori bolts off followed by Don and Gilbert, "What are you doing?! Leave him alone!"

Raul turns around as he lets go to give gravity its turn to drop the old man to the sidewalk. He's still alive but debatable on whether he's conscience. Raul looks at them, "Come on."

"What the hell are you doing?"

"Look around you, Lori. No one is around here." He points to Dan's. "There is perfect sight to Dan's where we went to hide. The only way they knew where we were was because of him."

"And you know this for sure?"

"Yes, as soon as I saw through his eyes. I knew it was him."

"You more aggressive than I thought," Gilbert says in an analytic voice. "You never showed that in all the years I've known you."

"I kept in check because of you and the running club."

Each of them stay silent until Gilbert commands, "Let's go."

"Not yet," Don says with an unusual forceful tone. Don turns back and walks over the defeated traitor into the darkness of the barber shop. The group stand there looking at each other wondering what the hell is he doing.

After, what seems 30 silent hours, Lori's impatience gets the better of her, "Hey! Where are you? We need to go!"

Don appears from the shadows without a beard, vest, shirt and wearing a new smile. He still has his full head of hair though. He proudly proclaims, "I am no longer Griffin. I don't want to be. We did our job. Let's run this race as a race and a team and not a distraction."

Without the disguise, Don doesn't look like Griffin. He still has the same body but has a much more a chiseled face and pointy chin. He keeps rubbing his face as it always feels so different after months of a beard is eliminated in two minutes. He feels relieved, happy.

"You realize that eliminates our ability to help Griffin, don't you?" Lori says.

"No. We did our job. Our whole purpose was to protect him and divert everyone's attention. Now the group that wants to kill him have found out so our ability to help is gone no matter what. We did our job enough to distract the crowds, media and the murderers for enough time to give Griffin his race back."

"He's right," Raul looks to Lori. "He or someone else has already called the news lady and she's reporting it. No matter what, we created enough chaos and distraction. Griffin and Sabrina are on such a different course we did what we meant to do. In fact, our anonymity may come in useful."

Coach Gilbert looks to the three, "Okay. Run."

CHAPTER 25

Does it Hurt?

"ALL RIGHT LADIES, call all troops here and quickly," orders Jimmy.

He is back to his cocaine confidence which means he wants another line. He holds up his index finger, "Stay here and I'll be right back."

Jimmy walks back into Dan's. He looks around to see the booth that needs the least cleaning. He takes his backpack off and sets it down on the table to unzip the main compartment. He wipes off the table with his hand then wipes it even cleaner with the bottom of his Hawaiian shirt. He pulls out the jar of cocaine with a smile.

Jay, Cheryl and Rob have self-initiated themselves as Jimmy's top soldiers so follow him inside. Cheryl has replaced her shotgun with Bone's AR-15. She views it as a symbolic 'I told you so' to Jimmy who best listen to her from now on.

He taps out a half-gram rock. Closes the jar quickly so no chance of spilling any precious cargo. He takes his name badge and places it on top and firmly presses down. The rock crumbles more and more in response to the pressure.

When he has the proper time and table then his cocaine line-to-be process is done to the most professional degree. On the last day of earth, he masterfully controls everything. Or so he has convinced himself.

He continues his well mastered art of cocaine preparation when he looks up at Jay, Cheryl and Rob, "You want a line?"

Jay looks at Cheryl then Rob not knowing what to say. Cheryl quickly answers, "Sure. Jay wants one too." She sees Jay's hesitation so answers for him. His body language has made it clear that he's never done it before.

Rob immediately follows, "Fuck yeah."

They each set their weapons down knowing it will soon be replaced with a straw and claiming this time as a party break. They relax their stance watching Jimmy continue as the line cook. Jimmy takes his name badge, turns it side-ways so the edge is now chopping the pebbles to a fine powder. In what seems excruciating minutes for the three waiting, he artfully creates four long lines.

He grabs his cigarette pack from his front shirt pocket, opens it up and pulls out his $1000 dollar bill and rolls it up in a thin, tight tube. He hands the bill to Jay. "Here. Use it like a straw."

Jay looks at Cheryl. He's nervous to almost a point of embarrassment. He's never done anything remotely like this in his life. "I just snort it up? Does it hurt?"

Cheryl looks back with a slight grin, "A little. First thing is to exhale all your breath out away from the lines." She says emphatically and with experience. Blowing away an hour of a cocaine high is a tough lesson to learn in the party world.

"Then hold one nostril with your finger then stick the straw down to the line and breathe up the line through your nose. That's why it is called snorting. And do it forcefully and quickly."

Jay still looks like he doesn't get it. Cheryl knows it's more his fear than interpretation. "In other words, inhale with one nostril. You'll see. Just a little jolt, that's it."

Jay holds the rolled-up bill with a wary look at the line not knowing if this is the right thing to do. Looks back up at Cheryl who is now smiling watching his internal debate. Jimmy is getting impatient. He holds out his hand, "Here, give it to me."

Jay is now feeling a little embarrassed for not knowing the snorting protocol and then gets even more embarrassed for being embarrassed. He's in full internal debate. He hands the bill to Jimmy who snatches it out of his hand and looks at Jay as his new student.

"Put the bill in one nostril while pressing down on the other."

He's pairing his words to his motions so Jay can see how to proceed.

"Let out a deep breath up above so you don't blow the caine all across the table. Bend down then inhale the line up quickly. And follow the line while snorting in."

Jimmy turns away from the table, lets out a deep breath, holds his left nostril, bends down to the table and snorts the line in an instant. He does it so easily and quickly, it's almost like a signature that's been honed down. It's more of an autograph motion than an addict move.

He looks up with squinted eyes and a nasally voice, "There, that's how it's done." Jimmy hands the bill back to Jay who gently takes it like Excalibur bestowed upon him. He looks at Cheryl who smiles slyly back. With Cheryl's approval, he does a quick nod.

He puts the rolled-up bill to his nose, exhales away from the lines just like they emphatically instructed. He bends down then places the bill on the surface of the table at the end of one of the three carefully sculpted lines. From his point of view staring so closely, the 6 inches of the white powdered line looks a mile long.

In nose combat mission, he takes one long inward breath and sweeps the line to nothing. Jay's eyes go wide that make the other three start laughing remembering their first time.

"Whoa. Oh. Whoa," he blurts out. "Jesus!"

Jay stands straight and starts walking around as if he's trying to put out a fire in his nose. He winces at the jolted pain shooting through his throat and nose. He keeps pacing around as the numbness starts seeping down while the pain slowly dissolves. He's noticing some deeper feeling and energy creeping inside.

His confused, irritated look is turning into eyes with light bulbs just turned on. He smiles at Cheryl smiling back then looks at Jimmy with a nasally voice, "May I have another?"

Now they all start laughing even more. Jimmy sagely advises, "Hold on there, cowboy. You don't need more right now. It hasn't even started to seep in. Just wait. Enjoy that line and in about 40 minutes then do another. Here."

Jimmy says to Jay as he ignores Cheryl and Rob standing there anxiously waiting their turn. And it looks like their turn may take way longer than they want. Jimmy starts fumbling around each pocket on his medical jacket then reaches into the side pocket. He drops his head in disbelief then looks up taking out his book of blank prescription notes.

"Of all the ironies to find my script pad. Unbelievable." He rips out one, puts it flat on the table. Grabs several good size rocks out of the jar and puts it in the paper then folds them tightly in it. Then wraps that into another paper script for safe keeping then hands it to Jay.

"Here. This is yours. You saw how it's done so when you're Jones-ing, just make yourself a line and have at it. What I gave you should be 7 to 8 really big lines or 15 good size lines so that will take care of you big time until the end. You can even share with that amount. But do each line 30 to 40 minutes apart otherwise you'll waste the rock and the high."

"I don't want to take all of yours."

"Don't worry, kid. The first rule of being the drug host is always keep a hidden stash or two so I'm fine. Do you have a straw or a dollar bill?"

"Uh, no. I didn't bring any money. Didn't think I would need any. Can I use one of these straws?" He points to the straw dispenser on the order counter.

"Yeah. Take one of those but cut it in half. Those are too long."

"Thank you. I really appreciate it. Truly."

"Polite kid, isn't he," Jimmy says to Cheryl.

"Where's our personal stash?" Cheryl asks.

"Not so polite girl. Have patience, my pretty."

"It's my turn," Rob interrupts pushing his way forward with full grin of anticipation. Jimmy just looks at him shaking his head with annoyance.

"Ladies first," Jimmy hands the bill to Cheryl.

Cheryl grabs the bill as it's now her turn to be knighted. She lines it up, snorts it with precision then hands the bill to Rob whose nose is twitching like an anteater. He snorts his line even faster. They too start walking around wincing at the jolts. Jimmy pulls out his liquor bottle and takes a quick swig giving him a look of another pain.

Following proper indulgent protocol of rock, liquor and cigarette, Jimmy pulls one out and lights up. Jay, Cheryl and Rob head to the door to meet the others outside. All of sudden, a motorcycle slams into the X men waiting outside.

CHAPTER 26

They're Scattering

T ANK LEAPS OFF HIS MOTORCYCLE letting it slide into the first of Jimmy's six X-marked soldiers flipping them over or sliding their bodies into the van behind them. Only one of them somewhat escaped the slam. A bearded professor like man with a McCallum High School Band tee shirt was able to keep grasp of his gun and staggers around to point at Tank's chest but too late.

With a forward up kick to the hand, the gun flies into the air. The kick is quickly followed by a right punch slamming against his face thrusting him to the light pole behind him. Tank picks up the gun and shoots him dead.

Tank quickly turns to the other five and with precision aim, executes each one before they could even stand straight up. Behind Tank, the rest of his troops ride up. They distribute themselves shooting any X army that fall in their sight. The surprise gave them quite the advantage, already 15 X men down.

Not enough though as a response happens as quickly as their attack. To their right, one of the X soldiers carries a weapon of mass bullet-fire destruction. Tank sees four of his men fall to the ground.

Jimmy and his three-man posse witness the attack stunned. Jimmy throws his cigarette to the floor and turns to run out the back door. Jay just stands there. It's one thing to say you're going to kill, it's another to witness it. Cheryl grabs him and they turn to follow Jimmy. Rob is already out the back door.

Tank ducks under the side of the car as the bullets fly. He looks through the car window and now sees the shooter but only from the chest down. He's not sure how many bullets are left in his *borrowed* gun but doesn't have time to check.

Tank carefully aims and shoots through the window to hit the X man in his right leg. Blood shoots out but he's still standing and shooting. Tank fires three more times and the man goes down. He's not sure if he's dead but he's down and not shooting at the moment.

Tank's bullets are gone so he goes to grab one from the other dead soldiers but is prevented by another X man approaching with a shotgun. He jumps up to the building pole, turns around when the double barrel fires hitting mostly the pole with some of the pellets hit the back of Tank's arms.

The shotgun cocks again but an empty click goes off. Tank quickly bends down to grab another pistol then turns around to shoot but his attacker is already around the corner. Tank turns back around and sees the machine gunner loading another magazine while laying on the ground bleeding to death. Tank shoots him in the head eliminating that danger.

The bulk of the chaos is moving down the street so Tank heads to his motorcycle laying on its side with the wheels slowly turning. All of sudden, Tank's gun is knocked out of his hand by a shotgun swing. Tank tries to turn around but is slammed into the car then has the shot gun thrown over his head to pin his neck in a choke hold.

Tank grabs the shotgun that is still hot so burns him slightly. He sees the attacker's hand holding a crushed up animal cookie box preventing his hands from burning. *Hadn't thought of that use for animal cookies.* Tank starts back pedaling as fast as he can. He's 'pushing the rope' leaving his attacker off balance trying to maintain control. Just where Tank wants him.

Tank rams his attacker into the brick building behind them rendering his attacker breathless dropping the shotgun. Tank picks up the shotgun from the sidewalk, turns around and swings the butt like a baseball bat into his skull dropping him to the ground either unconscious or dead. As long as he's not moving Tank doesn't care.

Tank looks around surveying his troops. Seven lay dead and another is screaming in pain. He stares at his wounded soldier for a moment shaking his head. At that time, Darren and Escobar drive up.

Tank picks up a pistol then looks at Darren and Escobar for an intense second then walks over to his injured soldier. Tank stares into his eyes with love and mercy and shoots him square in the head. His soldier is no longer in pain.

He turns back to Darren and Escobar emotionless. He starts collecting ammo and other firearms the dead X soldiers left. He needs to be armed with this many attackers. He picks up a deer rifle and shakes his head. *A deer rifle? Really?*

"Hey sharpshooter. You can have some help now. Escobar, go with him." Tank throws Escobar the rifle. "Jump on a roof or balcony and give us some cover. Quickly. We need to head down there and help the guys."

Darren eyes up the Driskill Hotel down the street that has a wide view from the third-floor balconies. Darren shoots off, "Follow me!"

Tank grabs his comm, "Martinez."

Martinez back, "Copy."

"Well, if we were to actually believe the news woman and 100 are out there then they are now 75 so log them down." All of sudden a rifle shot goes off. He knows it's Darren's.

"74." Another rifle shot. "73."

Tank looks at the back of each of his arms. They're both bloody with red welps glowing. And a hand that is nearly broken from a shotgun barrel slamming down it. He wipes the blood off on his newly made dress. "And, Martinez, we lost seven. Maybe more."

CHAPTER 27

Meet Your New Son-in-Law

"**H**I, MOM!" says Sabrina breathing heavier. The parents smile widely holding out their arms taking turns hugging her. Dad's holding two Gatorade bottles ready. Griffin takes one pacing back and forth nodding his head in sincere thanks for the needed drink.

Their course sent them into 'restaurant row'. Many of the restaurants used to be homes back in the 20s. Now they're mostly locally owned restaurants with a few law offices and interior design companies. Griffin made sure to create as pleasing route possible under the circumstances. This area is full of large Texas live oaks and elm trees giving a feel of long and peaceful lives.

Even in this area, though, several burned out cars scatter the street and a law office now burned to the ground. Probably from a former client who got screwed from a divorce or wrongful termination case. They're meeting underneath the spray painted "666" marker on the side of the Shells Italian Restaurant. Shells is one of theirs and the running clubs' favorite restaurants. Runners need their carbs and pasta is loaded with them.

On the brick wall, the 6s are painted thematically in red. The first and third 6 are much smaller so as to still mark mile 6 but also to add some of Griffin's sick humor. Sabrina looks at Griffin, "Really? 6-6-6?"

"What? I think on this day that presentation of our 6-mile marker seems appropriate, don't you?"

Sabrina just rolls her eyes then looks at her parents, "Meet your new son-in-law."

"Uh. Well. Okay," Mom says with a puzzled look.

Griffin chimes in, "We just got married. We're planning on two kids and counting on you two to watch them a lot."

Mom turns to Sabrina, "Are you pregnant, dear?"

"Geez, Mom. Just play along, will ya? You're already falling into the crazy mother-in-law category."

Griffin's having fun as the new son-in-law. "We're going to play a lot of Monopoly and doubles tennis."

Now even more puzzled, Mom responds after a pause, "Uh. Okay."

Dad's still on the sideline wondering if he'll ever be included.

Sabrina grabs her Gatorade and now Dad feels he finally accomplished something.

Sabrina continues, "You are just too easy. Wish the world would still be alive. We would have had a field day with you."

Dad finally interjects, "Now leave your Mother alone. She may be crazy but would be a great grandmother and mother-in-law." Mom turns to Dad who's grinning and gives him that 'we'll be having a discussion on this later' look.

"Couldn'ta asked for a better son-in-law," Dad sincerely proclaims.

Griffin's smiling, nodding while continuing his pacing and breathing, "Thank you. Likewise. I already think of you as my parents anyway."

Dad smiles, honored with the comment. "How are the crowds?"

"Not too bad. And are beginning to thin out as the race goes on. Our route overlaps several others so some spots can get crowded. Hopefully when we hit mile 17, the crowds will be thinned out enough to keep running a pace without weaving and dodging."

"Is that when you get back on the main course?"

"We get back on course at mile 23. I tried as hard as possible to limit our path with the pack."

"Come on, hubby. Let's go!" Sabrina commands.

Griffin looks at the parents, "Bye Mom. Bye Dad."

They each smile then Sabrina hugs each again, tears welling up.

"Bye. See ya at mile 13!" Sabrina yells as they resume their run.

"Bye!" yells Mom.

"Love y'all!" yells Dad. He turns to his wife, "Well, looks like your dream came true after all. Sabrina got married, planning some kids and settling down."

"Ha-ha-ha."

CHAPTER 28

Nice to See You Again

O N THEIR MOTORCYCLES, Joe and Ernie move slowly up to the corner of Congress and 6th. On their right, the State Capitol looms Texas proud staring down Congress Ave. Unsuspecting runners keep streaming through without a clue of the ensuing battle. Joe and Ernie have learned to erase them from their minds to stay focused.

On their left down on the corner of 5th and Congress, there are six X soldiers behind a white truck T-boned to a Cadillac SUV. It makes a perfect triangle for front and side cover. They're shooting up at the Driskill trying to get rid of snipers Darren and Escobar. Across the corner on their left, there are four X-soldiers behind a row of cars tipped on their sides shooting down Congress at Johnny and Dana.

Joe and Ernie back their motorcycles to the wall of the Austin Museum of Art out of sight. They dismount and walk silently against the wall.

Ernie is in front so gets first look. "Those across the corner are shooting at Darren and Scoba but because the SUV, we can't get a good shot. These down here…," he nods towards the sidewalk.

"…are a different story. If we get closer, they're sitting ducks but then we become sitting ducks for the six across the street."

Joe is looking back and forth at the two sets of firing X-men trying to formulate a plan. He has one but it'll take some finesse and is dangerous. He looks back to Ernie, "Come on. Let's take down these four then be the decoy for the six over there. They have to move at least six feet from the truck into the street to get a good shot. That could be enough room for them to be easy targets for Darren and Scoba."

Joe pulls out his phone and calls Darren. Darren answers on the third ring, "Yes."

"Darren, you two focus on the six behind the white truck. We're going to get the four in front of us then hopefully draw the six out enough for your sharpshooting asses."

"Okay. But do it quickly. There are six of them."

"Who's shooting below you?"

"Johnny and Dana."

"Call them to be prepared to move against them once we take out the four."

Joe turns to Ernie, "We're going down the sidewalk to get in range to kill those four then run as fast as we can to that truck for cover and to lure them out. We just have to get these four while we're on the move. Ready?"

Ernie nods. They turn the corner running stealthy to get in range. The existing gunfire gives them the distraction they need. Once they hit twenty yards away, they stop, plant their feet and start shooting.

The first two go down easily as their backs are against them. The next two go down but straight through the heart as they turn around. The six across the street turn to see the new attack.

Ernie runs for cover against the lone Silverado parked on the street. Joe stays to be open targets for the six looking for blood. But to be shot, the attackers have to leave their cover from Darren and Escobar. Joe's also counting on the shooters to be some schmucks who needed some excitement and aren't very good shots.

Darren sees a young Hispanic man with a Spurs jersey and an older white man wearing a sports jacket two sizes too small emerge from the cars pointing across the street. He whispers, "Three, two...". The Spurs player has just been ejected from the game. He shifts his gun to the older white man, "Three, two...". He, too, has been ejected. Joe runs behind the Silverado giving the sign of the cross that his risky move worked.

Escobar is not a sniper and has a deer rifle that is not his weapon of choice. He tells Darren he'll meet him downstairs as he pulls out his sig and heads for the stairs. The four X men left look like they are either from a gangsta rap band, a gang or both.

The four X men move to lean their backs against the brick wall needing to reload or take a breather. They are covered from gunfire except from east or west down 5th street. Their position also gives them the escape if they can keep Joe and Ernie in check to the north and Johnny and Dana on the south. They don't know about Escobar yet.

Escobar runs down six floors of the historic Driskill hotel to the lobby. He instinctively goes to the back and takes a left to run around the building's side where the shooters are.

He quickly looks down to see four X men against the wall. He sees the lead X man with a backwards Under Armor cap looking across the street for their getaway. It's a wide street so they need 30 seconds to get out of target range to fully escape. They know they're outnumbered.

Escobar's eyes go wide seeing them fully exposed. He ducks behind a white minivan to gauge their next move. They're reloading and Escobar can see they're about to bolt. Escobar and his fellow soldiers need as little enemies as possible. And in this instance, getting rid of enemies means killing them.

He sees their leader wave to them. It's now or never. He takes out his Glock 19 and walks out from behind the minivan methodically shooting straight at the four with one hand his sig, the other his Glock. It's still a block and half but enough of easy targets to at least distract the four if not wound or kill. His steel concentration and arm strength show his Apache fighting intensity that made him a natural for the police force.

As he marches down, he can see his aim is good enough watching their bodies jerk and blood immediately staining their clothes. But it's the distraction that counts.

Joe and Ernie run across the street behind a covered bus stop that give them the opening they need. They start shooting repeatedly to kill two of them. Johnny and Dana run into position to finish the job. Teamwork pays off.

They all gather around the downed X men's lifeless bodies. Dana consecutively shoots each in the head to ensure they are gone from this world. She looks up to see runners start returning.

They waste no time and start re-loading or rummaging through the dead soldiers' armaments to restock or add to their personal fire power. Dana looks down the street, "I can still hear gunfire where Tank is so let's go back there."

"Roger that," Darren says as he strolls up.

Dana starts a jog towards her motorcycle that's four blocks up where Tank should be. The rest follow her except for Joe and Ernie who are still reloading and their motorcycles are on 6th, a block up.

Ernie starts walking towards their motorcycles, gun in hand as he surveys the area. There are wounded and dead people scattered throughout. Some are moaning. Others barely breathing. He can't believe it. In his other world, he would have rushed to save them waiting for the ambulance to arrive. Now, it's a hierarchy of lives' importance. These on the street are the lowest and his team at the top.

"I need some more ammo. I think skinhead over there has the same as mine. I'll meet you at the motorcycles. Call Tank," Joe says to Ernie as he walks through the paved graveyard he just helped create.

"Okay. Grab as much ammo as you can. I still have room to carry more."

When Ernie turns the corner, his gun is kicked from his hands then front punched from Tanner, a tall muscular man with fatigue pants and a wife beater shirt. Ernie goes flying over a fire hydrant.

Tanner picks Ernie up and slams him into the nearest car. Tanner grabs him by the throat with both hands choking him. He stares intensely at Ernie whose eyes are fluttering being choked to death. "Hi Ernie. Nice to see you again," Tanner says with a matter of fact voice.

Ernie can't believe it. A ghost from his past is staring right at him. But the past reminds him that he too knows hand to hand combat.

All of sudden a bullet comes flying behind Tanner hitting the light pole ricocheting to the window of the store next to the two. Joe's shot distracts Tanner enough for Ernie to use both arms to swing upwards to his attacker's arms that free him for the moment.

Ernie lands a fist to the face then jump kicks him sending Tanner backwards fast. Tanner is surprised by the move and stunned for the moment. Ernie lunges and pushes him hard against the brick wall, grabs his shirt and throws him over the hydrant onto the pavement.

He wanted to land Tanner's skull directly to the retro metal lamp pole but Tanner was too quick so the resulting damage was minimal.

Ernie is still in disbelief and pissed. He positions himself in Seal fighting stance walking towards Tanner, "We should have killed you when we had the chance."

Runners are screaming and scrambling. Tanner knows there's a gun close by wanting him dead so he looks over to see Joe running up with gun in hand. He jumps up, grabs an unsuspecting runner and uses her as a hostage and shield. Ernie picks up his gun and turns to Tanner who's back pedaling with his newfound squeeze.

Both have their guns out looking for a spot to shoot him dead but he's one move ahead of them with his hostage. She starts hyperventilating pleading for her release. He keeps backing away until a group of runners pass where he throws her outwards. "Tell Theodore his time is coming." He maneuvers his way into the group then escapes down an alley.

"Who the fuck was that?" asks Joe. Both of them crouch down behind a car giving them cover for who knows what.

Ernie is coughing trying to regain his breath. "That's Tanner. Tank and I served in the Navy with him. We fought together in combat for many missions. We were close until…"

"Until what?"

Ernie is looking at the direction where Tanner ran making sure he's not back. "Until he murdered Robert, another soldier on our team. He and Robert didn't get along. They accused each other of cheating in poker or horseshoes or whatever stupid betting game they were playing. All of us thought it was gorilla chest puffing until they got into a real fight and I mean a real fight."

Ernie looks around and motions to Joe towards their motorcycles. "Just imagine two Navy Seals having a throw down. Not a pretty sight. One day, we were off duty just sitting outside in our lovely Afghani station. Some of us were playing spades. Others throwing the football, lifting weights, whatever.

At this point, Tanner is on his 10th beer or so and continuously taunting Robert for being a pussy. No reason. Just a pussy in general. Robert finally had enough and went after him. Robert was 10 beers short of Tanner so had that advantage and used it. He pinned Tanner down and was about to break his arm shouting that is neck is next. Tank and others pulled Robert off and ordered both to stand down.

Tank ordered disciplinary actions immediately. Disciplinary actions go on your record and your record is what helps you get promoted or not so both were not happy about any of this nor at each other.

They were forced to apologize and promised to behave otherwise further, more severe disciplinary action would happen. So they did, all while hating each other even more. Several weeks later, we were on a mission when we were ambushed by a group of Al Queda. It was intense. Hell, you may have seen it on the news.

They killed most of us but we fought back. In the skirmish, Tank and I saw Tanner quickly pick up one of the Al Queda's gun then turn to Robert and shoot him dead. He thought he got away with it and if they found out it was one our bullets then it's under the 'friendly fire' category which means it's either buried in the report with some sort of reprimand or not mentioned at all. But Tanner was smart and shot him with the enemy's gun.

Tanner, Tank and I were the only survivors and the count of their soldiers down was 32. As such, Tank and I were awarded the Navy Cross. Tanner didn't get it because Tank and I made sure he didn't. We reported his murder but couldn't prove it especially since the bullet wasn't ours. His only punishment was not getting the Navy Cross.

Ever since then he hated us and vowed his revenge. He left the Navy after that and we've never heard from him. Someone said he went back to his hometown in Minnesota and we just forgot about him. And now he's back."

"Notice he didn't have any weapons. Just him. That's o ne intense motherfucker. And who's Theodore? Is he talking about Tank?"

"Yes. It's Tank he's after. Tank was in command and the one who spoke up. When I corroborated Tank's story, they still didn't do anything. Didn't want a blemish on the Navy seals and we couldn't prove it."

They both get on their bikes when Johnny and Dana drive with Darren and Escobar right behind them. Tank follows up. His dress is considerably bloodier and tattered which shows why he was late for the party.

He explained he had to rip an entire strip of the dress at the bottom as a makeshift cord to strangle one of his attackers. Ernie said it turned his dress from an evening gown to a cocktail dress. Each of those who heard gave a laugh. Tank didn't respond.

Ernie grabs his comm, "Martinez. Log 18 down."

They hear the count so add to the tally.

"Count ten for me," Tank reports.

"Four more besides these 18," Johnny shouts out.

"Two more," Darren throws in.

"And four for me," Escobar adds.

Martinez squawks back, "Looks like we're up to 55."

Candy Man's army has scattered the area. Runners keep streaming through as if nothing happened. In their world, nothing did. They were four blocks away without a clue.

Tank looks around and across the street there's a Volkswagen car dealership with most of the cars missing and windows gone. Tank looks at them, "Come on. We can't stay out here in the open like this. Follow me."

Tank revs his bike and shoots across the street. He bounces up into the showroom floor and does a semicircle slide stop then waves to the others. His entourage quickly follow into the showroom floor. "We need to find out if Griffin is still alive."

His small army is turning into a small group filing into the VW dealership one by one. Joe and Ernie drive straight up to Tank and stop their engines. As they take off their helmets, Ernie looks at Tank, "Guess who I just ran into? Pun intended."

Tank pushes out his kickstand to station his bike. He takes his helmet off and wipes sweat off his forehead with part of his ripped dress. All of this while staring straight at Ernie with a stern look.

"Tanner."

Tank keeps staring, motionless and emotionless. "He says your time is coming."

Joe chimes in, "He almost killed Ernie. Caught him off guard and nearly choked him to death."

"Is he part of Candy Man's army?" Tank finally asks.

"Don't think so. Candy Man's army was long scattered before he showed up. The real question is how did he know we were going to be here. That we're even trying to hunt them down."

"I left a note on my door," Tank says now angry at himself. Joe and Ernie look at him with a quizzical look. "I thought some of our friends or cops might show up at our house so I left a note where we'll be. He must have gone to our home to kill me. Found the note then went to the bar.

Obviously left Martinez and family alone. Martinez just responded and didn't mention anything. Tanner must have just silently listened to Martinez talking to us and found out where we are. Tanner's smart. So that's another rogue element we or I have to be on the lookout. He didn't have a gun on him?"

"No," Joe responds.

"I guess for the end of the world, it's only hand-to-hand for him. One thing is obvious though, he hasn't forgotten or forgave us," he turns to Ernie. "How did he look?"

"Like a Navy Seal. Hasn't lost an ounce a fat. Hell, knowing Tanner, he's probably in better shape than he was."

"Well, no matter what his shape, I guarantee he still doesn't have it."

"Have what?" Joe is in detective mode.

Ernie turns to answer, "Yes, he's a Navy Seal. He's obviously fit as one. He's also smart as one. But, under all of those trophies, he doesn't have *it*."

Joe bugs his eyes out and asks again, "What?"

"The gut instinct when it comes to battle. He stayed alive because he survived them not because he won."

Tank shakes his head then grabs his comm, "Martinez, has the news lady said anything yet?"

"Not yet," Martinez responds.

"Do me a favor. Find KUTV's number and send it to me. Maybe she's answering."

Martinez smiles, looks back at Maria and Melia. They know the look. Melia starts typing away. She knows what to do and is better at the computer and the world wide web than Mom.

CHAPTER 29

Dress Up Day

J IMMY IS PEEKING AROUND the corner watching it all unfold. He is most intrigued from the bronze gladiator who shows up out of nowhere doing the dirty deeds he needs done. He turns around to look at Jay, Cheryl and Rob, "Follow me. We need that guy."

They start running down the street that backs up to Dan's and away where his pursuers are. They run down two blocks, turn right and run up to the corner and stop. Jimmy sees the four dead X men laying on the sidewalk behind the overturned car. He looks at their lifeless bodies with a hint of sorrow. He shakes his head with a quick erase of any emotion but rage and focus. Jimmy motions them to stay still as he takes a quick peek around the corner.

With one eye, he sees some of the cops in their pow wow and notices the leader or seems to act as the leader wearing an old western dress over his police uniform. He's more than a bit surprised. Looks brand new except that it has seen recent action. It's torn at the bottom and has fresh blood stains spread throughout.

He turns around to his group still not knowing what to think, "The cop has got a friggin' dress on. Do we have the head of the LGBT army after us?"

Jay peeks over his shoulder to see. He has to wait for a gap in the runners to get a good look. At first, he was skeptical but after careful observation he sees what Jimmy is grousing about. He pauses for a moment then turns to Jimmy, "Well, you have a medical jacket on. So, I guess it's dress up day. I think he has you beat at the moment."

Jimmy stares straight at Jay not knowing what to say to that comment. Cheryl and Rob smile while also peeking their heads out to look at Little Miss Gunslinger.

Rob, "He's cute and all but still looks like he could kick our asses in one swing."

Cheryl looks across the street down a block and sees Tanner standing in front of several X men. Tanner has his arms folded across his chest looking directly at them. It's obvious that Jimmy is part of his plan.

That gives Jimmy newfound hope besides the cocaine. He has a wringer plus an army waiting for him. But he has to cross a busy and wide-open intersection with the Lady Gaga cop and his army looking for him.

It's now a matter of timing and strategy for the four of them to cross the intersection without notice. But the intersection is at the cross section of two downtown streets so it is long without much cover.

They are in the middle of the race so runners are streaming through. The runners just look straight ahead as they dodge dead bodies and debris. The constant motion of runners may be just what Jimmy needs to cross unscathed. Jimmy turns around while the three look at him waiting for direction. He backs up to make sure he is fully out of sight. He looks at Cheryl as he takes off is medical coat and hands it to her.

"You're in charge of this until we're across the street. Be careful with it. I want it back. As it is."

Cheryl holds his jacket perplexed, "Why me? You run with it."

"Can't take the chance. They've got to know that they're looking for a guy wearing a medical jacket on. I'm a man with a medical jacket on raises two red flags thus one bullet to my head. Already taking enough of a chance running across the street this close."

"Then leave it here. Throw it in the trash can. Or let's go down another couple of blocks."

"No and no," Jimmy says emphatically.

"I need it. It's important. Take it with you. Please. And our army is right there. I'm not taking a chance of losing them."

"OK. Now I'm the target. And what the fuck does being a man have to do with anything, you pig?"

"She's got a point. Just fold it up and put it in your bag. This is kind of a stupid conversation," Jay interjects.

"Thank you," Cheryl says looking to Jay then back to Jimmy. She throws the jacket back at him.

Jimmy exhales, "Fine. I'll take it. And they're looking for a man is what a *man* has to do with it."

He starts folding his jacket up very carefully not to wrinkle it any. He looks up at the three of them. "What? I just didn't want to get it dirty. It's my lucky jacket."

Cheryl and Jay look at each other wondering if he's serious. Jay just shrugs his shoulders as Cheryl shakes her head in disbelief. Rob is enjoying the parlay. Jimmy gently puts his jacket in his backpack then pokes his head around the corner. That's when he sees all of the motorcycles start jetting across the street to the abandoned car dealership.

"Hey, hey, hey. They're going into the VW dealership. This is our chance." He's about to run then sees more motorcycles and cops driving into the dealership. *Shit.* "How many cops are out there?" He turns to his three, "Just cuz they're not looking doesn't mean they're not watching. So, be careful."

He peeks out again and with perfect timing, a thick group of runners come marching up. That's his cue. He bobs his legs, secures his backpack then smoothly runs out to join the group trying to blend in as much as possible.

He runs silently as he maneuvers through the group across the street behind the corner and out of gunsight. He looks back and waves to the group to follow his lead.

Cheryl looks at him then the others knowing he was lucky. Now it's her turn. Jay gets in front of Cheryl looks straight into her eyes and grabs her hand, "Follow me." Jay's initiative definitely surprises her. Cocaine has its confidence boost, that's for sure. Before she protests, he pulls her with him to cross with stealth. Cheryl is actually scared.

Timing is perfect. He follows Jimmy's lead and joins another group running through the street. They bob and weave into the running crowd. Runners are used to disruption from other runners with different paces so they just move out their way grumbling.

Jay leads Cheryl to the next block unnoticed. Rob is too dumb and uncreative to be left alone so he follows clumsily through the crowd. Maybe he looks so docile and unassuming no one cares even if he is brandishing a weapon.

They all join Jimmy as he is carefully unpacking his medical jacket and putting it back on. He sniffs in loudly and forcefully to see if any cocaine is left. At that time, Tanner and the others approach Jimmy.

"Who are you? Besides being my new best friend," Jimmy asks looking him up and down.

"Tanner," he says matter-of-factly.

Jimmy smiles nodding his head. "OK. Tanner. You're now officially part of the club. You deal with the cops. I'll deal with Griffin."

He then starts looking at the gang of about 10 behind Tanner and holds up his arm. "OK gentlemen," he turns around and looks at Cheryl who is glaring back at the Jimmy-the-chauvinist-pig. "And lady. I don't know who those people were but someone tipped them off. It definitely raises the flame on this fire to a whole new level. We need to regroup. Anyone see a good spot where we can hide for the moment? I need to call my agent."

"There's a group of us waiting outside that office building over there," a young skinhead blurts out pointing a finger down the block.

"OK. Good, and more soldiers. Come on, let's go."

They jog down the street then take a right that leads them through the entryway into a courtyard surrounded by three different office buildings. The courtyard is the central location that connects the office buildings that block cars and viewers from the four crowded streets surrounding. They have some privacy for the moment.

There are 12 others with their weapons in hand. Some are leaning against the glass walls smoking cigarettes, others are pacing back and forth. They hadn't expected Tank and his gang to add this new element to the hunt.

While they're still ready for battle, their eyes show a new-found fear of being the hunted rather than just the hunters. Jimmy sees some of the X soldiers are new getting the latest from the others. A replenishing army is a good asset to have. Jimmy waves and smiles as if they're getting ready for a softball game.

"All of y'all stay here. I've got to make a quick call," he looks at Cheryl, Jay and Tanner. "You come with me."

"What about me?" Rob says being slighted.

"Stay here and entertain the troops. It'll be just a moment."

They follow Jimmy into one of the office buildings. There are individual offices throughout the foyer. Everything from bank loans to spinal cord injuries and law offices. That's when he spots the law office of Crews & Kornin. *Perfect.*

He opens the standard office complex type of door to be presented with an upper scale image of a prestigious law firm. He knows what to look for—the conference room, standard at every law office.

He passes the reception desk looking both ways and immediately stops. The conference room is to his right. He walks in with the confidence that he's been here hundreds of times with the others following him. The conference room is even more posh than the reception area. It's the room where they seal the $550 per hour clients.

Jimmy throws down his backpack on the long mahogany conference table and pulls out his phone. He sees Jay closing the blinds to keep hidden. Jimmy looks at him with a furtive smile. He starts dialing and mumbling, "Fuckin' bitch."

"Hello," Janine answers.

"What in the fuck kind of game are you playing?" Jimmy growls.

"Have no idea what you're talking about." Janine's tone is not defensive but more indifferent and annoyed.

"That group you reported on, Griffin. They were decoys. The guy was a look alike. I think you set me up and making me look like a fool for your news show. And, are you also the one who called the cops on us?"

"I don't make news. I report it. What do you mean the cops?"

"Give me a break. You know what I mean. The vigilante cops that are hunting us down now. They've already killed 40 or so of my men. This has your name all over it. I should kill you if I didn't need you. Where is he?"

"Thanks for the news tip," she starts speaking out loud her news announcement. *"Candy Man strikes out as Griffin look-alike spoils his assassination attempt and vigilante cops come to Griffin's rescue. Our news station has also become a target of Candy Man's gang.* Got it." Janine hangs up. She starts scrolling through the social sites to find more detail.

CHAPTER 30

100 Million

L ARRY SITS SIPPING HIS SCOTCH watching the drinking duel of his two new friends and temporary co-hosts. On one armrest sits Veronica, a long-legged brunette somewhere in her mid 20s and on the other armrest sits Tiffany, a shorter blonde version of Veronica.

Larry is the happy referee counting down, "Okay. One, two, three." The two girls throw down their tequila as Larry's grin is about to break his face. The girls are perfect for the camera and definitely help viewership especially from the male audience.

Veronica has the tight-fitting black yoga pants on with a Houston Astros traditional baseball jersey. It's a unique combination but with Veronica's looks, it wouldn't really matter what outfit she wears.

Tiffany is going more party look with a short black leather miniskirt and a white silk blouse. The blouse is strategically designed to accentuate the upper body parts that deserve the exposure. Both girls are built, dressed and meant for the camera.

"Larry," Janine cuts in. "We have breaking news. Tell the Bimbettes their interview is over."

"Awww," Tiffany says as she sits up and pouts away. She doesn't miss the chance to blow a kiss to the millions of now adoring fans.

"Hey bitch! Who you calling a bimbette?" Veronica says as she walks away.

"Yeah, yeah. Go breathe some air or something," Janine responds.

"Bye-bye. Bye-bye. Don't go very far," Larry says smiling wide watching the two walk away. His grin now turns to irritation as Janine shooed his two trophy girls away.

"I have a direct report that the Griffin this station has been following is an imposter. Candy Man and his gang of thugs tracked down the imposter and found out it was a trick. We also have three confirmed reports that a group of vigilantes have come to Griffin's rescue already killing 75 of Candy Man's gang. At this point, Griffin's whereabouts are unknown.

We will keep you updated on the search for Griffin. And, remember, if anyone has a news tip on today's last race, please contact me through my twitter account #JanineSays."

The 'group of vigilantes to Griffin's rescue' makes Larry smile. His not-so-subtle call for help worked. "How many viewers now?" Larry asks.

"We're almost to 100 million. This is unbelievable. Somebody better find him quickly."

Janine's knack of elevating numbers of those killed or trying to kill is getting better and better as the clock ticks. Makes for better TV drama and keeps the viewers viewing. Janine looks at the ringing phone irritated but intrigued. "Larry, it's yours. Keep 'em entertained."

"Okay viewers. For the record, if you see Griffin or have a news tip just email me at LKMLawyer@gmail.com. It's been reported to me that her twitter account has crashed due to the volume of twits has following her so send them to me and I'll make sure she gets the information. Do not twit her but email me. That's very important. My email is LKMLawyer@gmail.com."

Larry is going to do everything he can to undermine Janine's mission to get Griffin killed. Steering information is one way he's doing so. Larry's stern face now becomes a smile as he grabs the scotch bottle and fills his crystal cocktail glass three-quarters full. He follows with the standard three cubes of ice.

He looks around, stops then smiles even bigger, "Ladies! Come on back over. There's still some Tequila shots for ya."

CHAPTER 31

Running This Circus

"D AD," Melia says staring at her laptop.

"What sweetie?" Martinez answers as he's popping open a beer.

"You got to come see this. The news lady knows. She just reported on our force going after the crazy men," Melia answers.

Martinez takes a quick swig and runs around the bar to look. He stares listening to her reporting then the screen shifts back to the old but pretty entertaining drunk.

"I gotta let Tank know. Did you find the number?"

"Yeah. Found several. This one looks like the best. Here," she hands him her phone. Martinez grabs it with a smile and a 'thank you' kiss on the head. He hits the comm.

"Talk to me," Tank answers immediately.

"She knows."

"Who?"

"The news lady. She just announced your crusade. Don't know if that helps or hurt but wanted you to know," Martinez holds up Melia's phone that has Janine's number, hopefully. "We got a phone number. Don't know for sure but try it."

Tank starts waving to his group, "Hey guys, write this down or remember it. Quick."

"Say it. I can remember it," Ernie responds.

"512-332-7852. Got it. If I talk to her and she reports it. Let me know what she says pronto."

He hangs up and immediately calls as Ernie repeats the number. She answers on first ring, "This better be good."

Tank's not the least surprised with her congeniality, "I want in the loop directly."

"Who's this?" Janine responds.

"This is the leader of the vigilante cops I heard you're now reporting on. It looks like you're running this circus so I want in the loop."

"I just report the news. How do I know you're the vigilante cops?"

Tank fires his pistol in the air, "Candy Man is wearing a physician's jacket. He's Caucasian with black hair and about 5' 11" and 180 pounds. He's with another Caucasian, 6' 1" 200 pounds, tan body, well built, wearing jeans and a white under shirt. We just encountered the group and killed approximately 50. They have dispersed and back on mission. How's that for confirmation?"

"I'll take it for now. What do you need?"

"Where's Griffin? And where did the crazy man go? Candy man or whatever you call him."

"Watch my news and you'll find out. And call me when you have something newsworthy." She hangs up.

Tank stays silent. He then clicks on his comm on his shoulder. "Martinez!"

"Yeah boss."

"Have you heard from Marian yet?"

"No boss."

"Just talked to the news lady so we're in the loop. I think. I hope. She'll now be reporting on each of our groups as she finds out. She has direct contact with us, the hunters and who knows who else she has out there. Let's hope Marian can shut her down but in the meantime she has the power and best information for all of the pieces so we need to monitor constantly."

"Roger that, Captain. Maria is monitoring the news. Melia is on social media and I'm central command."

"Doing what you do best. Tell the girls we all appreciate what they're doing and couldn't do it without them."

Martinez smiles as he turns to Maria and Melia who don wide grins of their own.

CHAPTER 32

TV Party

MARIAN'S WEAVING HER WAY through the dead cars and debris that lay in the roads for whatever reason or for many reasons. As she gets closer, the reality sinks in about her mission. *What exactly is she going to do to get into the control room without incident and with success?*

Tank is right. At this moment she broadcasts the news and who controls the news is in control. Just the way she wanted it and the way she planned it.

She turns the corner to get the first glimpse of the TV station and her initial instincts are more than correct. The building is a mess. How much so, she can't tell yet. Just enough to know that Janine is a target.

Marian slows her sportster down to a crawl far enough away to survey the area. She bumps over the curb to stop behind a large Texas live oak. It's a confusing site as some of the *debris* takes some time to digest.

Dead bodies and cars litter the area. There are several trucks that tried to drive up and over the construction berms protecting the station. Inside several trucks, dead men lean back or slumped over their steering wheels. Janine obviously knew this would happen and went to great lengths to protect herself. Marian parks the bike, takes her helmet off as she removes herself from the Sportster.

Being so far away, she doesn't have a full view so runs quickly, low to the ground to a truck a half block to the east. That's when she sees them and is completely baffled. She takes off her backpack and sets it down on the grass next to her.

About 20 yards from the station at the very edge of the grass, there's a large screen TV broadcasting the race with a group of what look like college students. There's a couch, some office chairs, approximately 12 men and women laughing it up, drinking vita water and two are throwing a football.

She grabs her phone and calls her husband and best friend. The phone immediately goes to voicemail. *Dammit!* He's either on the phone, battery dead or dead. She hangs up then calls Maria.

Maria answers immediately, "Hey girlfriend, what's going on?"

"You're not going to believe this."

"What?"

"I'm about two blocks away from the station. From this view I can see 15 or so dead bodies. Trucks piled up on the building and amongst all of this carnage, there's a group of what looks like college kids outside in a makeshift outdoor living room having a TV party at the very edge of the property."

"What? Are you serious?"

"Yeah. I'll send you some pictures when we hang up."

"This is way above my pay grade. Eddie, you need to take this call.

There's some weird shit going on at the station."

"Put it on speaker phone. I need to be paying attention and on call for Tank," Martinez replies.

"How do you do that? I didn't know this thing had a speaker phone," Maria responds rotating her phone looking for a speaker button.

"Mom, it's an iPhone. They can microwave your dinner. Here, give it to me."

She hands the phone to Melia where she taps the screen several times then holds the volume button turning it to its loudest. "Hey, are you there?"

"Yeah. Hi Melia. Eddie there?"

"I'm here," Martinez shouts. "What's up?"

"I don't know how to describe except Janine's not fucking around. There's those highway blocks of concrete surrounding the building. Trucks smashed into them with dead drivers in them. Then about 15 or so more dead bodies all over the yard."

"How were they killed. Can you tell?"

"Hold on. There's more. Then there's a group of college kids, I guess. At the very edge of the property watching the race on a flat screen TV, having what looks like a Super Bowl end-of-the-world pizza party. It's like an outdoor frat thing."

This report actually makes Martinez turn around. Melia, Maria and Martinez all look at each other. *Can this day get any weirder?*

"Do the frat party people have guns?"

"No. Not that I can see. They have a football they're throwing around."

That makes Martinez turn around again, "Do they have cover from the station?"

"No. They're in the wide open."

"And they're just hanging out amongst a group of corpses without a care in the world?"

"Well, they're at the edge of a long wide lawn so they're not exactly dodging dead bodies as they prance around. It's weird, though. Most of them are giggling or just laughing out loud. They're on something. It's got to be a hallucinogen. Acid or mushrooms. Maybe X."

"Do they know you're there?"

"No. I'm about two blocks away behind a truck just spying on them at the moment."

"Can you see where the people were shot?"

"The dead guys in the drivers' seats have been shot in the head. I can see two others with blood soaked shirts on their back. The others I can't tell. They seem to be mostly frontal wounds.

I can also tell that from the exit wounds that they are from different bullets thus different guns thus more than one person protecting her. And with that many dead bodies, there's probably a sizable group protecting her."

"Can you see inside?"

"No. It's too dark to get any sort of detail. Wait. One of the kids threw the football over another's head. He's going closer to the building to get it."

A shot comes from inside the building hitting the ground next to the football followed by a shout, "You know the rules! Stay behind the line."

"Yes sir. Just getting the football and back to the TV," answers a lanky blonde headed kid wearing skinny jeans, a yellow tee shirt donning one of those god-awful popular poop emojis. He grabs the football and runs back to the group without a care in the world.

Marian reports, "One of her men just sent a warning shot at him."

"Taking Janine out is important." Martinez pushes the comm button to Tank. "Boss, you there. Yeah. Looks like Marian has a serious situation at the studio. Yeah. OK. I'll tell her."

"You need to back away, girlfriend," Maria interjects as she's half listening to Martinez conversation with Tank. "Just back away a few blocks until some back up comes."

"Okay. Talked to Tank. He's sending Darren, Johnny and Dana," Martinez relays. "They'll meet you at Shoal Creek and Morrow. That's two blocks behind you. Go now and meet them there."

"You talked to Tank?"

"Martinez did," Maria interjects.

"Is he okay?"

"He's got some wounds but okay. Their bullet bag is definitely lighter," Martinez adds.

"Oh. Hold on." There's an eerie pause on the phone. Martinez and Maria look at each other with the 'eye-brow' look. "I'm going to definitely need some help. Oh Jesus."

CHAPTER 33

Excuse Me

I N A RARE MOMENT of running silence, Sabrina breaks it wanting some closure, "I didn't know you received a scholarship from Oregon."

Griffin sighs not in frustration but knowing where Sabrina is going with her question. "Yeah, I took high school state in Oregon for long distance so the Ducks offered me a full blown scholarship. The next morning, I left the scholarship, running, my childhood and my parents all in one swoop. My car was already packed and came to Austin.

My cousin let me bunk with him until I could find a place. He waited tables at Guero's. Told me to get a TABC license to be a bartender, or really a barback at that time, so I did. Got the job… "

"And that's when I met you," interrupts Sabrina. The missing puzzle pieces keep falling into place. "No wonder you were so elusive on your background. I remember you wouldn't answer any basic questions except you were from Portland and decided to go to the University of Texas."

"I lied, by the way. I don't know if you remember but you ended up staying at the bar the whole night talking to me while I worked."

"Of course. It was great night. That's how we became such good friends. You were so easy to talk to and enjoyed all the things I enjoy." Sabrina pauses. "And that's when I told you one of my favorite things to do is run with the Gazelles."

"Yes. I hadn't run for a year just bartending. The next day, I started running and beginning the process of applying to U.T. Got in, then building back up to 8 miles a day. Then graduated three years later with you."

"You're the one who brought up being a U.T. student. If you weren't, why did you lie?"

Griffin smiles, "You were wearing a U.T. cap." Sabrina remains silent. *How did I miss these signs?*

"Why do you think I took every semester I could? I had to catch up with you. Joined the running club and realized that I truly do love running—the camaraderie of a club, the races and you."

"Jesus. Why didn't you tell me all of this before? I had no idea. Hell, if you did, we would probably already had two kids."

"I spent all my years suppressing my own wants and needs from my parents or being scolded and rejected when I did. I guess I didn't want to take the chance. I thought if I subtly showed you going to the same university, joining the running club, being there when you needed me, it would be obvious to you."

"I'm so sorry," She drops her head. "I feel so bad."

"Stop. And don't. It's not your fault. I was too absorbed in feeling sorry for myself and punishing myself through you. I was using you to continue my pattern of rejection and not being good enough.

It's only recently, this has become so clear. I should have taken that scholarship. I should have waved the finger at my parents and walked on the track for me. Not for anyone else and shed myself from being controlled by my parents and begin my life—my life." Griffin says pointing his thumb at himself. He turns to her. "I'm glad now that I didn't."

"Why?"

"I would have never met you."

The two stare at each other running the same rhythm. Griffin reveals a small but sincere, deep smile.

"Excuse me," a tall man in his late 30s with his wife start running towards them at an accelerated pace. Griffin and Sabrina turn to them with a defensive glare.

"Hey," Griffin and Sabrina say at the same time. Both of their eyes relax and smiles return when they recognize them.

"Mike, Sarah, how's it going! So good to see you. What an odd deal to meet up with you," Sabrina says in complete disbelief that they ran into someone they know let alone some of their fellow Gazelles.

"Yeah. Sorry guys. Didn't mean to interrupt you. I saw you were wearing our running shirt and thought that was you two. Didn't recognize Griffin at first but saw you," he looks at Sabrina. "Hey, just wanted to say 'hi'. Can't believe we ran into you."

"Why are you on this route? Shouldn't you be with Gilbert and the elites. You're the star of this show," Sarah interjects.

Mike and Sarah are in their 40s without children and used the Gazelles for the past several years to get some pounds off and a social life. The running club was their only outlet that wasn't shackled by a spreadsheet and a ladder of bosses. Once their 'jobs' ended last year, they turned to the club for companionship and to run a marathon for their last hooray.

Griffin responds, "Just wanted some room to run and talk and not deal with the crowds. We split off and they understood. We'll see them at the end."

"Yeah, us too. Do you mind if we get a picture? I want to send it to my family in New York. They'll get a kick we ran into you two."

Griffin and Sabrina look at each other not knowing that when Mike says he's sending a photo to his family, he's doing so with his Facebook page that hundreds of others will see and share.

"Sure."

They pose in fun selfie mode as Mike captures them all in first thumb push.

"All right. Thanks guys and it was great to see you. We never really got to BS much with each other. Wish we had. You two were just way too fast for us. We'll see you at the finish where the club always meets. We're meeting at the same spot as always, right?"

"Yep. Sure am. See ya there. Great to see you two and keep that pace up. You're doing great."

"We had to use our running pace to catch up with you guys which is your jogging pace so we'll go back to our jogging pace and see you at the end. How did you guys pass us anyway? You should be way up there."

"We started really late. We didn't pass the start line until minute 18."

"Oh. That makes sense."

CHAPTER 34

False God Complex

J IMMY HANGS UP THE PHONE and starts swiveling back and forth in his newly claimed chair. He's inspecting the conference room with a satisfying grin. He knows these rooms all too well.

The long, dark mahogany conference table commands the room's center—the darker the table, the more intimidating. The table soldiers 12 black leather tall-back chairs from some European company that's name is unpronounceable or from the set of Star Wars. Parallel to the table of fear stands a skinny glass table flush against the wall still with a clear shine to it.

On the glass table, there are dozens of statutes of all shapes and sizes recognizing the legal achievements of the Crews & Kornin law firm. The three walls that are not windows adorn plaques, photos with elected officials and certificates of some made-up designation that warrants a higher fee. On any other day, this room would look most impressive.

As Jimmy continues to swivel, he asks out loud, "Know these guys?"

Cheryl and Jay hadn't really paid attention until the question so they start looking more closely.

"Oh yeah. These are those lawyers from the TV commercials. They're always looking for people who've taken some sort of bad medication," Cheryl says staring closely at one of the photos.

"They're kind of creepy," Jay adds. "They always wear the same suit and try to out angry-look each other. Bad actors. Hope they're better actors in the courtroom."

"They never go to court. They always settle. You know who pays them?"

Room stays silent.

"Big Pharma."

That gives Jay and Cheryl pause. Tanner stays standing, emotionless.

"Crews, Kornin or one of their 40 other lawyers troll the Medical Venture Capital world looking for newly formed pharma, medtech or biotech companies that could be a threat to the big boys. Most of these start-ups are funded by Vulture Capital thus fully beholden to their investors.

If the start-ups fit the C & K profile, they invest just enough to have the influence they need. They also make sure as part of their investment they provide free legal services. Gives them more power." Jimmy says the word 'free' while air-quoting. "They wait just before human testing then cleverly tip off the big companies to see if it threatens them. If big Pharma sees the start-up as a threat or opportunity they move in like a chess game.

Big Pharma send subtle letters of interest but more of threats. Makes the start-up nervous. That's when they turn to their Ole pal and loyal investor Crews & Kornin. That's when the fun kicks in.

If Big Pharma gives them money to buy them out then Crews & Kornin get a huge return. If Big Pharma begin legal proceedings claiming copyright infringement or whatever they can scare the shit out of them, the start-up has no choice but to turn to

Crews & Kornin to defend them but now the price to defend isn't free.

That's when they start calculating how much time it will take to either charge them legal fees to get their investment back plus extra. Or orchestrate a buy-out agreement that gets their original investment back, their legal fees plus the ROI of the buyout.

That's where I come in. I'm either an expert witness thus $750 per hour or a consultant which means $750 per hour and a piece of the buy-out. It's fool proof, really. You know the sad thing is many of these drugs never get tested nor go further because all that would do is lower Big Pharma profits. They just buried their competition.

Or, Big Pharma continues the testing and make 1000 times the profit while the original company walks off with a small return. Reason being? The original owners had to pay the investors first plus their return, their costs and then, of course, their lawyers.

Nine times out of ten, the VCs and lawyers make a shit pot full of money and the innovators get enough to pay some bills for a year then have to start all over again to then get fucked all over again. It's pretty smart. You got to hand them that."

Cheryl picks up one their crystal, oblong awards, "Well according to all of these trophies they seem to be successful."

"What are you holding?"

"This one says 'Crews & Kornin Named Top Lawyers of the Year'."

"Who gave it to them?"

"Austin Business Weekly."

"That's a receipt."

"What do you mean receipt?"

"They spent the most on advertising in their rag so they were named top lawyers."

Tanner interrupts the conversation. "Can we get down to business please?"

Jimmy swivels to Tanner smiling then points his hand at one of the board chairs.

"Sit. Please."

Tanner remains standing. Jimmy just looks at him, shrugs his shoulders. "So, Rambo, you want to kill cops. How about Griffin? Do you want to kill him?"

"I don't want to kill Griffin, just the cops. One in particular. Griffin's your problem."

Jimmy is a bit taken back by that response. "This should be good," Jimmy says as he picks up his backpack starts rustling around to pull out his jar of pick-me-up powder, the tupperwared canteen of whiskey and his plastic name badge. That gets Jay and Cheryl's immediate attention.

"So, I ask again. Why do you want to kill cops and a 'particular one'?"

"You and your army lured Tank and his brigade out into the streets. Thanks to you, I get my revenge."

Jimmy taps out a large rock on the table and starts the cocaine line dance. He's nodding his head smiling how focused Tanner is. "That's what I offer?"

"Yes."

Jay and Cheryl are focused but more on the cocaine crushing than Tanner and Candy Man's conversation. Jimmy now has the rocks small enough to start the chopping process to make the lines a fine dust. He takes a swig of whiskey and starts rolling out lines then with a sing-along voice asks, "Who wants some candy?"

Jay and Cheryl stand even straighter, eyes wider and in unison, "I do."

Jimmy looks at Tanner. He shakes his head 'no'.

"I heard you mention a name, Frank or something like that."

"Tank," Jay answers. That gives Jay a sneer from Tanner. Jimmy snorts up a long one. These lines are definitely super-sized. Now he's holding his nose up. Snorts hard and loud again.

Jimmy hands the $1000 dollar bill to Jay who snatches it up quickly and politely then goes to town on his line. Cheryl goes next but with a little more of girl-like elegance.

The three of them have their heads tilted back letting the coke drain by gravity looking like chicks in a nest squawking for more worms. Then with a nasally and whiney tone Jimmy asks, "Why Tank? Do you know him or something?"

"Tank and I have some history."

Now it's Tanner's turn. "What is your mission?"

"To make my contribution to mankind," Jimmy nasally responds still holding his head back. There's an obvious pause in the room as Jimmy looks at each one individually. "It's the False God complex. In the psychiatry world, False God complex is the narcissistic perception you're a god. In this particular instance, the world has projected the false god upon Griffin. That puts him in a no-win situation which is where I come in.

Killing Griffin resolves his problem. Thanks to Janine, he is responsible for millions of people's last salvation. He doesn't want that responsibility. Who does? You can see it in every interview he gives and the fact that he had a doppleganger pose for him just reinforces it that much more.

The fact that no one can find him or don't even know where he is shows how scared he is of being in this position. By killing him, I ensure that he becomes their 'God' while he avoids the pressure and responsibility so I'm doing him a big favor while giving me the stage for reason number two.

Reason number two and the real reason is what is called the "Ignorance Arrogance" syndrome. It means you don't know that you don't care or you don't care that you don't know. That they as a society and individuals have been so stupid and arrogant, they have put us in this situation.

And that's where Janine comes in, when I kill Griffin she will be salivating at the newsworthy murder of the false God she created. She will literally be dying to interview me.

Janine will give me the opportunity to tell a hundred million people that they are fully responsible for today and that they should have known, cared and prevented this many years ago. In religious terms so to speak, I am providing their day of reckoning. That which gives them the forgiveness to be admitted to their heaven or nirvana or whatever they believe.

And after I diagnose the world and provide them their salvation, I will murder Janine before those one hundred million people for the final hand of justice. But, none of this can happen if I don't murder their messiah Griffin first.

If I can make that happen then I will be able to fulfill my contribution to mankind. Something I have always dreamed of and I can finally say I have done. I know it sounds weird but killing Griffin and Janine is the best thing for every individual, the society, Griffin and me. I'm creating a win-win rather than a lose-lose."

Jay looks at him thinking projection. Cheryl doesn't get it and Tanner doesn't care.

Jimmy is snorting down the last remnants while swiveling back and forth in his boardroom chair with a victory smile that he sufficiently answered Tanner's question.

Before Jimmy can go further, Cheryl interrupts, "Time's ticking Candy Man."

Jimmy jumps up. Maybe too fast as he's becoming off balance and starts staggering. He leans against the wall knocking off several plaques and photos then looks at Cheryl that turns to a blank stare.

"You OK?" Cheryl says while motioning to catch his fall. *Here we go again.*

"Drink. Need."

Jay quickly grabs the whiskey and hands it to him.

"No. Water."

Jay fishes into his backpack and hands him his water. Jimmy just wobbles there trying to bring the bottle to his mouth. When he does, he can't drink as the top is still on. Jay grabs the water from him, takes the top off and hands it back.

Jimmy is able to take a tiny sip then another swig while his arm his shaking uncontrollably. He stumbles back to his chair. The sweat begins to pour down while he's blinking trying to grab some sort of focus.

He looks over to his backpack and slowly moves his arm to drag it towards him. When the backpack is finally in front of him, he stops and stares. He gropes around on the left side of the backpack to stop at one of the many side pockets. He obviously found the one he searches for, grabs the zipper and slowly pulls it open.

He is still detached from the world but enough to continue his directive. He reaches into the side pocket and pulls out a package of peanut butter granola bars. Jay and Cheryl are fully confused while Tanner knows what he's doing. He needs fuel.

Jimmy looking shit-faced drunk but the complete opposite of energy overload fumbles to rip open the bag. He lifts the dual granola bars exposed and takes a careful but large bite to start chewing with a face as if he's eating cardboard.

Cheryl finally interjects with as much irritation as curiosity, "What is he doing?"

Tanner responds even keeled, almost professor like, "He needs sustenance. He has so much cocaine in his body that if the drug has nothing to consume, it will start using his blood cells leaving him anemic thus unable to see, function and in the end, live."

Jimmy sits there chewing, slowly nodding his head confirming Tanner's analysis. While it's obvious he hates every bite, it is also obvious the food is feeding the cocaine thus his strength and the high that makes cocaine the drug of choice for millions of lost souls.

Tanner sits there watching not saying a word, "Are you up for this?"

Jimmy finishes the bars as his blinking slows to normal. He grabs his water and takes as big of a drink his body can withstand. He looks at Jay then Tanner and stops at Cheryl. He nods his head slowly.

After 30 seconds of silence and slow, painful chewing, the coke has its own food so takes back control. He looks up at Tanner with a cold intense stare and says with a dry, raspy voice, "Who's on Janine duty? What's that bitch saying now?"

Jay reminds him, "She and Larry are covering the race but they're fuzzy on exactly where he is. At the moment, they're focusing on Griffin fooling you."

CHAPTER 35

Real or Make Believe

"**Y**ES, HON. We're here waiting for Sabrina and Griffin at the half marathon spot." Mom waits as she listens to Janet. She furls her brow as Janet continues to talk. "What? You're kidding, right? How do you know this?"

Dad sees something is wrong and looks at his wife for information. She looks at him with that worried Mother look.

Janet likes to talk so yaps at a very fast word per minute pace. Mom's used to it so can keep up. Janet is relaying the grim news, "I just turned on the TV in the kitchen. No offense to Sabrina and Griffin but I haven't been watching the race until now.

It's all over Facebook, twitter, YouTube, you name it. There's a whole group of crazies hunting Griffin down to kill him. And it's all the news lady is talking about. When's the last time you saw them? I hope they're still alive. Are you going to see them? You need to find them. They need to go away. As far as possible."

Mom is stunned and silent.

"Mom. Are you there? There's another thing. Some group of cops or military people have taken up arms to save or protect Griffin. It's... I don't know. I don't know if it's real or make-believe. Find out what's going on. I'll keep watching. That's all they talk about on this news show-thingy. It's... just warn them. Call me after you talk to them. Find them. Now!"

Mom stays silent.

"The news lady also says there are like 100 million people watching across the world. This is surreal."

"Jesus," Mom utters back. "Love you, hon. I'll call you as soon as I talk to Sabrina." She hangs up with Dad looking at her bewildered.

He looks at her shocked face, "What is going on?"

"Griffin and Sabrina are being hunted down to be killed. Killed before 100 million people."

"What?"

"According to Janet, Griffin is being hunted down by a group of crazies. The news people are covering it. Another group is going to defend him and Griffin and Sabrina have no idea what's going on. She wants us to tell them so they can run away and protect themselves."

"Yes we will. We'll have them get in our car and drive as far away as possible."

Mom looks at him with a quivering voice looking blankly around, "I hope they haven't already found them, that we're not too late. This is horrible. We need to log in to something and find out what's going on?"

Dad grabs his phone and starts fingering away. He looks at the bars stopping half-way wondering if it's slow or not getting a signal. They both look at each other silently. The loud pops they hear all of sudden have new meaning.

He looks up at her, "Now I know why we came."

Coincidence doesn't exist.

CHAPTER 36

It's Our Time

"**M**OM, DAD, YOU NEED TO SEE THIS NOW,**" Melia says staring at her laptop.

"What," Maria says as she looks over her shoulder while Martinez walks around.

"Someone named 'He-Man' on Facebook just posted a selfie of himself, a lady named Sarah, a younger girl named Sabrina and Griffin. Wow, Griffin sure cleans up nice. Looks like they're next to Little Deli Restaurant over in the Brentwood area. The caption reads 'Look who We Ran Into!!'. So I guess it's Griffin and… a Sabrina running together."

Martinez immediately grabs his comm.

Maria looks down at her, "How do you know all of that? And how do you know where he is? You can barely see a background."

"This 'He-Man'," she stops and looks up. "What's a 'He-Man'?"

"Just a stupid cartoon. Go on."

"He-Man tagged the restaurant, Sarah, Griffin and Sabrina which is how I found it in the first place. I have Griffin's Facebook page on one of my tabs."

"How do you know so much about Facebook? You don't have an account."

"I don't have one that you know of."

"Excuse me? You're not supposed to have one until you're 12, young lady."

"Oh well," Melia responds with a smile. "Ground me."

Martinez on the comm, "Boss, we found him. Or should I say Melia found him."

Tank, "From where?

"Facebook post."

"You looking at it."

"Yep. He's all clean shaven, bald and running with a good lookin' chick named Sabrina."

The 'good lookin' chick' comment gives Martinez a snarl from the wife.

"This photo was just posted and he's next to the Little Deli restaurant over in Brentwood next to U.T. Not too far but well out of the way of the main route."

"I know where it is. I've eaten there before. Does the news lady know yet?"

"Not yet, but she will."

Tank revs his engine and looks around the group with a nod, "OK, ladies. It's our time. Get your asses over there pronto. And remember we're looking for bald and beardless and a good lookin' chick. Follow me!"

CHAPTER 37

Spies

WHILE THEY'RE OFF the beaten running path, gun shots and screaming still fill the ambient noise. Griffin blurts out, "Something's going on."

"What?" Sabrina turns to him in stride.

"Notice people are popping in and out looking for something? They're searching for something...someone."

"Well, no. Everyone is bat-shit crazy so I don't see any difference."

"See the Drag up there?" Griffin commands. "Take a right and let's weave through the U.T. campus. It's more hidden."

"What's going on? What do you know that I don't?"

Griffin jumps up on a three-foot granite wall bordering the south side of campus and grabs Sabrina's hand to join him. She jumps up and they stop for a moment to give them enough time to lift their legs over the two-foot ornate metaled fence into U.T.'s campus. There's enough foliage and buildings to shield them into the pristine campus where Griffin and Sabrina can hide for the moment.

Griffin continues, "I've now seen two people point at us in the last five minutes. Remember I told you I won state track for long distance? I also did cross country. And with cross country, you had spies.

"Spies?"

"Yeah. That's what we called them. With their stop watches and binoculars. It was standard in every race. Opposing teams needed to gauge the pace so they knew where they stood and how to adjust. And I can see it now. They're looking for us. We gotta get to your parents and have them scan the internet to what's going on."

"Why don't we ask one of those 'spies'?"

"I don't trust anyone at the moment. We need your parents. Let's go."

CHAPTER 38

Sign Language

I N AN ARMY-LIKE FASHION, five militants in full soldier gear emerge from the KVUT studios with semi-automatic rifles pointing forward scanning the area. The last of them carries a long, red extension cord. They methodically surround one of the dead bodies in full protective mode.

Their presence prompts the groupies to huddle behind the big screen watching intently. Marian instinctively moves behind the tire of the truck to block her feet from being seen. Another militant emerges from the studio running in a crouched form as if in a combat zone. He's holding two large desk calendars and runs up to a sprawling Texas Live Oak.

The militant stands over the corpse holding the extension cord rolled up noose style and puts it over the dead body's head. He moves forward a couple steps, looks up then throws the whole roll over a large overhanging branch. *They're going to hang that corpse from the tree branch.* And, with their next move, they begin.

Once the dangling body is fully lifted, the soldier holding the other end of the cord starts walking around the tree to tighten its grip to ensure the body doesn't fall. He ties a sailor's knot, wipes his hands then backs up looking at the hanged man nodding at himself for a job well done.

The body swings lightly in the air. This is the first time Marian notices that none of the groupies hiding behind the TV are smiling. They just gawk as if in a biology class seeing a dissected frog for the first time.

The militant closest to the trunk grabs a hammer and the two desk calendars and walks over to face of the dangling body with his back to Marian. The other militant grabs two nails from his shirt pocket and hands it to his accomplice. All while their armed protectors gaze from side to side in a 180-degree arc. The one thing she does notice is in all of their rotating gazes, they each seem to stop at her direction for one millisecond.

He starts hammering the first desk calendar into the dead body's chest then the next in the pelvic area. He nods to the group then hastily walks back to the studio crouching to avoid potential gunfire. The other militants walk backwards, guns pointing forward until they too wash away into the darkness. The last militant looks straight into Marian's direction. She quickly ducks hoping she wasn't spotted.

She waits for a moment then slowly lifts her head to view the area. Marian can't believe what she sees as it freezes her blood cold. The desk calendars have been turned into signs:

We Can See U—*We Will Kill U*

How do they know? And that's when she sees it. At the corner of the studio building under the roof ledge there hangs a security camera pointing directly at her. She looks side to side. The area surrounding her looks clear so she grabs her bag and starts running hunched down to her bike. While Janine is sick and twisted, she's also smart. Very smart.

CHAPTER 39

Get Ready

MARTINEZ IS WATCHING JANINE on the TV while Melia and Maria scan their computers. Janine's next broadcast stops all of them.

"Ladies and gentlemen, Griffin has been found. He no longer has a beard and shaved his head. He's still running the race and experts have him and a young woman somewhere around Neches Street heading south in the direction of the finish line."

Martinez clicks his comm, "Boss, she knows and just announced the general location. That means everyone will be going there. Get ready."

Tank and his team are weaving their way through the streets of runners and debris. Tank hears Martinez' report and answers, "Status report on engagement? We need to shut her up and shut her up quickly."

"I'll have Maria check in," Martinez says as he looks to Maria who is already speed dialing Marian's number.

"And what's the status report on our troops?"

"Throughout all of the groups. 12 of ours, dead. We estimate 75 of their brigade dead."

"Leaves us with?"

"You and your group then Marian, Darren, Johnny and Dana at the studio. There are others that are helping but we don't know who they are. They just took up arms and looking for the X men."

"I just sent a group of 20 to hunt down the X men so we have friends out there just no coordination," Escobar relays.

"How'd you find them?" Ernie asks.

"They found me. They saw I was a cop and asked what to do. They all had pistols, some rifles so I sent them down to 6th street to find any of those who escaped our first combat. They seemed ill-prepared, drunk and out of it so I gave them something to do but out of our way."

Joe jumps in, "We need to go and trust your wife's team is going to kill the Queen. And I mean soon."

CHAPTER 40

Technical Difficulties

MARIAN COASTS HER BIKE to an empty parking lot underneath an office building on Shoal Creek Blvd. She stops, parks and takes a cautionary 360 degree look around to make sure no-one is around or followed her.

She tilts her head down and rubs her eyes. This is not what she expected. Her phone starts to vibrate jolting her back to the moment. She quickly takes it out and looks to see it's Maria.

"Talk to me."

"The news lady found Griffin and is announcing to the world where to find him. We need to shut her down and shut her down quickly. What's going on?"

"Here waiting. Where are they?"

"Dana hasn't answered yet so we don't know."

"Hold on, I can hear some motorcycles. It's them. I can hear three and the sound of motocross Darren. I'll call you back when we have a game plan. Oh, before you hang up, do me a favor. Either you or Melia or both, open up google maps with the satellite feed and type in the address of the station and be on stand-by if we need you. Okay, thanks."

Just as she puts her phone back in her pocket, Darren, Dana and Johnny turn into the parking lot. They roll up cutting their engines off with that cavalry look that makes Marian breathe easier for the moment.

Dana grabs her comm that is dangling in front of her stomach, "Martinez, we're here."

"Good, we were getting worried when you didn't answer," Martinez squawks back.

"Technical difficulties. Look, I'm gonna have to sign off shortly so they don't hear the squawk box so be forewarned. I'll let you know before I do."

"Roger that."

Each start dismounting, taking their helmets off surveying the area. Johnny looks at her shaking his head, "We heard it's a combat zone over here." He looks around at the group with a frustrated smile. "Man, do I sound like a broken record."

Marian wipes her face of dust and sweat and just stares at him, "It's worse than that. It's fucked up, weird, surreal. I can't explain it. You need to see it for yourself. And we need to be careful, they have a small garrison there. Plus…" Marian pauses then looks at Dana. "Dana, Let me borrow that comm real quick."

Dana unhooks it and hands it over to her. She clicks and talks, "Martinez, do the girls have the station loaded on their google maps yet? Good. Ask them to close in on the station and look for any outside cameras. I know there is one on the northwest corner of the building overhang which should mean that another is at the northeast corner. Please look and confirm."

Martinez starts relaying instructions in the background. There's a slight pause as you can hear the girls in the background talking, "Melia says to remind you that these satellite maps can be anywhere from real time to several months old so you can't count on them being solid."

"I know. Just want to use every resource we have. Thanks. Oh, they're looking now? Must be Melia, she knows how to use that computer."

"They both can hear you, you know. Maria is getting a bit of an inferiority complex the more we keep Melia around."

That warrants a smile from everyone especially Melia.

"She says or…" Martinez pauses to look up at Maria with a sheepish smile. "They say there is another at the exact same location on the northeast corner pointing in the same direction as the other which would make sense. Other than that, that's what they have located so far."

Marian turns to Darren, "Hear that, sharpshooter? We need you to take out those outside cameras first. That's how they found me and then, well, you'll see."

Darren stares at her with a sniper's eye, "Martinez, can they tell what the best angle is to shoot them both out from one location? Any trees, branches, poles blocking?"

"I'm checking it now, Oswald. Looks like…your…northeast corner would give you the best angle for both. I'd go that route."

"All right then. Looks like that's where we're heading. Thanks. We'll let you know."

Marian hands Dana the comm back and looks at the group. Johnny finally chimes in, "Marian, how many of those grenades do you have?"

"Two of both. But I need one to blow the control center so there's only one to spare."

"How many men or women are in there?"

"What I saw was eight, all men. Looked like some of them could handle their weapons, probably ex-military or military wannabes. But they didn't look like the tip-top of physical shape. They probably wanted to hold guns and shoot on their last day and found this as good a reason as any."

"Hand me one of each. With those grenades, this first part of our strategy seems fairly simple. Just depends on the layout of the studio for the second part. Come on, let's go."

Marian leads them down through the complex that sprawl across three blocks connected through sidewalks surrounded by unkempt St. Augustine grass and rows of azalea bushes. The two-story office complexes host more than two dozen medical offices, dot com companies and a Tiff's Treats. All of the offices are pleasantly shaded by sprawling branches of Texas live oaks.

They're getting closer and the winding design of the complex gives them cover and comfort for the moment. Marian holds her hand out to stop the four. She turns around quietly while pointing in front of her. From this spot, they have the vantage point Darren needs.

She leans in and softly relays their position, pointing, "Just past that wall is the studio directly across the street. We'll be at an angle on the left-hand side of the studio. As you can see, it's a wide lawn and stretched out building. In that span, there's a lot of debris, cars, a man hanging from a tree branch and dead bodies. Oh, and a group of college kids playing football at the far end of the yard."

They all three just look at her with an unamused look. She looks back, "What? It's true. You'll see. I told you the scene is surreal."

"Hold on. I've got to see this for myself. Stay here," Dana bolts off and in a few minutes returns confirming Marian's assessment. "You're right. It's fucking weird." She turns to the group. "Here's how I see it."

Dana likes to lead and everyone is glad she does. "The cameras seem to be on one operating system. So, when one camera turns so does the other. That gives us an advantage. Usually, security cameras scan from side to side surveying their perimeter. Let's hope these are doing just that."

Johnny loves and respects Dana for just these moments. And it also turns him on when she takes charge. "Darren, wait until the cameras are all the way to the left, shoot out the first camera on the right. That should give Johnny and me enough time to run up right behind the white 4x4 that is half-way up the berm.

When Darren knocks out the second, I run over to the oak tree as my cover. That gives Johnny the view to mow down the fleeing guards and gives me the vantage point for any he missed or tries to run behind the building."

She looks at Marian, "Darren's second shot is your cue to run up to the 4x4 and stand behind Johnny with gun in hand. Once there, it's yours and Darren's responsibility to look out for other shooters that may come from the left, behind or the roof.

Now here's the fun point. As soon as all of us are in position, Johnny is going to throw the first smoke bomb into the studio to, well, smoke them out. If they flee Johnny and I are in position to eliminate them while you two give us cover. If they don't come out that means they're retreating which gives us even more vantage being on the attack while we get closer to Janine.

Ten or 15 seconds after the smoke grenade, Johnny," she turns to Johnny. "Toss the real grenade in. The explosion will either kill some that are still there or scare this shit out of them to retreat even further. After the grenade explodes, we'll have to make some quick decisions before we storm the studio. We have to see how they respond before we can pick the best option."

"Um, not to state the obvious but what about the group of drugged out kids?" Darren interjects.

"Fuck 'em," Dana responds. "Hope they run like hell."

She looks at each of them to make sure the plan is fully understood. They all look to her with pure confidence. She nods her head. "All right. Let's do it."

CHAPTER 41

On My Terms

G RIFFIN AND SABRINA REACH their parents at the designated spot. Griffin frantically waves them over to follow him while giving them the 'be quiet' sign. They hurriedly follow Griffin deeper into campus to an enclosed courtyard between Calhoun and Parlin Hall where no one can see them. Griffin's pacing back and forth as a marathon runner should while being chased to death.

Sabrina recognizes Griffin's worry but not why. She looks at her parents that reflect even more of a frantic look, "Mom, Dad, are we in danger?"

Mom in hysterics, "How did you know? Your sister turned on the TV to watch the news lady. She is reporting a gang is hunting you down to kill you. We need to leave. Now! All of us."

Griffin paces saying nothing. The dynamics of a last race focused around Griffin and, now, Sabrina watched by millions of people being hunted down to kill is difficult to process.

Dad breaks the silence, "There is also a small group of police looking to protect you. They've already confronted each other. Says they have lots of guns on both sides so all of the gunfire you've been hearing hasn't been just random craziness but direct combat."

That comment didn't help. Griffin breaks the silence, "Who's hunting me? And why?"

"Some guy named Candy Man and his friends, I guess. Janet didn't give much specifics. They don't like you," Mom weepily answers.

"Obviously."

"Do you want us to call Janet for more information?"

"No."

Griffin continues to pace while wheels in his head spin for an answer. Sabrina stops to grab a water from Mom. She watches Griffin intensely.

"I'll tell you what we're going to do. Sabrina stays with you. Go to the finish line and I'll meet you there. I'll take care of him."

"What?! What are you going to do? Run him to death?"

"Huh, never thought of that one, good suggestion. No, I'm going to finish this on my terms. I need to talk to that news lady. I need to get out a message."

Dad reaches into his pocket and hands Griffin his phone. Sabrina and Mom are staring at Dad like he's crazy. Griffin looks at him with a puzzled smile. Dad looks with a commanding response, "It's there. Just hit the dial icon."

Griffin hits the dial button then looks at Dad, "Is this her number or the general line?"

"It's her personal. You should be able to directly talk to her."

"How did you get this?"

"Our daughter, Janet, is very resourceful," Dad proudly says. Griffin has the phone to his ears. After the 10th ring, she answers, "What?" she not-so politely asks.

"Janine, it's Griffin. How are you doing?" Griffin says in such a polite voice that it is either sarcastic, patronizing or both.

"How do I know it's you? You're already the fifteenth Griffin I've heard from."

Griffin pauses. Has to think about that one. His eyes grow wider. "You know how Larry is drinking?"

"Oh so well," Janine dryly replies.

"Do you know where he's getting his ice from?"

"No. And don't care. Get to the point. Quickly."

"If you haven't shown his ice bucket on TV then I'll tell you it's a metal hotel ice bucket from the Driskill hotel. Has the Driskill logo on it. Call him to verify. That should narrow down your skepticism enough to listen to me."

"I'll call him to verify after we hang up. If you are the Griffin then what do you want?"

"Call this Candy Man and tell him I'll meet him outside the Independent Bank building. And call him, him only. I'm not going there with 1000 people wanting to kill me or wannabes wanting to be on camera."

"Why? What reason would I not report this to my viewers."

"If you report it. I'll turn around and run as far as away as possible and have a peaceful end with the girl I love and my great in-laws."

He looks deeply in Sabrina's eyes and winks at the parents. "I'll do you one better. We'll get in the car and be 20 miles from here in 5 minutes. Nowhere to be found and your story goes cold and bam! Nothing. You'll lose viewers by the millions every second, that's why."

"What time?" she says knowing he has the upper hand.

"Tell him to meet me in 15 minutes."

"OK. But, in return, I am going to have a cameraman there. I won't announce it. Just let him know one-on-one. If this is the great battle of human's last race then I want it covered properly."

"Fine. But don't tell the camera man what he's going to shoot. Pun intended. Have 'em show up and when we arrive, he'll know." He hangs up. Janine is getting a taste of her own medicine.

CHAPTER 42

Earth to Bartender

J ANINE IMMEDIATELY CALLS LARRY. Larry answers in a happy inebriated voice. General Janine begins barking orders, "Larry, find someone down there with a video cam on their phone and good signal strength to head to the Independent Bank building now. Have them call me on my direct number. I'll give them direct instructions. We have 15 minutes so do it now."

While Larry is drunk, he's still mostly in control of his faculties. He's had years of experience of this drinking game while being a sharp lawyer at the same time.

"Why?"

"There is going to be a show down with Candy Man and Griffin. I, and now you, are the only ones that know so keep it that way. Do NOT drunk away this secret otherwise we're screwed. Griffin doesn't show up, we lose our viewers and our spotlight.

Griffin agreed to a cameraman being there to broadcast the showdown. And the camera man cannot know either. We just need to tell them where to go. And that's it. Got it? So we need to find someone quickly. Where's your boy girlfriend? We'll even take him."

Larry pauses, thinking for a moment, "So you obviously talked to Candy Man or Griffin."

"Griffin."

"And now you're in charge of the battle of the end of the world." His wheels are turning.

"Yes," she impatiently replies. Silence follows. "Hello? Are you there? Earth to bartender. Hello?"

Larry responds in full confidence, "Sure. I can find someone. Give me a moment. I'll call you back."

He sits there for a full minute. His camera light is not on so he has time to think. He looks over to see Veronica and calls her over. She happily dances over and in her sweet talk voice asks, "What do you need, hon?"

"Do you know how to use the Facebook thing?"

"Of course. What do you need?"

"Do you know how to send private messages or poster wall it. Or however you call it? I need to get a message to the Austin Police Department and think this is only way. And a message that only APD can see. Is that possible?"

"Sure, hon. Give me your phone."

She takes his phone while handing her empty drink for the obvious refill. Larry knows the drill and happily plays bartender reaching below for the bottle. She starts swiping his phone screen looking for his Facebook app.

She has that puzzled look and finally looks at him, "I need your Facebook page. Where is it?"

"I don't have one. I don't even know how to use Facebook nor want to."

She tilts her head upwards with an exhaustive look. She puts Larry's phone on the table then pulls her out from under sports jersey and starts swiping away.

"Can you have Tiffany log on as well? This is important. And I miss her."

"She's right over there," Tiffany answers without moving her head frozen to the power of the iPhone screen.

"Yeah, ten long feet away. She needs to be right here with us."

Veronica smiles then calls Tiffany to come over and log onto Facebook. Tiffany saunters over with the same big smile and empty drink. Tiffany's sexy walk makes Larry forget everything let alone Veronica's drink. She has to mechanically clear her throat loudly to finally jerk Larry back to bartending mode.

"Go to your Facebook page," Veronica instructs. Tiffany gladly accepts Veronica's challenge and pulls out her phone from her pocket while looking at Larry adding a milliliter of water in her scotch.

Larry hands Veronica her perfectly made drink as she takes it with a smile and pats Larry on the head for her 'thank you' gesture. Larry is a happy puppy.

"I'm on it right now. Duh." Tiffany responds as she waves the phone to her.

Tiffany hands Larry her empty drink. Larry happily takes it and continues bartender mode. Tiffany looks at Veronica with that quizzical look for further instructions.

Veronica takes a small sip, "Find the Austin Police Department Facebook page and, uh, Larry? What do we post?"

He says without missing a beat on his strategic scotch pouring. "Send this message. Let's see if they respond." He looks around now talking to himself more than to the girls. "I need to find Leslie."

As he's looking around, he starts methodically relaying his message as if he was talking to some morse code messenger in World War One. Tiffany and Veronica respond with pure selfie generation agility.

Larry watches them typing away his message with a thumb speed that he didn't know exists. *We've been reduced to thumbs now? Hopefully they're opposable.* Tiffany hits send then looks at Veronica. Veronica hits send while looking back at Tiffany. She turns to Larry, "Is this for real?"

"Yes," Larry responds. "So don't tell anyone. The only people who need to know at this point are us and the cops so let's hope they read your post."

CHAPTER 43

Stay Tuned

MARIAN, DARREN, JOHNNY AND DANA look at each other for the last time and hopefully their last mission. Johnny and Dana nod Darren to the direction of the studio. Johnny looks back to Marian, "You ready?"

"Yeah. And why do I wait again? Shouldn't I follow y'all now?"

"You're the medic. Medics are always last in battle. You should know that," Darren interjects.

"With a gun in one hand and a grenade in my bag, I somehow don't feel like a medic."

"You have your medical kit with you so you're the medic."

"Okay. Wait. How do you know I have my kit with me?"

"Like I said, you're a medic. Medic's always carry their kit."

Marian's a bit taken back by that accurate assessment.

"Are y'all through playing 20 questions?" Dana interrupts. She looks to Johnny then down to the smoke grenade. "Have that armed and ready?"

He nods with mission engraved face.

"Good. Throw it in as soon as we get close enough. Time is ticking." She turns her head to Darren. "Go."

Darren crouches down and starts moving down the tree lined office complex with Johnny, Dana following and Marian a few steps behind. Darren leads them up to the final wall hiding them from the cameras and their eyes.

Darren runs up behind a black Nissan Sentra. Slowly and gently sets his rifle on the trunk, lowers his eyes into the scope. "Three, two…" The northwest camera goes flipping off its mount smashing to the ground. Johnny and Dana start running to the 4x4 while Dana scoots to the edge waiting her cue.

"Whoa! What just happened?" Janine blurts out looking at Building Monitor 2 go full static. "Ladies and Gentlemen, we're having some technical difficulties so let's see what's happening at the finish line." She hits monitor 2. "Larry, it's yours. Find a new drinking game and keep them entertained."

She goes back to her laptop and moves her finger to the comm button to the studio. Looks up and sees Building Monitor 1 go static. "Hey guys! Something is going on. Both cameras are out."

"Yeah, we know," a voice says over the speaker system. "Oh shit. What is that?"

"What?" Janine responds with a much more troubled tone. She hears a boom. Didn't sound like an explosion or a gun shot, more like something falling.

"What's going on over there? Status report please."

She hears hard coughing and breathing. "Tear gas, they threw a tear gas bomb into the studio. We need to evacuate."

"Don't! Stay there!"

Too late as the six closest exit the building where Johnny and Dana are gunning them down one by one. Janine can hear the gunfire.

"Shit!"

The melee finally wakes the students from their drugged out reality and flee the scene. *So far, so good*, Marian thinks.

She has cover so runs across the street up to the wall just behind Johnny with the F150 covering them. There are seven soldiers in the station whose positions didn't affect them as much. The soldiers heard the gunfire so know their options are limited.

Johnny and Dana can't decipher much of the guards' conversation inside but did hear the word 'trapped'. The guards are leaning against the back wall as the tear gas is naturally drawn out by the open windows. The lead guard loads a new magazine and nods to the others.

Before the guards go on the attack, another presumably tear gas bomb falls next to them but this one looks different. BOOM. The lead guard and two comrades next to him are blown to death. The three others are hit injuring them badly. This time Janine hears the indisputable sound of an explosion. *Shit!*

The remaining guards are breathing so much tear gas, they have nowhere to run but out the door. Limping and coughing, they evacuate the building as quickly as they can. Having three half-blind, coughing guards stumbling out the door gives Dana full vantage point to gun each of them down. Marian pulls out her pistol.

Dana turns on her squawk box, "Martinez, we're storming the building. Already have killed ten or more. Stay tuned."

At this point, Darren has moved up behind Marian and Johnny with pistol out and rifle wrapped around his back. The studio and surrounding area are eerily quiet. No coughing, talking or sounds of people moving around.

They wait another 10 seconds then Dana waves them to follow her. She runs to the side of the building and lays her back flat to the brick wall. Johnny and Darren follow her while the medic stays behind.

Dana does a quick peek into the building and doesn't see anyone. She takes a deep breath to move in quickly to ensure the area is clear. She enters with gun pointed in her sight. She turns her head right to a hidden mercenary pointing a gun at her. She whips her pistol to the stranger as he shoots her in the forehead for an instant kill shot. The mercenary shoots three more times forcing Johnny and Darren to stay put outside.

Marian sees Dana flat on her back and knows from the gunshot wound that Dana is dead. She looks around then lifts herself up to peer inside the 4x4 and sees a jacket next to the dead driver. She grabs it and starts wrapping the two bloody arm sleeves covering her mouth.

She runs up the closest concrete berm and climbs to its top and waits for the tear gas to thin out from the building. If she measured the angle of the bullet that killed Dana correct, she should have a clear shot. She peeks her head up quickly and sees the lone gunman cornered. He has a panicked look staring at the door with gun pointing at the entrance.

Marian figures he's probably waiting for the smoke to clear enough to run back behind the desk for better cover. He is trapped which means he has no choice but to fight. He can still take a couple more on his way out so Marian can't wait. She has a clear shot now.

She ducks her head to let more smoke clear and out of the shooter's sight. She pauses three seconds then stands up and starts shooting. Johnny hears the thump and rushes in to see him dead on the ground.

He rushes back to Dana to see if she can be saved. Marian jumps down to rush over knowing she is gone but not taking any chances and who knows. She has been in enough combat situations that reality is not always what it seems.

Janine is watching the events unfold and finally takes control. She pushes the switcher to the camera that broadcasts her. "Ladies and Gentleman, we have breaking news. The vigilante cops have stormed the KVUT building killing all of the supporters of our broadcast on a mission to kill me.

As the sole news reporter covering the event, it must be emphasized that eliminating this broadcast will harm the spirit of the race and the first constitutional amendment representing freedom of the press.

Those who believe in the Constitution of the United States should take arms to save me, the last remaining hope in the freedom America has symbolized throughout the centuries. I am at KVUT studios at Steck Avenue and Shoal Creek Boulevard. Please come save me now!"

Larry is in his seat smiling. *Freedom of the press, my ass. She asked for this.* Janine switches back to Larry as she smiles. At the bar, Martinez is watching her call to arms with a 'holy shit' response.

Marian, Darren and Johnny are in shock as the reality is sinking in that Dana is gone. Marian looks at Johnny knowing his reaction will be both intense and unpredictable. Johnny remains silent looking at his wife, holding her hand. He gently sets her hand on the ground then grabs his pistol, cocks it and puts it to his temple.

Marian's eyes go wide and grabs his hand. "No!" Her moves work well enough for the bullet to race off to the distance. Johnny regains control and returns to suicide position. This time staring straight at Marian.

"No. Please. She needs you to carry on her strength. We need you. Please. Janine is in there. Give her your next bullet."

He looks at her with the gun still firmly set to his temple. Darren is frozen knowing he has nothing to offer. Johnny stares at Marian, stands up and walks into the studio. The smoke has cleared enough to manage as well as can be expected.

He's doesn't look side to side for other guards. He doesn't care. His mission has changed from eliminate to revenge. Janine stares at Building Monitor 3 intensely as she sees Johnny walk into the studio gun in hand.

Marian's shock is interrupted by a text from Martinez. "Finish the mission. Just sent out a call for arms to protect her. Finish quickly and get the hell out of there. Now!"

Marian one-word responds, "Dammit!" *How does she know we're inside?* She runs in behind Johnny to look around and sees the camera pointing at the door. She points her gun and shoots the camera to the ground. Johnny quickly ducks. *What the fuck?!* He looks to see the camera bouncing down on the ground then looks back to Marian who returns with an apologetic face. Janine sees Building Monitor 3 go blank.

Marian turns around to Darren, "Stay out there. Get your sniper rifle and protect us. We're about to have company." Darren leaves the entrance grabbing his weapon of excellence. He scans the area to find the best spot and sees it.

It's the royal blue Prius that gives him the best 360 degree shooting position. It sits in the middle of the invader graveyard but close enough to the oak tree for coverage on the west side. And, morbidly enough, the hanging man providing additional cover.

Best of all, the little compact has a sunroof. Glass is much more stable to place a rifle than the flimsy polymers cars are made of. Why someone would drive a Prius to attack Janine is anyone's guess? Judging from the body outside of its front door, the old man didn't come expecting victory.

Marian looks to her left to see Johnny methodically inspecting each of the defender's weapons. He picks a semi-automatic on the ground. Looks like most of the make-shift army had the same weapons so the ammo necessary is plentiful.

Marian looks at him with urgency, "Come on. We need to finish this. She pulls out her second grenade."

Marian pulls on the handle and the door doesn't budge. *Janine locked her own guards out?* While it's a cold move, it's pretty smart. She added another layer to her protection.

"Why is there a lock on the door anyway?!" Johnny growls.

"Media attention will do weird things to people." Marian points to the grey scan box where approved staff wave their key cards to enter.

"If I remember correctly you'd be amazed how small news budgets are thus the equipment they buy. Back away for a moment."

Marian shoots the scan box twice watching it shatter to pieces. She turns the door handle and opens immediately. Marian ducks her head in quickly making sure the room is void of any more of her *guards*. They can hear Janine repeating the urgent news alert and her cry for help. Marian has had enough in so many ways. They're twenty feet from the door. It's enough distance to get an accurate grenade-throw with enough cover.

She holds up the grenade to communicate in no unequivocal manner of her intentions. Johnny nods in army-ready fashion. She lifts the grenade, arms it and rolls it to bump against the door. Whether the door is locked or not, who cares. Janine could use a jolt.

Martinez is on the comm with Tank letting him know about the invasion, Janine's announcement and Dana's death. He's shaking his head wondering why he did this. It's not like he could have saved the world.

He needed his last hooray of importance. And now his friends and comrades have been killed due to his self-importance. They could all be back at the bar enjoying drinks and memories.

At this moment, he has no choice but to finish what he started. *Otherwise, what's the point?* "Tell Marian to kill her immediately and get the hell out there as quickly as possible."

"I don't think it's necessary to give them the go-ahead to kill Janine. It's going to happen whether you say so or not," Martinez responds.

The grenade sits there at the doorway for six long seconds then explodes. They wait two seconds for the smoke to clear then rush into the studio looking forward to ending her world earlier than many. The grand studio is much smaller than what they see on television. TV has a way of doing that.

The explosion caused some damage and smoke but the pristine image of the TV news station remains. The backdrop, the elegant glass table and the ominous green screen sit there in a moment of stillness.

Johnny marches into the room with semi-automatic at full throttle gunning down the studio through the smoke without a care in the world what he hits as long as it has the name Janine on it. After his cartridge is spent, he stops with Marian behind him.

Marian has her gun out while Johnny is reloading. First go-around, they don't see her. The studio is in shambles from the grenade and bullets but enough to see it is empty of humans except for them. Nothing.

They scan the studio again. This was not a scenario they considered let alone a heart wrenching defeat they would never expected. Janine is alive and well. They can hear her over the TVs. She is still in control. And she has made them the fools and now the targets to be killed.

CHAPTER 44

Fool Proof

G RIFFIN LOOKS AT SABRINA and the parents, "I want to thank you for everything you've done. And Sabrina, you don't know how much I love you and cherish every minute I had with you. I have to do this alone. I don't want your last moments to be murdered."

As he turns, Sabrina yells out in a desperate plea, "Wait! What are you doing? What about death do us a part? I'm going with you!"

Griffin turns back still in rhythmic running breath, looks at Sabrina with a sincere smile and holds out his hand. Sabrina's parents are watching with dismay of what Griffin is signaling and their daughter's willingness to go.

"Don't you dare," Dad says as he grabs her shoulder.

"Come on," Griffin says to Sabrina with a calm smile and commanding tone. He looks at Mom and Dad as they're stunned by his response. "Meet us at the finish line so when we cross it, you're there. We'll be fine. We'll slay this dragon together. Trust me. Go on and we'll meet you there. Same spot."

Sabrina is a bit surprised on how easily Griffin is to welcome her. Mom and Dad are speechless. *So much for Texas chivalry.*

Dad turns to Griffin and sternly asks, "What are you going to do for God's sake?"

"To finish the race and join you and our friends in our usual joyous celebration."

"Yes. I know. You've told us, dozens of times. What about the part about the face off with the crazy man and his army? How can you possibly defeat them?"

"It's a fool-proof plan, actually."

Sabrina pauses waiting for the remaining explanation, "And that is?"

"To head down Trinity. Hit Shoal Creek to Congress then First to the finish line."

"Uh, that's nowhere near the bank."

"Yep."

"So, you just lied to the news lady and everyone else?"

"Yep."

"Wow. No wonder you're so calm. That's pretty damn smart of you."

"Yep. I have no obligation to the news lady or that freak chasing me. My whole goal is to finish the race with you and be there with the gang at the end. The news lady, the crazy dude, even the crowds have been trying to control me from the get-go when I never wanted this at all. You think I'm going start now? Nope. Fuck 'em. I'm going to beat them at their own game."

She runs to hug and kiss him. He smiles wide then looks to the parents with a wave.

"Why didn't you just tell us that you were never going to meet them in the first place and spare us this nerve-wracking moment?" blurts out Mom.

"Had to have some sort of plot twist. Otherwise what's the fun of this ending. We only have a couple hours left so thought I would fuck with y'all while I had the chance. Besides, if I'm your son-on-law for only a little while, I had to use my one 'get out of jail for free' card so as not to waste it."

Dad just shakes his head with a slow smile appearing, "Well you just damn used it there for sure, you little shit."

Mom interrupts smiling as well, "We'll see ya at the finish line, sweety and little shit of a son-in-law."

Griffin's smile is in full victory, "Okay. See ya there." Griffin waves as they start their pace again. Sabrina shakes her head smiling, "I'm glad I married you. You're awesome, you little shit."

Griffin looks at her and smiles even wider.

CHAPTER 45

Keep Janine Alive

W HILE JIMMY IS REGAINING his consciousness, Rob bursts through the door, "Boss! They found him!" Janine just reported it. But that's not all. The police are attacking the studio where Janine is. She's asking for help. She's about to be killed."

Jimmy shakes off his recent episode to catch the cocaine express. "Shit! I wanted to kill her but later on. At the moment we need her. Fuck!"

"That's why they're trying to kill her. Tank's smart. He knows if she's gone, we'll never find any of them," Tanner responds as their now self-appointed military advisor.

Rob looks at him confused, "Why? We found Griffin. He's over there near the U.T. fountain. Fuck her." Rob looks at the white dusty table then to Candy Man, "Can I have a line?"

"First, she may be getting bad information about Griffin's location. Second, U.T.'s fifteen minutes from here. Unless someone has him tied down, we still need eyes and ears. Griffin's on the run, remember. If I were you," he looks to Jimmy. "I'd send ten of your soldiers to protect her. Now."

"That'll severely deplete our army," interjects Cheryl.

"Again, without her information, it doesn't matter if we had 100."

"Rob, get 10 of those soldiers and send them to KVUT to keep Janine alive. Go now. Come back and I'll give you a line," Jimmy barks.

That's all Rob needed. He bolts out of the room. Tanner looks at Jimmy, shakes his head and follows Rob.

CHAPTER 46

The Drunk Guy

MARTINEZ IS SCANNING EVERY SCREEN, email, website while on stand-by for any communication from Tank, Marian or Dana. Maria is monitoring Janine's broadcast. Melia scans social media.

Melia has a methodical system of monitoring each of the popular social media channels—Twitter, Instagram, Facebook, Snapchat then some of the others. She has four separate windows open making it easier to monitor each and navigate to the others.

Melia scans each window then stops, "Uh, Dad. Whoa. Hold on. Listen to this," she pauses as she speed reads. Maria looks at her daughter and knows when she has that intense look, you better pay attention. Melia starts reading aloud.

"Hello Austin Police Department. This is an urgent cry for help. This is Larry, the on-air TV host. I have vital inside information regarding the safety of Griffin. Please call my personal cell number at 512-459-3880 immediately. Griffin desperately needs your help. And I have information that no-one else has. And, it's signed 'Larry'."

They immediately look at each other and say in unison, "The drunk guy."

CHAPTER 47

Protect Janine

ROB IS RUNNING OVER to what's left of the rag-tag army with Tanner striding behind him. Rob, huffing and puffing starts blurting out commands for them to go protect Janine. He's never felt so important in his life.

They're huddled behind smart phones trying to get the latest. They glance up for a quick look then back to the screens they go. "Okay. Candy Man wants 10 of you to go to the studio to protect Janine. Now!" They remain glued to their screens. Rob wouldn't have made a good motivational speaker.

"You know where the KVUT studios are?" Tanner interrupts. They stand to attention when Tanner speaks.

A brief pause then a grayish man in his early fifties responds, "I do but it's not that close. We need a car or cars if we want to get there in time."

Tanner looks at him nodding. "Go back to the VW dealership up the road. They still have a couple of lines of cars."

They each look at Tanner wondering if he knows something they don't. One of the X men sporting a Cushman & Wakefield dinner jacket pipes up, "Where are the keys? Do they leave them in the cars?"

The obvious silence captures the moment then a young Asian man speaks up, "I know where they are."

They all turn to him. He returns their looks with full confidence. The last day of earth will do that to you. He has spiky dark hair that doesn't-move-no-matter-what stillness wearing dark rimmed glasses. He pauses savoring the moment. "I used to work at a Volkswagon dealership. I know where they hide the master."

Tanner nods his head, "Go."

"I don't' think that's the best idea. That's where the police are," interjects the grayish haired man.

"They're gone. You can't protect a moving target staying still." He looks back at the Asian man, "Go."

The Asian man takes command. He looks to his fellow soldiers closest to him, "Come on, follow me." Another group in this last race has found a purpose with perceived importance.

Tanner and Rob watch what's left of their army disappear leaving them with two dozen or so stragglers. Rob's lightbulb goes off remembering he has a line of coke waiting for being a good boy. He rushes off for his candy.

CHAPTER 48

Harry Truman

L ARRY IS STANDING NOW wobbling like a bowling pin after a split. He keeps his left hand steady on the chair and drink in the other. He calls the play-by-play of Veronica and Tiffany playing tequila jeopardy with the crowd surrounding them. He's the color commentator for the game grinning largely having an excuse to watch Veronica and Tiffany closely.

He turns to the camera, "Here's how their makeshift drinking game goes. Volunteers from the crowd waiting in that long line wait for their one trivia question from Tiffany or Veronica. If they answer correctly, they get a long French kiss from both of the girls. If they answer incorrectly, a shot of tequila is mandated then the next sucker is up."

Veronica was astute enough to make it mandatory for participants to hand over their phones so no cheating. They must stay true to the spirit of the game for the participants' ignorance of mindless trivia.

With those parameters, it is no wonder that the line is 100% men. And with the looks of Veronica and Tiffany, the line of men is long. Add the fact to this mindless event, the number of liquor bottles next to them grow larger with every breathtaking moment.

While it's called tequila jeopardy, the makeshift coordination of a tequila-only game is a bit difficult on the last day of earth so their arsenal vary from tequila, bourbon, gin, vodka, schnapps and Baileys.

Janine would have cut him off 10 minutes ago but the viewing numbers keep growing. She chalks it up to the mindset of the world's TV viewing population.

The problem is, and no one has called them on it, Veronica and Tiffany don't know the answers to their own questions. But to this point, it doesn't matter as long as they act like they know.

They're looking at each other giggling as their previous victim exhales a full breath of fine tequila that tastes exquisite while fucking him up to the next level. The crowd goes wild celebrating this loser. The next contestant steps up to the plate. Veronica looks at Tiffany signaling it's her turn to come up with some random and unanswerable question.

Tiffany smiles and starts reaching out to her thoughts, "Ok. Um… Uh. Ok! Who was the 33rd President of the United States?" *Hopefully there have been 33 Presidents*, she thinks. She's proud of herself that she came up with a legitimate question so quickly when the average looking man immediately answers, "Harry Truman."

Both Veronica and Tiffany look at each other with the odd feeling that he may actually be correct. Add to the fact that the Office Max looking manager seems so confident in his answer. Veronica starts thumbing away on her Iphone to see that Harry Truman was, in fact, the 33rd President. They look at each other slumping their shoulders that not only was he correct but they have to uphold their line of the deal. The dumpy, goatee'd, middle age man just got his last day's wish fulfilled.

Tiffany and Veronica look at each other with the revelation of 'what the fuck?'. Let's have some fun and make this man's wishes come true in full form.

Veronica walks slowly with a seductive trance staring Happy Man without a blink. She gently grabs his face to serve him his happy meal of a slow, long French kiss that makes him almost faint. The crowd goes wild.

She slowly releases and looks him in the eyes with a Playboy stare. She smiles, tweaks his cheek and turns around. She makes sure to turn around and give him a wink to ensure he's fully examining her body from behind.

Now it's Tiffany's turn. She mimics the same walk as she high fives Veronica passing her both smiling knowing the power their looks possess. Tiffany wants to out-do Veronica so walks up with a seductive stare. She doesn't do anything but give Happy Man a small kiss. He's a bit disappointed but that quickly vanishes.

She emotes a playful smile then takes both hands to gently flow through his mildly balding head that strategically lands into a close embrace at the top of his neck where she has full control both sexually and physically. He now looks like he is seconds away from passing out.

She pulls him closer for another small but much more passionate and longer kiss. She pulls up again and tilts her head staring straight to his libido then lands one long, lasting full tounged kiss.

Happy Man just stands there blinking blankly. The crowd goes even louder. She strokes her hand down his left cheek, pats it lightly then blows him a last kiss. Tiffany won this round.

Larry is fully enjoying the moment. He has two beautiful girls at his disposal, a camera broadcasting him to the world while playing human chess with Janine, his estranged, crazy broadcast 'wife'. And last but not least, trying to protect Griffin, his self-adopted son. If there was a last day of earth, today is a good one.

Larry looks down at his phone as it's ringing the theme to "Walking on Sunshine". "Oh! I gotta get this. Switch to the other cam will ya?"

"No. Who are you talking to?" Janine is not happy with her direction being challenged.

"This is Larry," answering the phone looking at the camera with an irritated eye. "Hold on." He takes his hand off the recliner trying to maintain balance. "Hey gals, will you entertain our viewers while I take this call please?"

Larry points to the camera, "If that light is red then you're on. If not, then you're not so keep a close eye."

Janine is fuming.

"Sure," Veronica says with a big smile. Tiffany waves at the camera with a seductive smile then looks at Veronica. "Okay. Let's tease some more men." She turns around to see the salivating line of men.

Larry stumbles off camera. The scotch is finally beginning to show. He puts the phone back to his ear, "Sorry about that. Had take care something quickly. Who is this?"

"This is officer Martinez with APD. I'm the point contact for the police officers wanting to protect Griffin and his runners. You said you have some information you want to share."

Larry's eyes bulge wide open. *His message worked!* "Yes. Griffin's running into a big bear trap at the Independent Bank building in like 15 minutes. He's going to meet that Candy man there for a showdown but is going alone while Dandy man will have all of his gingabread men to make sure Griffin doesn't walk away alive let alone finish running th' race. He needs y'all there."

"How do you know this?"

"Griffin called us to set it up."

"Roger that. Thank you for the tip. You're a good man. I'd buy you a drink for your help but not enough time, you know."

"No. But have a drink with me down here at the finish line with Griffin and all else when you save his ass and finishes. How's that?"

"Sounds like a plan. I've got your number. You have mine. Let's stay in touch. Gotta run. And thank you very much."

Larry hangs up and turns around to see Tiffany and Veronica hamming it up to the camera. He smiles wide and shuffles back to his chair.

CHAPTER 49

A Message

JIMMY, JAY AND CHERYL pass Rob on their way out laughing at Rob's nose twitching like a rabbit. Out the front door, they see around twenty men left watching Tanner inspect their weapons.

So much for an army. Jimmy surveys the remnants of his crusaders. *If we can keep Janine broadcasting we have an army then that should be enough.* Jimmy, being a psychiatrist, knows how powerful perception can be.

Jimmy's phone rings. His attention alters, takes his phone out of his pocket, looks at the caller ID and raises an eyebrow. "Well, hello news lady. We were just talking about you and have a little gift we're sending to you."

"I have a message to relay," Janine instructs. Jimmy's a bit taken back how she's ignoring his message and the fact that she's about to be killed.

"Relay please."

"Griffin just called me. Says he wants to meet you at the Independent Bank building at West and 4th in 15 minutes."

"Why?"

"I don't know. I'm not his psychologist. He didn't tell me."

"Good reporting there Janine. Investigative journalism at its finest. Aren't you about to be killed, by the way?" *How can she be so calm?* He pauses wondering what Janine is up to.

"Are you there or not? Need to know so I can confirm with Griffin."

"Yeah I'm here. Didn't know it was going to be this easy. I'm almost disappointed." Jimmy responds hanging up the phone. He turns to his gang, "I don't know what's going on with her. She doesn't sound in danger. But the important thing that she is alive long enough to let us know where Griffin is. Let's go. Follow me."

CHAPTER 50

Let's Ride

"WHAT? WHEN? ARE YOU SURE?" Tank responds. Martinez is on the other end briefing Tank on his conversation. "I just got off the phone with Larry—the drunk guy broadcasting at the finish line. They talked to Griffin and that's what Griffin told them. Griffin's the one who is setting this up.

And here's the kicker. Griffin thinks it's a showdown just between the two of them but you gotta know that's bullshit. We need to be there."

"OK. The Independent Building in 15 minutes. Gotcha."

"Could be quicker. Don't know how late the information is. I'd haul ass if I were you"

"Good work. Keep monitoring. We'll let you know from our end."

Tank clicks off the comm, stands up straddling his motorcycle and turns to Escobar, Ernie and Joe.

"I have some information that their gang has a meeting with Griffin in 15 minutes at the Independent Bank Building. Make sure you're fully loaded with extra ammo at your disposal. This could be a blood bath. Let's ride."

CHAPTER 51

The Today Show

L ARRY SHUFFLES BACK to his chair. Veronica stands up and holds her hand out for Larry to grab. Larry takes it to steady his balance to plop down squarely in his chair without incident. Veronica is a physical therapist so Larry's drunk ass is right up her alley. Except for the inebriation part, usually it's a car crash or chemo patient she tends to.

Larry pulls a key out of his front pocket to unlock the chest holding his precious reserve. He pulls out a fresh bottle. He sees Tequila Jeopardy has been cancelled due to loss of alcohol so random chaos surrounds Larry's world again. Larry calls out to the girls, "Where's Leslie? Seen him?"

"Just saw him ten minutes ago," Tiffany blurts out excited she's a contributing member. "He was over near the finish line handing out joints."

Larry looks over but there's too many people and commotion in the way. He turns to the girls. They know the look.

"We'll find him," Veronica says with mission. She waves to Tiffany to join her.

"Please. Bring him to me. I have a very important task for him."

He smiles. He can't help it with beautiful women taking care of him. He sees the camera light is not on so knows Janine is stirring up some sort of trouble. At the moment, it's fine with him. He has a drink to fix.

Tiffany comes short-stepping up constrained by her miniskirt with her playful smile. "He's coming over right now. "

Just on cue, Leslie saunters through the crowd as if he and his garb are the norm. The thing is, it is. "What's going on? Fans asking for me?"

"Always but for now we need your help," Larry says in a more commanding tone. "We need you to be our on-camera host at the Independent Bank building."

Leslie's thinking about it. You can't really tell if he's thinking about the request or just trying to think in general. He's just that way. Larry's impatience forces his choice of words to a different strategy.

He slows his words down to present a more gratuitous tone. He takes a small sip to give him the commanding pause then casually looks at Leslie, "We're above 100 million people tuned into the race now."

"I'll do it."

That sealed the deal.

"Do you have a phone that can broadcast video?"

"Uh, no. I don't own a phone." Larry forgot he's talking to a homeless man.

Veronica hands hers to him, "Here. Use mine." She hands it to him then walks behind him. "See here. This is the KVUT app that has a broadcast now button but has to be activated on their end so I think Larry will tell you."

She looks over to Larry for confirmation. Larry's silently impressed at Veronica's technical skills being as good as her looks.

He wakes up from his salivation. "Janine will instruct you on that."

"What am I recording?" Leslie nonchalantly asks.

"Janine will instruct you on that."

"Call this number and talk to her directly." Veronica takes the phone back and starts typing Janine's phone number as Larry relays the number. She figures that will save at least ten minutes of valuable time for her to input it. Leslie stands there grinning excitedly waiting for 100 million viewers. Veronica adds Janine as a contact then hands Leslie back the phone.

She points to the address book app, "Any time you need to call her, push this phone button and her name will pop up and hit the number and that's all you need to do."

Larry relays to Janine that Leslie is the new addition to, as Larry puts it, "this crazy fucking version of the Today Show hosted by Janine, Larry and now Bicycle Leslie."

Leslie dons an excited smile to Larry and the girls as they watch him mount his bicycle to merrily pedal his way to the showdown and his death.

CHAPTER 52

What About You?

J IMMY'S MEN ARE CRAMMED in two VW Golf cars slowing down to the KUTV studio. Looters must have thought that VW Golfs weren't worth the effort so left them unscathed. Marian, Johnny and Darren stand at the doorway watching the midget cars approach knowing the closer they get, the more they are cornered. The scene would be comical if not the fact they are targets to be eliminated.

Darren has his rifle out. "If I can shoot the right person at the right time in the right order then we can get out of this fairly quickly and easy. As soon as I shoot, run across the street."

"What about you?"

"Don't worry about me. I'll get there." He stares in his scope, "Three, two…" The first bullet hits the driver of the car on his left. As the driver is now a lifeless 200-pound crash dummy, his body slumps down towards the passenger seat.

The car follows his lifeless arms up on the sidewalk hitting a telephone pole sending the seatbelt-less passengers flinging to the front of the car. There was a good reason seat belts were mandated to wear in the old days. Some go unconscious, others disoriented.

Darren quickly turns to the other driver but the driver saw what happened and veers off to the lawn on the right with at least a pecan tree to help shield themselves partially. It didn't help one of the backseat passengers as Darren's sharpshooting skills removed his gun from the fight.

"Go!" Darren shouts.

Marian and Johnny bolt. Darren's kill shots give Marian and Johnny enough time to run across the street unscathed. Marian jumps over the short wall into the complex where at the moment she is safe.

She looks to her side for Johnny. But he's not there. She turns around to see Johnny standing in the middle of the street shooting his semiautomatic rifle to the wrecked car picking off the easy targets. The Xs on their bodies ended up being a bad idea.

Darren doesn't know what to do. With the other car reacting as it did, Johnny is open season. Darren doesn't have the angle to protect him. He looks across the street to see if Marian has the angle but she's not there. *Dammit!*

He has no choice. He runs. Johnny's through killing the passengers in the wrecked car so turns to the other to car to eliminate them. Before he starts shooting, he's hit in the upper left chest. It's not a kill shot but close. He regains as much balance as he can and starts shooting in the direction of his killers.

As Darren crosses, he grabs Johnny to take him but Johnny still has enough strength to push him off. He turns to Darren, "Take care of Marian." He turns back to shooting in somewhat the direction of the remaining attackers when a bullet hits him dead center in the chest slamming his body to the pavement. He lies there open armed, motionless.

Darren, now on the other side under cover watches Johnny fall. He can't tell if he's dead but his instincts tell him to follow his dying wishes to join Marian and escape.

The remaining four attackers start maneuvering their way knowing they have the advantage. The only way Darren can escape is to stand and run. If he does, he's fully exposed. He has no choice. He grabs his pistol, jumps up and starts firing to give him some sort of cover.

One of the X men knew this would happen so waited patiently behind an old Camaro. Darren is clean in his sight when the X man meets a bullet in the head from Marian's pistol. She used the time and distraction to go around the complex to give her perfect surprise vantage point. She may be a medic but she's still a soldier.

Now it's three to two and Darren has enough time to get in position. They're distracted with Marian and forgot about Darren at the moment. He drops down to lay his rifle on the edge of a brick planter and sets his target clearly. "Three, two…"

The female dressed in all black falls instantly. She was on the side of the tree shielding her from Marian's bullets but not Darren's. Now, it's two against two.

That kill shot gives enough distraction for Marian to run across the street and hide behind a Mazda C3. The X man is a middle aged white trash looking mercenary, the stereotype white supremacist Hollywood would use.

He is now focused on Darren's angle. Marian may not have the angle for a kill shot but enough to hit him at the shoulder. She fires and pierces him high in the shoulder causing debilitating pain.

It didn't kill him but maimed him enough to get in survival mode and run. That gives Marian the opportunity to finish him off with a shot in the back. There's one remaining.

The last X soldier is a Mohawk-wearing girl who should have a mic in her hand on stage rather than a gun in a battle that has no meaning. She looks around. The KVUT building is long and 20 feet from her position. She stands and fires through the window enough to run and jump through.

Marian turns and runs as fast as she can to the motorcycles where Darren meets her. It ended up being an empty mission but more than 20 of them are down. Two dozen adversaries gone helps no matter what. They don't realize though that their failed mission changed the momentum of the battle to their advantage.

CHAPTER 53

It Works

C ANDY MAN TROTS UP to the front of the Independent Bank building. It is locally known as the Jenga Tower as it is stacked uneven vertically to the sky. It's the tallest building in Austin and next to the state Capital and U.T. Tower, it's become a fixture of Austin's skyline branding.

Because of its newfound fame, the owners were smart in pushing the building as an attraction making each side its own experience. The side Griffin selected is where the entrance is somewhat of an enclosed courtyard with office buildings, a Maudie's Tex-Mex dive and a Schlotskey's sandwiches surrounding the courtyard giving it some cover.

Jimmy looks around understanding why Griffin chose this spot. It's somewhat hidden, far enough yet close enough from the finish line. You can hear the race announcer in the background through the many cheers and music playing at the finish line.

His gang starts filling up the front entrance looking around to see if Griffin is already there. A few random people are in the courtyard. Two are reading a bible and four others are lying in the grass talking quietly. They look up to see Dr. Frankenstein in his physician's jacket surrounded by his monsters and quickly leave as they can see these newcomers are armed with eyes ready to kill.

Jimmy sits on a bench and pulls out his thermos and takes a quick gulp of water. Then he takes out his other thermos of whiskey and throws a tug on that one. Next, he pulls out the jelly jar of rock for another line. Jay and Cheryl are behind him wondering if he'll blank out, maintain his madness or just keel over.

He twists the top open, grabs a rock then looks around to see where he'll line this one out. He stares at the bench's arm rest, shrugs his shoulders with a 'this'll do' look and begins to crush the rock with the butt of his pistol.

This line is more of a gravel road line rather than the fine dust of masterfully sculpted one. Jay starts looking around for a spot where he can surreptitiously craft his own line without Rob, the cocaine jackal, around.

Tanner is leaning on a marble column above Jimmy watching as he snorts it up shaking his head in disgust. Candyman finishes then lets out a war cry of euphoric power.

He puts his pistol down and walks up to Jay who is startled by the unannounced visit while uncomfortably holding an AK 47. Cheryl smiles at Jay's nervousness.

"Is it ready? Does it work?"

"Uh, yeah. I guess. Haven't shot it." Cheryl upgraded Jay to an AK 47. She thought the pistol made him look like a pussy.

"It works," Cheryl interjects.

"May I have a look at it?"

Jay hurriedly hands it to him showing full deference, "Yeah. Sure."

Jimmy grabs the rifle then adjusts it to firing position with a tight grip from both hands. He puts a wide grin on his face then turns to the Independent building and starts shooting indiscreetly at the glass doors and windows lining the entrance floor of the 690 foot-tall office building.

Many shots nearly hit his own army but he's having too much fun to care if he loses a man or three. His people scramble quickly watching his lunacy. Glass is shattering and falling while bullets fly from his adrenaline and further entry to insanity. Cheryl stands there grinning ear to ear. Jay is rattled.

CHAPTER 54

A Total Bust

DARREN AND MARIAN know more people are on the way to kill them so they're throwing away caution to the wind and acting like it's the last day of earth and in danger of being killed. Oh wait, it is. They hit Shoal Creek on high gear to get some space. After a mile, they see a major intersection up ahead and see runners. It's around the 10-mile marker.

Marian doesn't want to get mired in that mess so looks around and spots a Sonic drive-in. She nods to Sonic's direction so both peel off into the parking lot around the back to a stop. Marian takes out her phone and calls Tank.

Tank and gang are weaving their way on Neches boulevard. They're in the student housing neighborhood so maneuvering through a narrow street full of cars on both sides. They're close to the race but far enough to get to the Independent building without racers stopping them or slowing them down.

Tank feels his phone buzzing. He grabs it out from inside his torn dress on his vest pocket and sees it's Marian. He quickly pulls over. The rest of the crew follow in line. "Love, what's going on? Where are you?"

"We're at Sonic on Shoal Creek. Janine's alive. She wasn't even there. It was a total bust."

"What?!" Tank looks at Joe and Ernie shaking his head. They've seen that look before and know it's not good news.

"Johnny and Dana are dead. Darren and I escaped. We killed every one of her guards, stormed the studio and it was empty."

Tank repeats Marian's report as she is talking so Joe and Ernie are in the know.

"She's broadcasting remotely," Joe whispers. "Fuck."

Hearing Joe and Tank give status Ernie grabs the comm, "Martinez, is Janine on TV?"

"Yeah. She was pleading for help saying she was being attacked but Larry is on right now with two fine chicks. I wonder if that means she's been cut off. Have you talked to Marian? What's going on?"

Ernie relays the news to Martinez. "They stormed the studio. Killed everyone to find Janine's not there. It was a bust. That's why I'm asking. Her distress call was a good move. Split us up and gives her and the freaks a bigger advantage. And," he pauses. "Dana and Johnny were killed."

That leaves grave silence from Martinez. Tank's listening to both conversations then abruptly asks Marian, "How many did you kill with Xs on them?"

"Ten. Or at least that's how many came to find us. They were the ones that came at the end. As for as Janine's guards, we probably killed 15 or so."

"They need Janine as much as we do yet they only sent ten? Maybe they're not as strong as they say they are. Or what Janine is reporting."

Marian's looking around as she is talking making sure they weren't followed while Darren is reloading.

"What now?"

"Head for the Independent Bank building downtown. That's where Candy Man and Griffin are having their showdown. We're almost there to hopefully end this thing once and for all."

"How do you know that? Janine report it?"

"No. The drunk guy on TV messaged us so we could help save Griffin."

"We're pretty far from there so we need to leave." She says that as she looks at Darren. He revs his engine signaling his readiness.

"This might sound stupid but go down to 35 and go that route. It may sound a round-a-bout way but the highway has enough room for your motorcycles to go through quickly and you'll be able to flank us from the east without dealing with any of the race routes."

Marian stays there with a removed stare of concentration. She looks down at her receiver, "Okay, but if you're wrong we're going to be late."

CHAPTER 55

Once and for All

G RIFFIN AND SABRINA are running west on Yates road. It's back in the U.T. neighborhood but not on campus so they're out of sight for the moment, "Guess we're not going to break our record after all, huh?" Griffin says as he's looking side to side for spies or attackers.

"No. I just want to finish," responds Sabrina with an exhaustive voice. "Get with our friends, my parents and celebrate our time together. Like the old times."

"What? When we weren't being chased to death? Have a minimal time on this planet? Or being turned into some demigod just because I like to run? Is that what you mean?"

"Exactly."

"Good thing though is I planned the starting time to give us enough time to do our after-race celebration. At first, I was going to time as best as I could so we finished the race at the exact time."

"Why did you change?"

"Cuz I realized the real value of running these races are those who I run them with. The journey and the close connections we've built is the real meaning of life."

"You know it's weird that we're actually living the stupid cli-ché' of spend your time as if it was your last. Mom always sent me those godforsaken emails that only old people send with the inspirational stories or photos or videos.

I would always roll my eyes when I would see the captions and that they came from her. Maybe I should have paid closer attention."

Griffin smiles as he was on her mother's same email list.

They run up to another crossroad and look both ways. It's clear so they continue on. Two blocks in front of them a group of motorcycles rush by. Griffin does a double take then stops to look at Sabrina.

"Did you see that?"

"No. What?"

"I swear it was a guy with a leather outfit or a cop's outfit wearing a dress."

"Well, it is Austin and the last day of earth so I'm not going to argue with you. Maybe it's the cops Mom and Dad were talking about who want to save us."

"It may be Austin but we're not that weird to have a cross-dress-er as a cop."

Sabrina just shakes her head, "You can be really naive some-times." Griffin ignores her on that one.

They've done 22 miles so they can feel it throughout their body but they've hit the stride where it's become robotic. They're breathing deeper and harder and the pain is numb now. They cross another block and Griffin stops again.

"What now?" Sabrina says with a little frustration but full stop. She looks at him waiting for revelation, direction or a sar-castic observation while running in place.

"There it is," he says pointing down the road. She looks far down and sees what he's talking about. It's the race route—the official one.

CHAPTER 56

A Tootsie Pop

L ESLIE IS WEAVING HIS BICYCLE through the cluttered streets talking with one hand and steering with the other. "So what exactly am I filming?" Leslie asks Janine again.

"Griffin agreed to an interview before he finishes the race. He said to meet you at the Independent Bank building." Janine hopes her bullshit story will work.

"How do you know this?"

"I talked to him. He's close to finishing so he's now ready to tell the world. Just make sure you are videotaping him running up to the lobby so we have a dramatic entrance." Janine holds her breath.

"Okay."

Janine has him hook, line and sinker. She has to hope he stays far enough away to video without getting shot but close enough so the viewers can see the final showdown.

Leslie pedals away as if it was a Sunday afternoon ride appropriately humming "Tick Tock" from Stevie Ray Vaughn. He can hear a machine gun in the area. As he gets closer the sound of gunfire gets louder. He furrows his brow for a moment but keeps whistling away.

He turns the corner screeching to a halt as he sees a black haired man in a physicians' jacket screaming at the building. He looks around to see a group of soldiers hiding from the bullets with white Xs on them and eyes grown wide. He grabs his phone, "Janine, we may have a problem. Those people looking to kill Griffin are here."

No response.

"Janine?"

No response.

"Well, forget this. I'm going back to the party."

"Leslie. Hi. Sorry about that. I was on the air so couldn't answer," Janine relays completely lying hoping he would be brave enough to stay. "Do me a favor and start recording the area so I can test the broadcast."

"I'm not sure I want to do that. Just across the street there are angry people shooting guns. I wonder if they found out Griffin's coming so are here."

Leslie is still clueless which has been part of his charm through the years. He has a duality of being dazed and confused while being extraordinarily insightful living homeless as a thong wearing side show. His antics worked though. Fed himself every day sometimes with enough money for a Dirty's burger or Threadgills chicken fried steak.

"Don't worry, Leslie. They're not going to hurt you and the guns they have are just for celebration," Janine relays hoping to comfort and continue her ruse.

"Uh, okay. But I'm not sure about this. I hope they don't start shooting at me."

Leslie climbs off his bicycle and starts walking up carrying the iPhone chest level broadcasting. "Is it working?"

Janine looks at her monitor as she is now in full view of Candy Man and his loyal Orcs. She sports a wide devilish grin. "Yes, it is."

As Leslie approaches, an X-er spots him instantly. He starts approaching gun in hand as he loads a bullet in his chamber. Leslie seeing a gun pointed at him looks up and starts running. The X-er follows him with his gunsight when his arm is quickly pushed down.

"No! Don't hurt him. He's here on our behalf," Jimmy says startling the X-er looking at him confused. Jimmy quickly turns and starts running after Leslie. "Whoa, whoa, whoa…slow down. We won't hurt you. He thought you were someone else. Don't worry. We were expecting you. Our fault, want a drink or cocaine or something?"

Leslie turns around suspiciously but he's been living off of offers his entire life that he is conditioned to stop and consider such gifts whatever they may be. The whole time Janine is yelling at the phone for the X-er to not shoot. This futile gesture doesn't work but loud enough for Jimmy to hear and now the devilish grin is his.

Leslie looks at him now with a more trusting view, "Do you have a Tootsie Pop?"

"Lift the phone up and keep shooting," Jimmy says with a sweet polite tone asking for a favor. Leslie smiles and does so as instructed. "Thank you. Great job. Thank you for doing this," he continues with a grateful expression then Leslie's request hits him.

"A Tootsie Pop?"

"Yes. I love Tootsie Pops. They're my favorite."

"Uh, no. Let me check," Jimmy turns around to his gang.

This is too much for Janine to resist. She switches the broadcast feed to Leslie. The Jimmy/Leslie conversation is now live. The hundred million viewers including Larry, Veronica, Tiffany,

Martinez and family at the bar are joined into the request for a Tootsie Pop.

"Hey, any of you have a Tootsie Pop?" Jimmy can't believe he's asking this question but it is the end of the world.

They all shake their heads. Some even check their pockets for some unknown reason thinking that one is magically stowed away.

"I have gum," Jay shouts back.

Jimmy turns back to Leslie with a generous look and tone, "Gum? You want some gum?"

"What kind?" Leslie asks.

Jimmy turns back to the gang, "Watcha got?"

"Bubbalicious," Jay yells back then another call from the ranks. "I have Jolly Ranchers."

Jimmy turns back to Leslie still videoing. He raises his eyebrows in a welcoming gesture. Larry, Martinez and one hundred million other viewers are now realizing that Candy Man is the lead character of this video segment. And the irony that he is offering gum and candy is received by just as many.

"What flavor? The Jolly Ranchers," Leslie asks.

Jimmy turns back to the gang. The one offering heard Leslie so yells back, "Cherry."

Leslie smiles, "Ooh. Can I have both?"

Jimmy smiles back, "Of course you can. Anything for our camera man." Jimmy turns around and waves the two to come down for the sacrificial offering. Janine is looking at the monitor still grinning ear to ear. *I couldn't have scripted this any better. Now where's Griffin?*

CHAPTER 57

Pizza, Coke and a Salad

T HE AVENGERS, as Jimmy dubbed them, is as far of an accurate description as can get. They're four white men in their early 30s that look like they just got out of their chess club meeting. Each have short, recently cut hair wearing newly bought polo shirts and blue jeans.

The shirts are nice except for the large painted white Xs on the front and back. From the looks on their faces, they're not too happy with ruining their almost matching outfits. The only distinct difference is one is wearing a brand-new rebel flagged baseball cap and another dons a new Mr. Gatti's Pizza polo'd shirt. Such a nice Mr. Gatti's collared shirt must have been for the store manager or above.

They are near the 24-mile mark standing in Shoal Creek Park near the 15th street bridge. They are the first line of defense as the other two groups are a mile down the road. Each have the same G17 long slide pistols furthering the image of a group of friends who want to play army as their parting shot on earth.

Hank, the one in the rebel ball cap, turns to Deke, "I still don't understand the Mr. Gatti's thing. Of all shirts to wear."

Deke rolls his eyes again, "It's the only time in my life when my responsibility was a pizza, coke and a salad for that one meal on that one day. Just a simple but rewarding task. No coding. No meeting. No follow up. No report. No review. No ever present CYA.

It was a time in my life that the only thing I cared about was girls, D&D and pizza. The shirt brings me peace."

"As you're holding a pistol looking to kill a man."

"Yes, a simple task."

"How rewarding is that? A fucking slice of pizza?"

"Did you ever leave a pizza joint unhappy?"

Hank stands there silent.

"That's what I thought."

The other two Avengers are people-watching as racers stream by. They don't think they'll see Griffin let alone kill or capture him. But they have a militant purpose on this day that is in the real world and not on the internet or some video game. They are fulfilling their fantasy.

Lori looks up to see they passed the 24-mile marker and the spot where Lamar Street is in a straight line so can see a quarter mile down the race route. She is just behind Gilbert and next to Don and Raul. They haven't talked in the past several miles each wondering if Griffin and Sabrina are okay.

When she looks up, she sees four X men close to the end of Lamar before it makes a wide dog-leg turn, "Guys, look down over there. There are four X men. What do we do?"

"We continue run," Gilbert responds. "I don't think we've done enough for Griffin and these guys with their Xs are beginning to turn me angry."

Lori and Don do not like the sound of that. Lori turns to Gilbert, "What is that supposed to mean?"

Don agrees, "Yeah. What are you saying?"

"Slow our pace, guys," Raul instructs.

"Shut up," Gilbert instructs. "I coach, you listen. You slow pace. I fast pace." Raul is not happy with that answer. "Trust me. This will be for the best. For all of us."

Gilbert ups his pace creating a bigger gap between he and the three. As he approaches the Avengers, Gilbert stops. "Oh! Glock pistol. Brand new too. Our soldiers in Africa had the exact same. Let me look."

Hank and Deke are surprised at the bold interruption from one of the runners let alone a tall lanky African. His stature offers no obvious threat, they think. The two X men in the back stand up from leaning on the trees to walk up to the conversation.

Don, Raul and Lori stop still 20 yards behind. No one notices them.

"May I have look?" Gilbert asks.

Hank looks at him with suspecting eyes, "Hey, aren't you the running coach who supposed to be with Griffin?"

Raul starts his jog again as Hank and group scan the crowd. Raul doesn't want to look like a group so subtly waves his hand behind him gesturing to Lori and Don to back away. Lori bends down to look like she's fixing a shoe while Don runs in place acting like her running partner.

"No. I am one of the many African runners on the race. What? Are you saying we all look alike?" Gilbert says with a sarcastic smile. That comment gives a laugh and eases the tension for the moment.

Raul passes by Gilbert who purposely ignores him then starts hopping as if he twisted his ankle. He's walking in circles feigning pain while watching closely.

"Haven't held one since the wars of years ago. It would give me great pleasure." Hank still isn't buying it but Deke is enjoying the attention and some new conversation so hands Gilbert his.

Gilbert gladly accepts it. He holds it up admiring its beauty and checking to make sure it is locked, loaded with safety off. He looks at them to give the gun back but aims it straight to Hank's head and shoots him dead. He turns a slight right to claim Deke's life while the other two hold up their pistols to gun Gilbert down simultaneously.

Before they can get their shot off, Raul slams into Mr. Gatti's man with a blindside of sacking a quarterback. They go tumbling down to the pavement. Runners start shrieking away. Mr. Gatti's man drops his pistol while flying into the dirt and rocks. Raul picks up the gun.

Lori yells as she and Don come upon the skirmish, "Freeze!" Why she did, she has no idea but it gives Gilbert enough time to shoot the third dead. Another bullet shot goes off from Raul eliminating any delivery from Mr. Gatti's.

Don looks incredulously at Gilbert, "What the hell was that?! Were you going to tell us?"

Gilbert just stares back, "No. I had full advantage of surprise and didn't want any you in danger. I knew it would be easy and we would help Griffin and Sabrina once again."

"You know you were wrong. You should have been killed if it wasn't for Raul."

"Yes, I know. Miscalculated their response time," he turns to Raul. "Thank you for saving my life. You too, Lori and Don. Very much indebted."

Raul smiles holding his now claimed pistol. "How did you know it was locked and loaded?"

"I did not lie. Those were types of pistols used in my war torn country. When you live in war, you learn how to use weapons no matter what age. Come now. Finish race. Be with Griffin."

Gilbert throws his pistol as far as he can into Shoal Creek Park. While those pistols saved his life, they also killed friends and family. He wants no part of any type of gun.

Don, Raul and Lori are stunned once again but continue on. They just eliminated four X soldiers so they feel better about their role in this last race. As they run by the Tavern restaurant, they do not notice the X man carrying an AR-15 nor does he notice them.

Raul now runs with a loaded pistol in his hand. He wasn't about to throw his away.

CHAPTER 58

Kill Him

TANK, ERNIE, JOE AND ESCOBAR are weaving their way out of the U.T. campus into Austin's downtown going as fast as they can which is still slow. Rapid gunfire in the background is getting louder. Tank hopes that's not Griffin receiving those bullets. He can hear glass smashing so it sounds more like a gunfire tantrum of fear, anger or fun.

"You know Tanner will be there, don't you?" Ernie blurts out. Joe and Escobar look at each other.

"Yes," Tank responds. "I've gone down the same logic as you have. The only way he is sure to find me is to be just where I am heading."

Joe joins in, "If he is, what are you going to do?"

"Kill him."

"What do we do if he is there?" Escobar asks.

"Stand back and cover me. He's going to want to fight hand-to-hand so I'm going to need cover from whatever army Candy-man has."

"Why don't you just pull out your gun and bullet him right in the forehead? Problem solved."

"I will. After I beat him one-on-one and he lays unconscious on the ground. We have some unfinished business that doesn't include bullets. I've been waiting for this moment for years. I covered for him disrupting our company, our missions and creating conflict that wasn't there. Then he got away with murder, literally.

So it's time for justice. The worst thing that could happen to Tanner is if I beat him at his own game in hand-to-hand in front of everybody then execute him. That would be due justice."

Escobar is still shaking his head, "Why didn't you kick his ass back then? Hand him justice then?"

"He was his commanding officer. He can discipline him but not in that way. Has to be within the rules and code," Ernie chimes in.

Tank interrupts, "I could have and I should have. Most COs do. I'm just too much of a rules guy."

"You know you're saying that while you're wearing a dress, don't you?" That gives the group a laugh. Tank ignores them.

"I got tired of disciplining him with jumping jacks and sit-ups. Why do you think I was merciless of his murder during the hearings? And, yet, he still got away with it. So, I had to just sit there and keep my mouth shut and hope this day would come. I didn't think it would be this type of day but here we are."

A moment of silence follows. Tank shakes his head back to command mode, "We need to find out which one is Candyman. We don't even know what he looks like."

"We do now, boss." Martinez says in the comm. Tank smiles as he forgot about Martinez perpetually being a part of their conversations. "Check your text."

Tank quickly pulls over as the three follow behind as if being pulled in by a magnet. When he pulls over, he can hear the race announcer and the crowd cheering off in the background.

Tank puts his feet on the ground to steady his cycle. He turns to the others. "Check your text. Martinez sent us a picture of Candy Man and the link to the broadcast."

Out come their phones. Each are pushing buttons, sliding thumbs and brushing fingers on their rectangular wands.

"He's wearing a doctor's jacket?" Ernie calls out.

"That is so Dark Knight," Joe comments.

"What do you mean?" Escobar says trying to get a clearer picture.

"The Joker in the Batman movie. He blows up the hospital wearing a hospital uniform," Tank explains staring at the phone. Escobar shakes his head with a confused look.

"So all of that shooting over there is from Candyman?" Joe asks.

"Probably or from one of his minions."

"Well, here we are. Now what to do?" as Ernie states the obvious.

"I'll tell you what we're going to do. We're going to get a little help from our friend Janine."

CHAPTER 59

Leftovers

L OCK, STOCK, BARREL AND CURLY stand guard at the
Tavern Restaurant and Bar doing their lazy but self-im-
portant job of making sure Griffin and Sabrina do not finish the
race. Lock and Stock watch Janine repeat herself or the drunk guy
hanging out with two beautiful girls. They like Larry and the girls
better. They're more entertaining and easier on the eyes.

The Tavern is a popular bar/restaurant designed as a German
beer joint that serves the popular pub grub menu with meatloaf
and chicken fried steak as local favorites. It was very crowded
until Lock, Stock and Barrel decided to clear the audience with
bullets in the air or in the head. Now they have the place all to
themselves.

So far, it has been non-eventful except for periodic bullet
shots in the background, some explosions and general mayhem
a final day of life will create. They are becoming immune to the
outside chaos and more in tune to the TV, beer and exquisite
food.

In their 40s, Lock and Stock both look like they are professional TV watchers. Sitting on their bar stools, they're the live
version of Norm and Cliff from Cheers. They sit there with warm

beers silently watching Janine and Larry banter while adding their own commentary eating a bowl of assorted shrimp and tuna courtesy of Curly's hunger games.

With their 1970s haircuts, these single white males needed something to do on their last day. Why not watch TV and perhaps watch someone kill another close up?

Barrel is outside standing on a bench holding his AR-15 looking down Lamar Boulevard as the runners stream by. Being so tall and lanky, he can see far up the race course.

He periodically steps into the restaurant for updates, a swig of beer or a crab cake bite otherwise he's taking his job the most seriously.

Upstairs, Curly is enjoying a gourmet scraps dinner meant for a king he found at the Ruth's Chris steakhouse next door. From the looks of his protruding gut, it's safe to say he's had a couple of those in his life. It's also ironic that he was dubbed Curly as he has no hair and that cherubic face. Jimmy either got lucky dubbing him that name or it was blatantly obvious.

Earlier, Curly was so hungry he went into Ruth's Chris hoping for a miracle. Maybe a hidden steak or lobster tail. It was worth a shot. And there it was. In the private dining room, he hit the jackpot. It must have been his lucky day or something like that.

Someone hosted a feast last night and never cleaned up. There was a long table that fit 20. Nine on each side and one at each end. The plates remained on the table and there were plenty of leftovers. Who in the hell is going to clean up on the last night of existence?

Leftovers from Ruth's Chris are gold especially after months of hoarded Corn Flakes and Ranch Style Beans. At this point and on this day, he could care less about the flies. There was steak and plenty to grab and plenty to choose.

He grabbed one of those big family platters and started inspecting each plate. Some were licked clean others had half their steaks, lobster tails and ahi tuna waiting for his belly. He didn't like seafood so he grabbed the best of those for Lock, Stock and Barrel.

For him though, it was a heart attack special. He grabbed a bit of each—porter house, T bone, Filet, Ribeye and New York Strip. He spent time cutting each prime piece so they were independent of any teeth marks.

He added potatoes au gratin, asparagus and French fried onion rings. Then the crème a la crème, a butt load of bearnaise sauce. At this point, he almost doesn't want to see Griffin as his last wishes of a kingly feast have come true.

The stretch up Lamar Boulevard is a half mile long so it gives them plenty of real estate to monitor. Curly has binoculars next to him to make sure Griffin doesn't slip through but the only tools he's using at the moment is a steak knife, fork and his shirt as the napkin.

The other two volunteers from Candy Man's three stooges group, Larry and Moe, would be there but decided to do rum shots and play Russian roulette until two of them killed themselves. Curly won so he's still alive and on duty.

Curly takes a sip of his diet coke for a one-second break from his ribeye to let go a loud belch and hold up the binoculars to the crowd. He scans quickly up and down Lamar Blvd. then puts them down to finish his five-star dinner.

As he is about to cut a bite, he glances up through the window to the stretch of runners streaming through. He looks back down then freezes. He snatches up the binoculars and looks a quarter-mile up and there he sees them. Or, at least, a couple that fits their description perfectly.

"Guys," he yells down. "I think I have them. They are in the middle with runners around them. They're a c ouple o f b locks away."

A silence follows. They w anted t his m oment b ut n ever thought it would really happen.

"I see them," yells Barrel standing still focusing through the crowd. Lock and Stock look at each other. *We're really going to have to do something?*

They grab their guns to exit but can't run too quickly as they have to jump over or run around dead bodies. Curly is racing down the stairs.

"Don't be so obvious!" Barrel yells at them. That sends them into nonchalant mode as if they were window shopping that makes them stand out even more especially with Moe holding an AR-15 in the air.

He turns to them and tells Lock and Stock to run to the other side of the road. Lock and Stock head across the street trying to shield the guns in their hands.

Griffin and Sabrina have just passed mile 25 and feeling good about it. One mile left and plenty of time to celebrate with everyone waiting. They are in the middle of a small pack that share their pace.

Griffin is shaking his head laughing at some memory Sabrina recalled when all of sudden their surrounding runners split like racked pool balls just getting hit. Sabrina and Griffin look up to an AR-15 pointed right at them. They look side to side to see two pistols and a rifle pointed at them and nowhere to run.

"Call Candyman and tell him we have a present for him," Barrel instructs. Curly pulls out his phone and dials in looking straight at Griffin.

CHAPTER 60

Eeny-Meeny-Miney-Mo

M ARIAN AND DARREN are speeding as fast as they can down Koenig Lane. Koenig Lane is an east/west road that is also Allandale Road, Northland Drive that turns into Ranch Road 2222 to the west and Hwy 290 to the east. It's the exact same damn road with five different names that drive out-of-towners crazy.

Original Austinites, or unicorns as they are called, just roll their eyes when they hear the carpet baggers bitching about the local nuance of the five-named road. Austinites mentally answer the out-of-towner's frustrations over a street's name 'that it is just as easy to leave Austin as it is to arrive'. But Austinites can't say that because it's not the Texas friendly way. They can still think it though.

At that part of the road, Koenig Lane is more residential and well out of the way of the race route so they're able to go 40 miles per hour up to IH 35. Tank was smart for the recommendation.

At this speed, they'll make it in time to join the fight. Now it just depends on IH 35's congestion. They hope the open lane decree is still being honored. Government leaders and friendly Texans made sure to keep at least one lane open on both sides of

IH 35 so Texans could have paths to Austin's marathon, the gladiator games up in Dallas, the fiesta in San Antonio or the beach party in Corpus.

They are nearing the spot of IH 35 towards downtown Austin where the driver has the choice of the lower lanes that have many exits and entrances or going the upper level fast lanes. The top lanes are elevated thirty feet in the air with no exits until downtown at the U.T. exit.

From their vantage point, it doesn't look like a single lane is open on both levels. When it comes to the last days or months of civilization, it's hard to count on civility and order. The guarantee of easy passage may no longer exist.

Darren and Marian slow down at the spot where the driver has to choose which route to go. They look down at the lower level and see debris scattered through the lanes. The upper level looks free at this angle but cannot tell for the full 4-mile stretch.

No matter which direction they choose, they do have the advantage of a motorcycle and its ability to maneuver through or over obstacles quicker and more easily. They look at each other with the "eeny-meeny-miney-mo" look and choose the upper level that looks more open.

Both hit the gas to the 40 mph speed for the first mile then see a block of cars that forces them to stop and assess. As they approach the pile up, they see nowhere to go through. They look at a domino yard of cars in random crash formation. Marian shakes her head and whispers aloud, "The one-lane order wasn't followed very well."

Darren looks to Marian, "Do we go back or try to go over?"

"Let me look." Marian gets off her bike and jumps into the bed of a crashed Chevy pickup. She stands on the back of the bed's rail to get a full view, "If we can go over then let's do it.

There's a small pile-up up ahead but looks like we can get through then looks wide open."

"I've got the dirt bike so let's see if we can find or make a ramp to get over these cars. I just need that first lift and jump."

They start looking around to see if there is any debris, boards or makeshift ramps. Marian looks at the Uhaul that seems to be the culprit to this whole mess then a light bulb goes off. She jumps onto a Chevy Malibu and hops onto the hoods of an Explorer then a Camry to the Uhaul. On the back of Uhauls, each have a sliding ramp that pulls out to help roll items up into the truck smoothly and easily.

She wiggles in between the Camry and the Uhaul to pull the ramp out, lifts it to its highest level then pushes in to unhook it. She slides it out as an independent ramp to take where ever she pleases. Perfect for what they need. Now where to put it?

She throws the ramp over the two cars forcing Darren to move backwards to avoid being hit. Marian cringes in embarrassment and yells a quick apology. Darren rolls his eyes. She jumps back over to the motorcycle watching Darren get off his bike to pace the edge of the domino'd car boneyard. Marian's inspecting the edge of the cars as well but more interested in looking at her watch as time is against them in more than one way.

Darren turns to Marian, "Okay. We put the ramp on the bumper of this little guy." He says pointing at a red Dodge Charger. "When I drive on the hood, I'm going to have to turn to the right to drive over the Camry. Once I hit the Camry's trunk, I quickly gun it. Drive over the roof to the hood, pop a small wheelie to land both wheels on the pavement and then I'm on the other side."

He turns to Marian, "You're going to have to leave your bike here and hold onto me for the rest of the way otherwise we turn around."

He looks at Marian with that 'reality check' face, "If we turn around and have to go back to the underpass and the side roads, we'll lose 15 to 20 minutes just to get back to this point. And then we're still 10 minutes away depending on traffic so to speak."

He turns around to point to the second pile up 20 yards away, "Otherwise, we try this little trick and we'll be there in five to ten. I just have to make sure I don't break the bike."

Marian's anxious as these conversations and decisions leave Tank and team even more exposed as time goes by. Marian looks Darren then claps her hand with full confidence, "Let's do it. You've been riding since your childhood so I guess all of that daredevil-ness prepared you for this moment."

"Can you leave your backpack behind?"

"No. It has my medical equipment in it and we're going to need it."

"Hope not," Darren quietly says. He grabs the ramp and puts it on the bumper securing it under the grill. He stands on the ramp and jumps up and down on it several times to gauge its stability. "Stay here until I make it. If things go wrong like a weak hood crevassing or a tire slipping, I may have to let go which means the bike will lunge out of control so I don't want you anywhere around."

Marian nods her head as Darren revs up the motor bike and guns it in neutral a couple of times. He moves his butt to the back of the seat, puts it in gear and heads up the ramp. He guns the throttle just enough to lift the front wheel to jump onto the Charger. Does a quick turn to then throttle enough to pop up, over and bounce off the Camry to land both wheels on the pavement.

Well, that was easy. She kisses the tips of her fingers and taps her motorcycle goodbye. She jumps onto the Charger and follows the same path to the swaggering, smiling moto-cross champion.

"Get on. Let's go. And you better tell Tank about this. I don't want to brag so you have to do it for me."

"Never stopped you before."

"Ha ha."

He winks at her then rolls the throttle to weave his way through the graveyard junkyard.

He passes the last truck that will leave them wide open spaces to the rescue of Tank and Griffin when he abruptly stops. They both look and it comes crystal clear why there's a large pile up on one side and a wide open pass on the other. Half of the highway is gone.

CHAPTER 61

The Conference Call

THE PHONE RINGS TWICE before Janine picks up, "What?" Tank is used to Janine's demeanor so gets right to it, "I need you to call Candyman or give me his number. I need to talk to him."

"Why?"

"I think he has an old friend of mine that has some unfinished business that we need to take care of. I need to talk to Candyman to get to my friend so we can resolve this and move on to the real business of Griffin finishing the race."

"What's in it for me?"

"If you have cameras over there, which I'm sure you do, then your viewers will get to see the fight of the century. We're both ex Navy seals and black belts who literally will fight each other until one dies. Like I said, we have some unfinished business."

"What's in it for Candyman?"

Tank looks at Joe. "If Candyman and his army let us fight then I will walk away." Joe, Escobar and Ernie all look at him in full surprise. Tank lifts his finger to his mouth to shush them quiet.

"Hold please."

There's silence on the phone. Tank's wondering if she hung up on him again but the phone's timer is ticking.

Janine comes back on, "Okay, Tank are you on?"

Tank looks around wondering if this is a trick question. "Yes."

"Candyman, are you there?"

And then he hears his voice.

"Yeah. Here."

Tank's eyes go wide open then looks at his gang. He hits the speaker button.

Janine continues, "Before you begin these negotiations, I want to let you know that 100 plus million people in the world are listening."

Tank rolls his eyes in exasperation while the others just shake their head. *She has no shame.*

"You have got to be kidding me," Jimmy says as he starts pacing back and forth shaking his head. "You are unbelievable."

"Shut up, Candyman. And ladies and gentlemen you just heard it straight from the man's mouth. I now have Candyman and the leader of vigilante gang I have been reporting on the line for negotiations that involve trading Griffin's life for another man's death."

Janine looks at her numbers escalate another 5 million. Larry starts to interrupt when Janine slams the mute button on Larry's comm without interrupting her pose. The last thing she needs is Larry getting in the way of her exclusive.

"So, please. Vigilante man and Candyman, the stage is all yours. Candyman, why don't you start?"

Janine hits the switcher button to Leslie's camera so viewers see and hear the words straight from Candyman. With the camera off her, she is able to smile ear to ear.

"First of all, Janine, I want to thank you for being such a cunt and demented bitch that I am without words to say that you are such a cunt and a demented bitch."

Jimmy is waiting for a response but Janine is not taking the bait. She watches the drama unfold and her numbers skyrocket. *It's working like a charm.*

Tank cuts in, "Candyman, is Tanner there?"

That takes Jimmy by surprise as he turns around to Tanner. Tanner starts walking towards him. He knows what's going on.

"Yes, he is. That's pretty astute of you. Where are you? And where's Griffin. Have him stowed away for me?"

"No. I thought you had him or are going to have him."

"How do you know that?"

That comment has even Janine wondering. *How in the hell does he know?*

"I have my sources. If you leave Tanner and me alone for our fight to the death as Janine so eloquently puts it then I'll walk away." Tank holds up his hand up to his three mouths on the ground staring at him showing that everything is in control.

"Why? You've already killed 50 or so of my men. And now I'm supposed to believe that you're going to walk away? What gives?"

"Tanner killed my best friend under my command. I have a settle to score. You and I have no personal beef but Tanner does so for my last wishes, it is to kill him. Surely you most of all, a doctor, should know what it means? Think about it, I could shoot you and Tanner right now and walk away without you ever seeing me."

That statement makes Jimmy start looking around wondering how close Tank really is.

"But, what's the fun in that? I want Tanner all to me without you or your bozos interrupting before, during or after our fight. Do we have a deal?"

"So for Tanner, you walk away from helping Griffin."

"I walk away. Yes." Tank looks at his gang. They notice how he chooses his words. Classic tactics in negotiations.

Tanner grabs the phone from Jimmy, "I'm sorry it took the last day of earth for my revenge but so be it. Where are you? How long do I have to wait?"

"I'm closer than you think." Tank hangs up the phone. "Come on, let's take a look to see how many men he has and the layout of the plaza."

They get off their bikes, pull out their pistols, check their ammo and load up. They start running silently through an out-door courtyard surrounded by four office buildings. They hug the wall to get to the office building closest to the Independent building.

The first floor's main entry way is wide open with elevators on each side. The view is clear to the other side of the small delivery street to the main plaza where they can see Candyman pacing. Tanner stands statute-still scanning the area.

They hide behind the walls of the elevators. Escobar and Tank on one side. Joe and Ernie on the other.

"I count 15, maybe 20 soldiers," Ernie whispers.

"If you can call them that," Escobar responds. The remaining X soldiers are either those that hid well enough to not get shot or those that have the skills not to get shot.

"There's a couple of them that we need to take out first. They look like they have some fight in them."

Tank looks across to Joe and Ernie. He points back to where they came from. They slip outside and back to their bikes. Tank looks at them, "Get as close as you can without being seen. That building is perfect just as long as you're not spotted getting up to the front windows. It has that desk to hide behind.

Use the other two buildings for the second and third spots. This way each of you have a certain vantage point. After I kill Tanner, I'll walk away two steps then start shooting down Candy Man and his army. That's when you storm the plaza and take them down."

"We have to storm the plaza," Joe emphasizes. "We don't have any rifles so we have to be much closer to do our job."

Tank looks around, "We need a rifle. We need Darren and Marian. Where are they?" Tank grabs his phone and taps his top favorite while Escobar calls Darren. Tank thumbs off after a short pause, "Voicemail."

He looks to Escobar, "Same."

Ernie takes out his phone and taps the screen. Martinez answers.

"Heard from Darren and Marian?"

As Ernie listens to his response, he shakes his head. "Okay. Keep trying and let us know. Okay, bye."

CHAPTER 62

Through It

"**Y**OU THINK I CAN MAKE IT?**"** Darren says looking through the 20' by 30' foot hole in the upper deck stretch of IH 35.

"Jumping over this hole? You're nuts. There's no way," Marian says astonished that he would even suggest that option.

"I'm not talking over it, through it."

"What?!"

"Look, see that Fedex truck there," Darren says pointing down at an abandoned Fedex delivery truck crashed into a black Range Rover on the lower deck.

"I just need a little room here to drive to this edge. Pop a wheelie and land on the top of the truck with both wheels.

As it is in the air, I let go. Both the bike and me land on the truck. The bike keeps going over the truck then crashes into those cars. I jump down, get the bike and we're off to help the gang."

"You're crazy. You'll kill both yourself and the bike."

"Think about it. The Fedex truck is really tall so it makes for a 10 foot drop. No different than dirt bike racing. I can handle a ten foot drop. Yes, the bike crashes but we don't need a bike that looks good just working."

"Then just drop it on those cars below," Marian says pointing directly down from them. "We jump down onto the Fedex truck. Recover it. Then we go."

"It's too far of a drop for those small cars. That's a 20 foot drop.

The Fedex truck is a ten foot drop. And, if we just drop it here then we're assured the bike won't be able to run.

It has to land on two wheels for the first drop then roll onto the cars to either crash into the cars or on the pavement. That reduces the damage significantly. Hell, those fiber glass cars in front of the truck would probably help buffer the fall."

Marian remains silent as she inspects the hole. "This was obviously done by a demolitions expert."

"How do you know?"

"It's a perfect horizontal line just over the support which is why the hole fell like a trap door leaving the debris all in one area over there," she points down to the ground where the concrete debris are scattered in the same area. "And why it broke just at the next support over there," she says pointing across the divide.

"Good," Darren says. "That just helps us and I don't really give a shit at the moment. Can we move on? Time's ticking"

She turns around to see the pile up and knows that will be another ordeal to crawl over to return. They could leave the bike there, climb back over and take hers but that takes 20 minutes away from their mission.

"We really have no choice but to try," Darren's looking into her mind churning while becoming anxiously impatient. He needs to convince her quickly without demanding. Marian is her own master.

"If it works, we're off to save our gang and Griffin. If it doesn't then you go back to your bike to pick me up but we lose valuable time. If we don't try, we're screwed. If we do, we at least have a chance to complete the mission."

"I get it. I'm wondering about us. We need to make sure we withstand the fall without breaking too many bones or dying."

"You have your medical kit, don't you? Do you have any pain killers?"

"Even better, I packed T train and Adderall." Darren looks at her with that 'I don't know what you're talking about' look.

"It's a combination of prescribed speed and opiod. Toradol kills the pain and Adderall amps you out. It's what the NFL and combat troops use. They numb your body so much that you don't even know anything is broken yet you still have full mind to go back to battle.

Ruins peoples' careers and bodies in the long run but works for that several hours you need." She exhales and looks at him. "Let's do it."

Darren claps his hands with the confirmation he needed. Now it's his turn to inspect. He's measuring time, speed and length to the truck.

"I just need a little more room to get enough space and speed to jump long enough. So, let's put this car in neutral. Push it off and that should give me enough room especially with the space open behind."

Darren is saying this as he is going under the car to release the wheel locks tow truck drivers use to get parked cars onto their chains. He crawls back up, waves to Marian to get behind the car with him.

"One, two…"

They start pushing the Ford Explorer. It doesn't move at first but as they plant their feet hard to the pavement, it starts moving. With each step, it moves enough to give them hope and the reason to push harder. The tires start rotating into a continued motion to give them the motivation they need. When it gets close to the point of a happy ending Darren yells, "Now!"

They plow with enough speed for the Explorer to have its front wheels fly off the ledge, flip over and crash to the ground. Darren winks at her then heads to his bike. "Here's what I want you to do. Climb over that truck over there to get on the other side."

Darren points across to a white Chevy truck with just one back wheel dangling over the side. It looks stable enough to climb over without the truck plummeting to the junkyard below.

"Once over the truck, walk over to be directly over the Fedex truck. You can see the Fedex truck is aligned perfectly with the edge of the hole to drop squarely down on the roof. When I'm down on the roof, you're going to drop the rifle to me then your backpack."

He turns to Marian making sure she is fully understanding his plan. They both know they are going off a ledge on this one, literally and figuratively, so better be fully aligned on each part.

"You're going to sit down on the ledge then crawl down off it to get a grip on those exposed rebars. This way you're hanging down to reduce your drop from ten feet to five feet. You just have to make sure you hold tightly to those poles so you don't immediately fall. Let yourself dangle until you're not swinging so you drop with as much precision as possible."

He looks at her again. She stares back beginning to understand the delicacy and danger this part presents. She nods with full confidence in her face but he can't read her mind.

"Okay. Let's do it."

Darren gets on the bike and starts backing up while Marian starts weaving and climbing her way to the other side. Darren revs the engine, closes his eyes and does the sign of the cross. He opens his eyes, looks straight ahead, releases the clutch and shoots off.

Marian's still climbing over the truck so doesn't even see him go. Darren pops the wheelie just as he hits the ledge and goes flying in the air. He hopes he gunned it with enough speed to reach the Fedex roof.

As the bike is in the air, he lets go just as in those photos of the dirt bikes jumping over the dirt mounds on their racetracks. The bike hits the roof perfectly with both wheels then goes flying off into the pile of cars and concrete debris below.

Darren lands onto the roof and does his drop and roll perfectly except that he has too much momentum so rolls right off the front of the roof falling down to the cars below. Fedex trucks don't have a front extension for their engine so it's a straight drop down.

Marian is on the other side so she sees Darren drop onto the hood of a Range Rover then bounce down in between it and a black Mercedes SUV. She can hear his pain with a scream of an 'Ow!' and a 'Fuck!'.

Good news, he's alive. Bad news, he's hurt. Now it's a matter of how hurt. It may end up being really smart to bring those pain drugs. She can't see the bike as it went flying beyond her ledge. She can't drop down until she knows the bike and Darren are alive enough to move forward with this plan.

"Hey!" She yells. "You okay?"

She sees him crawling up to stand and start hopping on his left leg.

"Yeah. I'm as okay as can be expected from a 20 foot toppled fall. I fucked up my knee and wrist pretty bad. Don't know if they're broken or not."

He looks down at the pavement at his phone that's split in half from the fall. "Looks like I did break my phone though. I hope yours is still working. I may need those drugs after all especially for my wrist. It's my trigger hand and it hurts like hell."

He's starts rotating his wrist and spreading his fingers trying to assess the level of pain and dexterity remaining. He's slowly shaking his hand to gauge the level of use when he suddenly stops.

He feels a presence. On this day, presence can easily mean death. Instinct overrules analysis and unsheathes his gun with lightning speed and excruciating pain pointing it straight to his right at a portly gentleman approaching him through the wooden fence of a backyard.

The black-haired man in his early 40's stops and stares directly to Darren's eyes as he holds a large antique bible. He has a puffy face with a pouty, gentle smile to him that somewhat disarms Darren.

"What do you want?" Darren coldly says. Marian can hear Darren talking to someone so stays strategically quiet.

"You're trying to help Griffin the runner, aren't you?" the bible man says.

"What's it to you?"

"I will pray for you."

He opens his bible that has large leather covers with a ribbon bookmark set at a specific passage. The bible and Bible Man have an unusual mystique and power that dominates the moment.

Darren has been thinking in the back of his mind about how good it would be at the bar celebrating these last hours. Strangely enough though while pointing a gun at a stranger's head, he feels better taking this path for the last day of earth. He has purpose.

"Pray all you want. You move so much as an inch I will kill you in an instant."

Bible Man ignores Darren's comment. He begins with the passage from Romans 12:19, "Do not take revenge, my dear friends, but leave room for God's wrath, for it is written: 'It is mine to avenge; I will repay,' says the Lord."

Bible Man looks up with vacuum eyes. He starts thumbing through his bible looking for his next verse. Darren shakes his head and lowers his gun. Marian remains frozen quiet. He starts walking towards the bike as he yells up to her, "It doesn't look too bad from here."

"Who are you talking to?" she yells down.

"Who cares." Darren doesn't feel like explaining another weird encounter.

She exhales as he walks out of her sight. A couple of seconds later, she hears the engine rev up a couple of times then returns to her sight.

"It runs. Has some broken bones like I do but it works. Now it's your turn." Marian takes off her backpack and tosses it onto the roof of the Fedex truck. There's nothing too delicate in the bag so didn't need Darren's help. The rifle on the other hand.

"You're going to have to get on one of these trucks or something so the drop of the rifle is as short as possible," she yells out.

"I know. The Fedex is too vertical and my wrist is too sore to get back on that one. There's the SUV that should give us enough room."

Darren approaches the black SUV where its front is crushed into a candy purple Hyundai Sonata. *Who would buy something painted like that?* He shakes his head then jumps onto the Sonata's bumper to step up onto the SUV's trunk. He does a quick jolt up the front windshield then looks up, "Okay, go ahead."

She moves over to be directly above. She grabs the rifle by the strap and lets dangle as far as it will stretch to make the distance as short as possible with the butt pointing down.

"You do have the safety switch on, right?"

"Yes. Thank you for your confidence."

She lets it dangle for a moment then lets go. Darren catches it but with an added bonus of grimacing pain. Marian winces for him then walks over to the ledge where the drop is directly below the Fedex truck.

She turns around gets on one knee then the other just above the point of the exposed rebar and the Fedex truck below. She lays down on her stomach and starts slowly sliding her feet over the ledge and rebar.

"Careful. Careful," Darren yells.

"No shit," is her response.

She now has her stomach over the rebar. It's holding her weight so that's good. She grabs the corrugated bar with her left hand holding it tightly knowing it has to hold her hanging body. She then takes the right hand on and grabs the exposed rebar a few feet over.

She scoots her stomach to the best point where each hand is equal length to spread the weight as evenly as possible. She slowly bends her elbows to halfway down to get into the key moment of the drop.

She stops to test her strength to see if she can maintain the hold. At this point, the position feels good. She lets gravity take the next step as she lowers her body to a full stretch of the arms. She dangles there holding the rebars feeling pretty good about her regular trips to the gym all of those years. Now comes the real test of landing on the roof without too much pain and injury.

"Careful. Careful," Darren repeats.

"Would you shut up please."

Darren offers an apologetic look.

"Okay, here I come." She looks down knowing the moment of reckoning to help her husband or not is here.

"One, two, three." She drops landing both feet with bended knees. Darren looks at her with a big ole grin and fist bump.

"That was great! See, I told you it would work. Come on. Time's wastin'."

Marian just rolls her eyes. *We got really lucky is what happened.*

She looks across the highway to see Bible Man release his latest passage. Without a beat, Marian dryly calls out to him, "Will you shut up please?"

Darren wasn't expecting that comment, "What's wrong with a little bible passage. It can't hurt."

"Yes, it can. That book is a big part of why we got here."

"Well, that was uncalled for. The bible is how good people live their life."

"Yeah, well I guess everyone forgot to read it. It's a book just like the Koran. Basically the same book just 'insert prophet here'."

Darren steps back with a surprised almost defensive posture, "What's your beef with the bible? I had no idea you had such issues."

"It's not the bible I have issues with. It's its use. And just like the other. I spent years in the Middle East listening to both sides quote a book that contradicts itself passage to passage. While in the end, all of those that I watched die ended up calling out to their family and friends as their dying words."

"So?"

"From my experience, when it comes down to defining one's purpose everyone whether Muslim or Christian had the same wish—to be with family. Why couldn't we focus on that commonality rather than the difference on how two books were written?"

Darren stands there in pure silence. Bible Man keeps finding passages to recite. Marian quickly blocks him out to open her bag. "Let's take care of you. Let me give you a couple of happy shots then go see my husband."

CHAPTER 63

You're Going to Die

T ANK RIPS THE REST of his tattered dress off. "Won't need this for hand to hand." He looks to the three, "Ready?" They all start checking each weapon making sure they're fully loaded and ready.

"They're going to be looking at all of the entry ways for me to arrive so inside those buildings should give you a good view and an advantage.

Tanner doesn't care about anybody but me so if he sees you creeping around, it won't matter. I don't think the others are smart enough to think about it or look for you. Go ahead. I'm giving you three minutes to get in position."

That's all they need.

Tanner and Jimmy stand out in the middle of the plaza close to the entrance but still in the open at the top of the steps. Most of the X mercenaries remain lined up against the wall of once-was windows while the others are scattered throughout the plaza.

Cheryl is right behind Jimmy. Jay, as always, is right behind Cheryl. Jay keeps sniffing making sure he is maximizing his most recent snort. Rob is behind the granite reception desk in the far back railing out his current line.

There are two X soldiers outside standing guard up on the ledge of the limestone walls to the building's fountain pools. The two skinheads are obviously hungry for a fight scanning the area for anyone who's worthy to gun down.

Both are in their late 20s, skinny and wearing mismatched militia gear. One has Marine camouflage pants and an army green tee shirt with the sleeves torn out. The other is in police riot pants and boots with a Navy jacket. Those too have the sleeves ripped out.

One's holding a Glock and the other a Beretta. Both have additional pistols tucked away in shoulder holsters and their tandem movement, look and intensity reflect a pair that are either close friends, brothers or lovers.

What's even more strange and could be problematic for both parties, people are beginning to show up. Those viewers who recognize the plaza from Leslie's camera are now joining them to view the fight in person. This new dynamic makes for a more complicated scene. All of Candyman's platoon are beginning to pace. Tanner remains stone-cold still.

And the moment happens as Tank enters the line of sight from the street to their south. The two soldiers standing on the ledge stop their scanning and smile. The one in riot gear motions for the other to follow him.

Leslie moves in closer to video Tank in a more dramatic style. He is obviously taking his assignment seriously. Janine's smile is about to split her head in half. She remains uncharacteristically quiet.

The one soldier with a scimitar tattoo on his neck and a thin goatee starts walking along side of Tank on his right. The other X man who has so many tats on his body that he looks like a walking comic strip bodyguards Tank on the left.

The X man on the right points his Glock two foot away from Tank's temple. Tank keeps walking unmoved staring straight at Tanner.

"You're going to die, motherfucker. Right here, right now," the skinhead says loud enough for all to hear. He cocks his pistol surprising the other skinhead. Tank still remains unmoved. Tanner smiles as he knows what's about to happen.

Tank continues to stroll then with lightning speed grabs the wrist of the skinhead holding the Glock with one hand and an upper cut grab to his elbow. The X man's elbow immediately breaks and drops his gun. He uses the two handed grip on his arm to swing him around into the X man on his left while screaming in pain.

The X man gets hit so hard he falls to the ground. On the ground, he turns to shoot Tank but Tank has his human shield that is now taking one, two, three bullets killing him. Tank throws the now dead body directly on the shooter then picks up the dropped gun.

The shooter is pushing the dead body off him revealing more of his body for Tank to shoot. Tank shoots the leg that is exposed. He screams while pushing the skinhead further off of him. All that does is expose his body more. Tank shoots him in the shoulder.

Without a shoulder, it's harder to push a 180 pound body off of you. That gives Tank enough time to saunter up and put a bullet straight in his head. *Two down.*

The two quick deaths scare Jimmy so much he quickly retreats inside the building behind the reception block where Rob is now hiding underneath. The rest of the soldiers take cover and the newly arrived onlookers exit the scene as quickly as they arrived.

Tanner remains standing, eyes locked on Tank. Leslie holds the camera down to look with his own eyes the horror he just witnessed. He starts backing away.

"Leslie, stay there and continue to shoot them!" Janine yells out from her studio. *Bad choice of words*, Larry thinks as he and the girls are watching the events on their monitor in shock. Leslie reluctantly lifts his camera back up but stays further away.

Holy shit! Janine recognizes the leader of the vigilantes is Tank Miller. She is stunned and overjoyed. She can't stay quiet for this. "Ladies and Gentlemen, as you can see, the vigilante out to protect Griffin is Austin's own Tank Miller, the elected Chief of Police. He is obviously committed to being the peace keeper in this town.

He has already killed two of his attackers and has clearly shown why he is a decorated veteran and the leader of the Austin police force. The once crowded plaza is now clear and tensions are now in full boiler."

"Hey!" Jimmy yells out from behind the counter. "There's supposed to be a truce here until you kill each other! That was the deal."

Tanner responds with a small smile staring at Tank, "They asked for it."

Tank drops the gun and resumes his OK Corral march to battle. Jimmy is pissed, now wondering if Tank's word is for real. At that moment, Jimmy's phone starts buzzing. Must be Janine. *Geesh.* He looks at his phone and doesn't recognize the number but answers anyway. He doubts it's a sales call from India.

CHAPTER 64

Long Time, No See

TANNER WALKS DOWN the steps onto the small street as Tank walks off the curb to be directly across from him, "Long time, no see."

"Too long," Tanner retorts as he starts circling him. Tanner gives him a quick one-two swing with his fists then a follow-up kick towards the stomach. The first two swings are misses then a forearmed defend swipe to Tanner's leg swing attack leave Tanner a little unbalanced.

The small tip of imbalance gives Tank enough room to land a glanced body blow to Tanner's side and a right jab to the face. Tanner blocks the punch but knocks him back a couple of steps. Tanner regains control.

"So much for small talk," Tank says circling Tanner's move in their war like dance.

"Time's a little short today so don't want to waste any."

Little by little, more people keep showing up. New audience members who didn't see the first two murders have no context how dangerous of a position they put themselves in by kibitzing.

Leslie is doing his job shooting the fight while not getting in the way. Janine is letting the fight carry the broadcast. Jimmy has disappeared.

Tanner's first move was textbook. He's with his teacher so the moves were on purpose. A warm-up for the real fight. Now that he got a small pop in the side, the fight is for real.

Tanner quickly advances with a side kick move to the head. Tank quickly moves to block and grab his foot to throw him to the ground and pummel him on his back. *This is too easy.*

But Tank took the bait and the kick was a fake and Tanner takes full advantage with Tank's arms reaching out with a one-two swing punch to his unprotected head. The first punch lands 100%, Tank ducks the other.

Shouldn't have fallen for that one? Tank's face definitely tells himself he needs to up his game. Tanner has. The advantage is Tank has been in this exact situation hundreds more times than Tanner. Now it's his turn.

It's almost the hidden ball trick in baseball. There's a runner on first base watching the pitcher and first baseman walk away from each other after a short discussion of baseball strategy for the next hitter. The pitcher acts like the ball is in his glove but it is really in the glove of the first baseman to tag the runner out when he unknowingly steps off the bag for his lead off.

Tank is about to give Tanner his signature move. Just what Tanner was expecting. Tank advances as if he's going in with a high jump kick which is a difficult move that Tanner expects.

With Tank, the move is a guarantee hit. The question is where and how hard. If it lands directly, the recipient is gone. The best response is a deflect but a deflect will still hurt. It's Tank's signature move but zaps a lot of energy so can be used only a few times in a drawn out fight.

Tanner prepares but Tank never jumps. Tanner's already blocking a phantom kick that leaves the side of his head open. Tank just does the obvious and clobbers him with a one-two boxing punch to the face that leaves some stars for Tanner to ponder. Touché.

Tanner changes tactics and sport going in full UFC with two sidekicks, two head jabs that leads to an attempted head lock. Tank received some body blows but nothing significant. What did happen is when Tanner went in for the head lock, Tank was quick enough and ducked Tanner's grab to his neck.

That gave Tank the opportunity to turn around and grab Tanner from behind in a full nelson. He lifts up Tanner to then jump in the air to smash Tanner onto the pavement front first with Tank's weight on top.

But Tanner is quick enough to shift the fall to his side rather than his face. While it saved a lot of damage, Tanner's right shoulder and ribs absorb the drop and pain.

Tank fell on his right arm giving Tanner enough elbow room to thrash his way out. He rolls over and jumps up to standing position. Tank mirrors the same move so now they are staring straight at each other once again but a little more damaged.

Joe, Ernie and Escobar are in position watching the melee. Joe is behind the bar inside Maudie's. Escobar stands behind the entrance wall in the ransacked Schlotskeys. Ernie remains in the office building behind the front desk next to the front doors so has quick access to a frontal attack.

More people keep showing up getting closer to the fight. Joe thinks he saw more X men show up raising their army back to 20 or more. Not good, he thinks. Except for Rob who is still hiding behind the reception stand, the X soldiers are front row center with guns out. *Are they there to make certain Tank doesn't leave alive?*

Cheryl is grinning enjoying the show holding her AR-15 in one hand leaning it back on her shoulder. Jay is behind her. He's not nearly as amused.

Tank and Tanner's tango has amped up in volume and speed. Exchanging swift kicks and extended punches. None of them are direct hits but still do some damage. The real damage is their constant jabs are wearing down their stamina. It may end up being a battle of endurance unless someone makes a mistake which Tanner does.

CHAPTER 65

You're Free to Go

J IMMY PUSHES HIS PHONE to end the conversation to stroll quietly out the side of the Jenga tower. Everyone is distracted with Tank and Tanner duking it out.

He holds his head down so none of the streaming onlookers recognize him as he exits and takes a left. His stride turns into a fast walk as his grin turns to a smile. Taking a left amplifies the boom-boom sounds from the race's finish line as he can hear the festivities with a new volume.

He walks through a large Austin art bat installation outside the Zachary Scott Theater then goes through the 'employees only' door. The doorknob has been blown out so he just pushes it open to look straight into the eyes of Griffin. They meet at last.

While Griffin doesn't show it, he's in full shock. Of all things in the universe to be wearing, his hunter is wearing a doctor's coat.

Now knowing the backstory of Griffin and his father, Sabrina looks at Griffin. Griffin turns to her for a brief moment as they lock eyes. *Coincidence doesn't exist.* This time, though, Griffin looks this doctor straight in the eyes.

Lock, Stock, Barrel and Curly surround them pointing guns at each of their heads. Sabrina has a gripping fear locked on her face. She and Griffin are breathing hard. Twenty five miles of heaven and hell will do that to you.

Jimmy can't believe it. It has come to be and now he's got to make the most of it. He looks at Sabrina, smiles and offers his hand, "Hi, my name is Jimmy. My stage name is Candy Man but wanted to introduce myself properly. Very nice to meet you."

Sabrina is in twilight zone not knowing what to do. But with four guns pointed at you and your husband, you do what you have to do. With a very confused and scared look, she slowly raises her hand as he shakes it firmly with a welcoming smile. The four bozos holding their guns are silently laughing at his gesture.

Sabrina slowly shakes his hand, "Hi, I guess."

He maintains his attention to Sabrina still smiling. "You're a very pretty girl." He turns to Griffin, "You're a lucky man. Jealous of you."

Griffin looks at Jimmy then back to Sabrina who's shaking her head. *This can't be happening.*

Jimmy turns back to Sabrina, "You're free to go. No need to be here. No need to witness what's going to happen. Please. Go finish the race and be with your family, friends or whoever you have."

Lock, Stock, Barrel and Curly are stunned. Sabrina looks at Griffin then Jimmy wondering what the trick is.

"Go. Seriously. No one is going to hurt you. Please."

Griffin takes control, "Sabrina, Jimmy's right. Go. And please tell Grammy that I will always thank her for everything she has done and left for us while we were here."

Sabrina gives Griffin a blank stare. Griffin turns to Jimmy, "The organizers of the race were kind enough to let my grand-mother open the race so she's there waiting for us."

The gun! It hits Janine as hard as the gun hit the pavement. Maybe Grandma blowing her brains out was the best thing that could have happened. Coincidence doesn't exist especially on this day. Griffin nods in a quick up and down bob willing her to understand his reference. She's already there.

"Of course! She's waiting just where she was when we ran past her. I'll go be with her if that's want you want."

"Please. I'd like that."

Jimmy smiles as he strangely feels good that he's helping someone stay alive and help with their departure. She looks at Griffin then Jimmy, "Thank you." She turns around and bolts out the door. *I hope it's still there. And still loaded.*

Jimmy turns his full attention to Griffin and holds out his hand, "And now let me properly introduce myself..."

CHAPTER 66

The Distraction

ERNIE HAS A GOOD VIEW being at the front window but still seems too removed for his liking. He's behind the reception desk with a fake Ligustrum plant blocking his upper body. More people enter the plaza and he can see several of them with Xs painted on them. Tank has to end this quickly before they're overrun with Candyman's added army.

He can't see Joe or Escobar but know exactly where they are and know they're thinking the same thing. He knows they can't interfere. That would start the Hunger Games and leave every-thing to chance. The last thing a soldier or cop ever wants to do.

That's when it hits him. *A cop?* He quickly sets his gun on the table and takes his vest off then starts unbuttoning his police shirt.

Ernie being shirtless amongst the crowd of Austinites as if it was Halloween on 6th street on steroids, no one would ever know or care. He picks up his gun and slides it behind him in between his bare back and dark pants. He opens the door and walks out.

Ernie weaves his way through the crowd to get a closer look. He may be in his 40s but a former Seal and current cop keeps him fit in a noticeable way. He gets as close to the make-shift UFC fighting ring as he can without Tanner seeing him. He hasn't seen

Tanner so close since the murder investigation. It is a weird sight and feeling.

Tank and Tanner are in the middle of a fighter's break. Tanner spits out a wad of blood holding his ribs while Tank pedals back a couple of steps. Tank stares through Tanner's eyes to his soul to make sure. Tanner still doesn't have *it*.

Now it's time for Tank to use that to his advantage. "How's Robert? Seen him lately? I know he's been calling you. Wakes you up. Wanders into your thoughts uninvited. I heard he followed you home. Are you roommates? Still mad at him?" Tank has done enough volunteer PTSD counseling to know how avoidance manifests itself especially in these circumstances.

Tanner's breathing heavily staring at Tank with a newfound rage. Tank knows. He's counting on it. For Tanner to wait until today to come thousands of miles to kill Tank is not a coincidence. Murdering Robert. Being *robbed* of the Navy Cross have caught up to him.

If Tank can break his emotions then he has him. Tanner will attack mindlessly without strategy or thought behind it. He'll be a predictable robot and Tank knows every one of his moves. Half of which he taught him. All he has to do is watch how he pivots his feet, waist and shoulders. With that knowledge he can block or avoid every swing, punch and kick until Tanner expends all of his energy. That's when Tank can use Tanner's exhaustion to his advantage and take him down.

"Robert told me the Navy was wrong and you have been awarded the Navy Cross for your bravery and loyalty. They sent it to me to present to you. All you have to do is come and get it." That's when Tank pulls his Navy Cross medal from under his shirt and proudly dangles it in Tanner's face.

And that's all it took. The dam broke. Tanner lunges with rage and in foolish manner that years of training teaches you to avoid at all costs. Tank goes into boxer mode and dodges each swing or neutralizes with a swift block.

While Tank is in pure defense weaving and blocking, he's still able to strategically throw in swift jabs to Tanner's ribs. *That's where he'll get him.* Body blows aren't sexy for the TV shows but it's how the smart fighter knows how to defeat their opponent.

At this moment, Tank starts counting in his head waiting for the exhaustion to catch up. It's that pause of the body telling itself it needs at least a one or two second rest. It's at that fraction of a second, Tanner's body will distract the mind for Tank's counter-attack.

And then it happens. Tanner pauses for that one moment and Tank erupts to throw a frontal kick to Tanner's open stomach leaving him breathless enough to welcome two punches straight to the face. He swift kicks him in the head then a direct body blow to Tanner's right side leaving him breathless for another even harder shot to the exact same spot breaking a rib or two.

Tanner lets out a grunt showing he is wearing down to the point of full exhaustion. Tanner's wobbling, holding his ribs when Tank lands a right to Tanner's face stumbling him several steps.

Ernie's adrenaline is pumping watching this long, overdue fight. He moves up to the front to see the final seconds Tanner stays alive. But Tanner still has some fight left. Tanner blocks one of Tank's two punches and lands one himself. Not a full hit to Tank's mouth but enough to know Tank has a little more work to do.

When Tanner approaches, Tank makes it looks like he's more hurt than he is so takes advantage and ducks Tanner's kick then stands to land a frontal punch. Tanner's nose goes broken and he stumbles back falling down but turns around to catch himself with his two arms out holding himself up on the pavement.

He quickly pushes up to get his balance back and looks up to see Ernie staring at him. "That one was for Robert."

Tanner freezes with a look of guilt, shame and rage that gives Tank the moment for a full kick in his already broken ribs. Tanner screams in writhing pain. He backs up trying to regain his fighting stance. Tanner is badly hurt and Tank has had enough.

Tank sets his stance for his signature kick. Tanner is not falling for the fake kick trick again. Tank and Tanner know if another rib is broken or pushed further it will puncture the lung leaving Tanner fully incapacitated.

Tank moves in while Tanner quickly lowers his arms to block his ribcage while Tank's right foot lands the knock-out punch straight to Tanner's head watching him tumble to unconsciousness or death. Looks like his signature kick wasn't fake at all. Tank saved his best for last.

CHAPTER 67

Is He Alive?

C HERYL HAS HAD ENOUGH. Especially now that Tank has won. Tank is walking over to Tanner for the insurance kill shot when she drops her AR-15 and shoots Tank hitting him in the shoulder. Being 30 feet away and a moving target, she can't tell if it's a kill shot or not.

Tank clenches in pain falling down onto the steps. The crowd disburses screaming and blocking Cheryl's line of sight. Cheryl rolls her eyes irritated that she didn't get an instant kill shot. She waits another second for the crowd to vacate then lowers her gun to Tank's head.

All of sudden Jay jumps from behind and pushes her several feet to the side forcing her bullets to the open air. Cheryl is both surprised and pissed. She turns around to kill Jay when a rifle shot pops in the background that lands a bullet straight into the back of Cheryl's head.

Ernie turns around to see Darren at the far end of the plaza with his sharpshooter's rifle propped on the ledge doing what he does best. Darren and Dana are alive and back.

As the chaos raised another level, one of the X men just starts shooting at the crowd randomly knocking one by one off before

Ernie puts a bullet straight to his heart. Leslie starts running away leaving Janine screaming at the monitor for him to stay.

She switches the camera to herself, "As you can see, ladies and gentlemen, we lost our cameraman or woman. If any of you at the race can get to the fight and broadcast for all of the millions of viewers you will be doing the last race its finest contribution ever."

Janine looks down at her monitor and sees Leslie is still streaming the showdown but in an odd way. From what she can see Leslie must be pointing the camera without looking at what he's actually shooting. Which he is.

Leslie is crouching behind a stone ledge with his two hands on the camera phone pointing it over the ledge without a clue what he is videotaping or what's going on. Janine figures out what he's doing so begins to direct him, "Leslie, turn the camera to your left."

He starts turning the phone.

"No. Your other left."

He stops then starts turning to the left.

"Stop! Keep it right there."

She turns the broadcast back on Leslie's camera.

Larry is so sick of Janine and this whole fucked up mess, he shakes his head in disgust and gulps down a full glass of scotch that almost knocks him out. Tiffany and Veronica drop their glasses to prevent Larry from passing out and falling out of his chair.

Joe and Escobar bolt out of their buildings shooting X men retreating or attacking. One of the X men close to Tank walks up and points his pistol straight at his head when the gunner's head jerks back from a bullet shot ten feet away from Marian's pistol.

Marian drops down and turns Tank over. He's bleeding badly from his right shoulder while his body tightens up into a ball. She takes out her medical kit and starts wrapping him up as quickly as possible hoping she is not too late.

Escobar runs up to Ernie to give him cover as he stands over Marian and Tank selectively shooting any X men he can see. Ernie turns to Escobar, "Get cover. I'm not leaving." Escobar knows Ernie won't leave. Which means Escobar won't leave either. That's what police do. They cover each other.

Ernie looks to Marian, "Is he alive? Can we get him out of here?"

"He's alive but hurt badly. We can't move him just yet. Keep me covered if you can," she yells out over the chaos.

At that moment, Darren sees three X men sneaking up on the side of Ernie and Escobar for their kill shots. He yells to them telling them to cover but doesn't know if they can hear. He sets his sight on the far right and let's it loose as that X man goes down. The other two stop and start shooting at Ernie and Escobar.

Ernie drops. He heard Darren and saw the two approaching so dropped to the ground to shoot one of the X-ers leg. X man drops to the ground where Ernie follows up with a shot to his throat leaving him gurgling to death. Darren takes care of the other.

Joe sees Escobar on the ground with blood filling his shirt. He rushes over to administrate. As he bends down to stop the bleeding from his chest, he sees Escobar staring at him with a far-away look and that's when Joe realizes Escobar is dead. Ernie stares back to the pain of war, hatred and today.

All of a sudden, the plaza turns strangely quiet. You can hear the race in the background, some painful screams but that's it. A second later a loud voice shouts to the crowd commanding the moment. Ernie, Marian and Joe look up while Darren looks directly into his scope.

CHAPTER 68

Under. The. Stand.

"**E**VERYBODY CHILL OUT!**" Jimmy yells as he escorts Griffin in front of him with a gun behind his head. Griffin is staring straight ahead with a stoic look unafraid of the guns pointing at him.

Lock, Stock, Barrel surround Griffin and Jimmy with their guns pointing straight at Griffin. Lock and Stock on each side while Barrel is in the front with his back to the crowd. Add the column just behind Jimmy and he is fully covered from the many bullets that want him dead. Curly is leading the group as if they were a marching band at the Thanksgiving Day parade.

Jimmy's smiling as he has everyone's attention. The silence is broken with a gunshot to Curly's head as he falls to the ground immediately.

"I said chill, goddammit!"

Darren quickly reloads his rifle with a sneer on his face whispering to himself, "Oops."

"Okay, okay. Everyone chill and we'll take care of a little business then go our separate ways," Jimmy starts looking around. "Leslie! Where are you?"

Leslie slowly stands up still holding the camera phone. Janine pounds her fists on the table with a gleeful shout, "Yes!"

Larry is having a hard time keeping his head up to watch what's going on. He's having to close one eye to see anything otherwise it's a drunken double vision. Veronica and Tiffany remain quietly next to him, watching the events unfold on the monitor in front of them.

Jimmy sees Leslie, "There you are! Thank goodness. Now come on over here and get a better view of what's about to happen." Jimmy looks out to everyone. "Now leave Leslie alone. He has nothing to do with this. He's just the camera... ." He turns to look Leslie up and down. "Uh, camera person. So let him do his job so I can do mine."

Leslie walks around the wall and quietly walks up 15 feet away videoing the surreal moment. Janine is smiling ear to ear knowing she is responsible for all of this story-boarded death ride that a hundred million viewers are glued to.

"Okay Griffin, wave to the camera please."

Griffin stays statute still looking straight ahead showing no fear. While all of the attention is focused on Jimmy and Griffin, Marian quietly gives Tank a shot of the powerful pain killers so Tank can move and feel no pain. Then she gives him Adderall to get his cunning back. Tank's stiffness is softening and clenched jaw loosening up.

Ernie and Joe are pointing their pistols in Jimmy's direction. They don't have an open shot but are in position to take advantage of one if the opportunity presents itself. Darren has his sight on the back of Barrel's head knowing he needs to drop him first if they can get to Jimmy and the others to save Griffin.

Larry's bobbing his head trying to see as much as he can but his attention and consciousness is fading fast. As he lifts up his head as best he can, out of the corner of his eye, he sees a racer wearing a cap run up to the starting line. He vaguely recognizes her then realizes it's the girl who interrupted their interview before the race.

Sabrina is scrambling around the scaffolding trying to look on the ground as much as possible but this is the four-hour mark from the start so is the heaviest flow of people finishing. Runners keep bumping into her or cursing her for being in the way. Sabrina is in full panic. *Where is it?!* She's desperate knowing that it may be gone.

Larry sees her frantically looking around as if she lost her wedding ring. While his mind is swimming in scotch, the adrenaline of the last hours still keeps the brain neurons firing. He lifts up his head towards Veronica, "Hey."

Veronica quickly looks at Larry but not enough as she is glued to the monitor. He tries again. This time with as much oomph as he can muster.

"Hey!"

Veronica looks down at Larry with an impatient but thoughtful response, "Yes, Larry. What do you want?"

He nods towards Sabrina's direction and slurs again, "Tell her, look under, stand."

Veronica looks up at Sabrina who has her hands wrapped over her cap breathing heavily pacing around looking for something. Veronica gives Larry a quizzical look and repeats his question, "Tell her to understand what?"

Now with all of his might, Larry tries to utter as clearly as he can, "No. Look. Under. The. Stand. Tell her."

"Oh, okay."

Veronica looks up to Sabrina in her panicked look and has to know that's who he is talking about. "Uh, excuse me. Excuse me!" Veronica yells politely at Sabrina trying to get her attention. Sabrina looks up.

"Larry here says you need to look under the stand," she says pointing at the scaffold tower that Grandma stood on when shooting herself. Sabrina's eyes go wide. *Someone may have kicked it under the scaffolding skirt.* She quickly bends down, pulls the skirt up and there it is. She grabs it and jumps up to look at Larry and Veronica with a lit up, thankful face.

Veronica is taken back as she is now holding a gun. Larry is one happy drunk as he gets to help another pretty girl. His smile turns serious to hold up his index finger. Sabrina's thankful look turns confused.

Larry demonstrates as much as he can the motions necessary to put a bullet into the chamber of the gun. He's cupping one hand over the other hand moving it back and forth. Both Veronica and Sabrina have no idea what he is doing.

Larry does the hand motion once again but with much more theatrical force. Sabrina looks down at the gun and realizes what he's trying to say. She may not know anything about guns but she's seen enough movies and television to know what she needs to do.

She grabs the pistol's frame and starts pulling but it barely moves. She realizes that it may look easy in the movies, it's not so easy in real life. She tries again but still not enough.

This can't be happening. Veronica starts going over to her to see if she can help. At this moment, Sabrina lets out a deep breath looks up to the skies for divine inspiration. With all of her strength and will to save her husband she pulls the lever all the way back and loads the chamber.

She and Veronica share a smile of victory together. Sabrina quickly runs over to Larry and gives him a kiss on the cheek and whispers the sincerest of a 'thank you' then bolts off to save Griffin.

Larry's still awake enough to let out a big grin. Veronica turns around to kiss Larry on the other side letting his grin stay even longer. She knows who he just helped. Tiffany hasn't noticed one thing this whole time staring at the monitor.

CHAPTER 69

Runner's High

RAUL IS PACING BACK AND FORTH trying to cool down from finishing the 26.2 mile last race. He's still holding his newfound gun. It's loaded with the safety off. They've gone through too much not to. Lori stares at Raul never seeing him this way especially with gun in his hand.

Typically, after long-distance races, especially a marathon, a euphoric sense of clarity sets in for the runner. That's why it's called the 'runner's high' and so many people are addicted to running. That's also why Lori doesn't know how to react to Raul. Is his clarity along with the last hours of earth taking him into a Charles Whitman high to free all of us from our fears?

Lori does the only thing she knows what to do and goes over to Raul to ask him. Don and Gilbert stay pacing watching closely. Raul knows she's there but stays in his own world. When she is about to ask him, she notices a runner behind him running the opposite way with a gun in her hand and she could swear it was Sabrina.

"Was that Sabrina?" she blurts out. Raul jolts his head up to see what she's talking about. Gilbert and Don hear her as well and jog over there. Raul starts weaving through the crowd to get any kind of glimpse.

And through the masses of people standing there cheering, running or cooling down, he sees the girl with a gun in her hand. And Raul knows what to look for—the hat and it's brand new.

That's all he needs to see so bolts after her. If she is carrying a gun, Griffin is in trouble and needs help and he's the one to do it. Lori, Don and Gilbert think the same thing and sprint through the crowds to make sure they do not get out of their sight.

CHAPTER 70

Do It

T ANK'S MOVEMENTS are slowly coming back. *Thank god for drugs.* Marian checks his bandages and sees they're holding. Tank slowly turns on his side to get a more frontal view of Griffin being surrounded.

He slowly glides his hand down to grab his hidden pistol wrapped inside his boot. He takes it out as if in slow motion. He does not want Candyman nor his posse seeing him holding his firearm.

"Okay everyone!" Jimmy yells to the crowd. He turns to Leslie and looks directly into the camera and in a calm voice tells his millions of fans, "The moment of truth is here. Thank you, you've been a great audience."

Griffin unexpectedly with full deliberation turns around to stare Jimmy directly in his eyes and the barrel of his gun. This bold move silences the crowd to a vacuum of noise and movement with only the ambient sounds of the race in the background. Jimmy's stooges tense up.

The move even takes Jimmy by surprise as he backs away a few steps. The only ones moving is Tank's army but in stop-motion stealth mode.

Each of the police know that here and now, in a split second, their mission could end and fail with Griffin's life. In the meantime, though, their training has them taking full advantage of the distraction Griffin caused. Jimmy and Griffin stare at each other in a world just the two of them. No Janine, no runners, no pandemonium, just the two of them in their own silence.

Everyone packing in the plaza has their guns out pointing in Jimmy and Griffin's direction. Janine is aching to say something but knows better. The drama is too good with the silence.

Joe turns to Ernie and whispers, "I can't get a clear shot unless I move ten feet to my side."

Ernie responds, "Me too. Glide slowly and quietly. I'll take the stooge on the left, you on the right."

Joe looks over at Tank who is the closest at a 45-degree angle to Jimmy so may have the best shot. He sees Tank slowly laying his pistol down behind one the stairs hoping that conceals it enough.

Darren is creeping his way along the wall looking for his kill shot. The pack of lions are setting up their attack formation.

Leslie moves in closer to the face off to get the best close up he can. Janine is impressed and keeps glancing over to her viewer numbers that are now over 120 million and counting. She can't quit smiling.

As Leslie moves closer, he's helping block Ernie and Darren's line of sight. Their protection of Griffin keeps getting more complicated. Leslie is not a target but if he's in the way so be it.

Lock, Stock and Barrel hold their guns steady as they can. Lock has a shake to him. Barrel is sweating to the point it's about to get into his eyes and Stock has the calmest look of the three but still doesn't say much. One thing for sure, they are getting tired from holding their guns up and the pressure on them.

Stock keeps scanning the area and out of the corner of his eye, he can see Joe is more in view. He yells out, "I can see you! Quit moving!" Joe and Ernie reluctantly stop. Ernie glances over to Darren who is no longer there. Darren is rushing upstairs of the office building to get high enough for a clear shot.

Tank knows he may have the best shot so keeps silently sliding to get solid ground for a steady aim. Marian leans back to sit straight knowing Tank isn't feeling the pain and trying to position himself. She has basically the same angle so moves her hand slowly in her jacket to grab her pistol.

Jimmy and Griffin stand there as motionless statues. Griffin nods his head as if a decision has been made, and so it has.

"Do it," Griffin says in a quiet, assured voice.

Jimmy is surprised by the comment and the tone. He tilts his head using body language to ask Griffin if he's serious. The stooges rock back and forth in full angst exchanging glances wondering what to do.

Only Marian and Tank heard the request. They look at each other while Marian pulls her gun out for quicker action. She glances over at Ernie then Joe with a look of urgency and nods her head for them to move in position.

Each start stepping sideways for a better angle. They can tell something was said up there that calls for urgency. Darren opens the roof door and runs to the ledge to see the chess pieces trying to position. He looks down at Candyman and sees he has a clear shot.

"Do it," Griffin repeats this time in a much louder, commanding voice. A loud enough voice for the 120 million viewers to hear. Janine is in heaven.

Where are you, hat girl? Larry thinks. Veronica and Tiffany now have fist full of Larry's shirt wadded up in their angst filled hands. Larry doesn't mind as it's helping keep his head up.

Darren hearing the conversation for the first time quickly kneels down and places his rifle on the ledge to get Candyman in his scope. Joe and Ernie are no longer being stealthy as each get in position for an open shot.

Raul is running through an alleyway getting closer when he sees a sniper on the roof pointing down. He stops not knowing whether he is friend or foe. It's too confusing to know who the bad guys are in all of this. One thing he does know is where to go. Exactly where the rifle is pointing.

He runs to an open courtyard where he sees Griffin and the doctor that let them go in their stand off in the middle of a crowd in still-life poses. He is in a scene that even the end of the world couldn't script. He backs to the edge of the wall where he holds his fist up like the marines in a movie silently ordering Gilbert, Don and Lori to stop.

"Do it, you fucking pussy!" Griffin shouts as he takes a step towards Jimmy's pistol making sure there is no way he can miss. *I dare you.* The step leaves all to readjust their aim losing valuable time.

Jimmy stares at Griffin with the lifeless eyes of a shark. He responds nonchalantly. "Okay. You asked for it."

Veronica lets go to hold her mouth in complete horror. Her hand gone from Larry's shirt relieves Larry's drunken head support to fall so all he can experience is a lone gun shot in the background.

CHAPTER 71

The Moment of Truth

J IMMY THOUGHT LONG AND HARD to Griffin's demands. Thought about this moment, journey, day, wife, child, life and now his decision—the moment of truth. Jimmy looks at Griffin with pure conviction to pull back the gun and turn it to the side of his head. Jimmy stands at full military attention and in an instant, shoots himself dead and falls lifeless to the ground.

To Griffin, it was all in slow motion as he now looks at the column right in front of him and the dead psychiatrist below him. He is in utter silence and can only think of the weight off his shoulder, the race and most of all Sabrina. His silence is quickly shattered when he hears Tank.

"Now!"

And in trained, ordered formation response gunfire from Joe, Ernie, Darren, Marian and Tank release dropping Lock, Stock and Barrel to the pavement and their deaths.

There stands Griffin alone on the entryway with his back to them surrounded by five dead bodies almost to a comical scene. He only notices Rob running at full speed out the door like a cockroach when the lights turn on. Griffin turns around to first look at Leslie.

Griffin holds his hand out gesturing for his phone. Leslie looks up and slowly hands the phone to Griffin. "No!" Janine yells out from her studio. "Keep shooting, you freak!"

Griffin takes the phone and throws it dead center in the nearby fountain. The show is over, at least from that camera. Janine quickly switches the camera to herself. She looks at Monitor 2 and sees Larry is even a more idiot drunk. He can't even lift his head. She hits the monitor that broadcasts the real star—herself.

Griffin puts his hands on his hips and looks down to start laughing in an exhaustive but relieved manner. He looks up then waves to everyone not really knowing what to say to these strangers. "Thanks, whoever you are."

Those words make everyone laugh. If there were any X-ers left, they're long gone now with the Candyman gone and Tank's soldiers there to eliminate anyone who tries.

Tank stays laying down looking to the sky knowing he gets to go out the way he wanted, to serve and protect. Joe and Ernie trot over there to help him along with Marian. Darren is rushing down the stairs to join the victory.

"Do you mind if I finish the race now?" Griffin yells out. "I'd really appreciate it if you join me. It's just a quarter mile or so and I'd like your company." He looks at each of the remaining police force and smiles big, "And your protection." The all start laughing at that one. But it turns out, he's going to need it.

CHAPTER 72

Not Again

TANNER WALKS OUT from behind the column and quickly grabs Griffin in a headlock with one hand and the other holding a gun to his head. He starts dragging Griffin backwards into the building waiting area behind them.

Not again! Griffin thinks. He has had enough—these past hours, days, months. It's enough. "Kill me."

"What?"

"Just kill me. You won. You're now the second person I have asked and it still hasn't happened. Either let me go to be with my wife or kill me now. I'm not going to resist."

"Don't worry. You'll get your wish but I want it shown to the world. If I couldn't have killed Tank then I kill what he and his men died trying to preserve."

Not only is Tank not dead but so are four of his soldiers and they are still in serve and protect mode. Joe and Ernie help Tank get up as they begin to stealth up the stairs using the same column to block his view.

Raul, who just exhaled a sigh of relief, is now watching his best friend dragged away with a gun to his head once again. He has had enough and starts walking straight towards Tanner and Griffin with gun in hand.

Raul's about 30 yards way at the 3 O'Clock position. He can see the cops strategizing behind the column. They don't notice him brazenly walking to the front of the building.

The building lobby is empty. The only things remaining are shattered glass and a lone reception desk that he drags Griffin to give him some additional cover. Tanner groans with each step holding Griffin while limping backwards closer to the wall. His pain is not unnoticed by Griffin.

Tanner pulls out his phone, but it's out of power. "Shit!"

He hurls the phone across the lobby. He looks around for options and turns around to see a female runner enter the lobby to his left. He thrashes Griffin around to face her with gun pointed.

The runner quickly turns around begging not to be killed. She is fully vulnerable with only a sports top on, running shorts and a cap.

Tanner barks out, "You have a phone?!"

"Yes."

"With video capabilities?"

"Yes."

"Then turn around and if you video this, I'll let you live."

"I'll have to get my phone and log on first. Please don't kill me."

"Get it then, log on. Quickly!"

Tanner jerks Griffin tighter around the neck for safe keeping with gun now pointed at the girl's back. Raul reaches the top of the stairs twenty yards away. Tanner's back is almost fully exposed for a bullet. He slowly lifts his revolver but Tanner starts jerking Griffin around that he doesn't want to take the chance.

Tanner keeps kneeing Griffin outwards while maintaining a chokehold. *His ribs must be really hurting*, Raul observes. He's seen it too often in his football playing days.

The girl stops fumbling around with her hands. And with a second of silence, she alerts Griffin with an odd observation. "Griffin, your shoes are untied."

That takes Tanner by surprise. *How does she know that's Griffin and his shoes are untied?* Tanner instinctively looks down. At that instant, Griffin jams his elbow as hard as he can in Tanner's ribs that sends a jolt of excruciating pain throughout Tanner's body. Griffin feels Tanner's grip go limp so he pushes Tanner's arm out as he stumbles away falling down.

Sabrina turns around to shoot Tanner in the forehead just as he looks up. Tanner's head and body jerk backwards onto the cold marble floor. She walks up to Tanner lying lifeless ready to shoot him again.

She knows he's dead so really wants to look closely at the human that put her in a position of being glad she was responsible for his death.

Tank and gang rush the lobby to see Tanner flat on his back. Tank looks up to see the girl who he assumes has been accompanying Griffin for these 26 miles there with a gun at her side. Tank holds his hands up while smiling in deference and respect. Tank's army or what's left along with Raul, Don, Gilbert and Lori just drop their heads with a sigh of relief that could equal a silent breeze.

Griffin gets up as quickly as he can wiping his his shorts cleaning himself from the stench and evil of Tanner. He looks at Sabrina with the most thankful eyes, "Goddammit, I told you! I tied my shoes!"

Sabrina drops the gun and jumps into his welcoming arms as they hug for what seems an eternity. When they finally pull apart, Griffin looks into her eyes, "Thank you. I love you. And does this mean we can finally finish this fuckin' race."

"Yes, it does. Or I hope so. Who knows with what we've been through."

"Don't worry," Tank speaks out. "We'll make sure you finish this fuckin' race."

"Yes, we will," Raul says behind Tank with Lori, Don and Gilbert standing right there. Griffin smiles to each of them with the utmost appreciation while Raul calls out, "The finish line is just around the corner. Let's go!"

CHAPTER 73

Soldiers of the Apocalypse

THE CROWD AT THE FINISH LINE is on edge and eerily quiet. *Griffin should be here by now.* With Leslie's camera out of order, no one knows what's going on and the suspense is killing them especially Larry and the girls.

As a minute passes the silence deafens even more. In the background, motorcycle engine sounds start creeping within ear shot getting louder by the second. Then around the corner, the five police soldiers of the apocalypse appear escorting marathon runners Griffin, Sabrina, Raul, Gilbert, Don and Lori to the finish line.

This time, though, Marian is lead motorcycle with Tank bandaged up holding onto her with one arm and the other still clutching his shoulder to keep the bandage tight. Leslie remains in the back merrily riding his bicycle without a care in the world.

The crowd and 120 million watchers worldwide erupt in perfect unison watching Griffin and company cross the finish line. It is a finish that only the last day of humanity could create with the world celebrating in singularity. Tank and his four smile wholly as they achieved what they were meant to do—to save the good guys and defeat the bad guys.

For the first time, both Griffin and Sabrina smile in a deep and complete way that hasn't happened for a long, long time. Griffin starts waving to the crowd then Sabrina follows his lead. And with all of this madness, joy and "surreality", Sabrina can take no more.

She bends down and starts balling like there's no tomorrow. With long distance races especially marathons crying at the finish line is a common response. The adrenaline, runner's high and exhaustion combine to break the dam and let the tears flow. On the last day of earth and being hunted to death, it's magnified that much more.

Griffin's eyes well up and walks over to comfort her in their victory. She's bent over crying out loud seizing the crowd's emotional attention leaving them in the same state. Griffin looks up to see their time is 4 hours and 47 minutes, the worst time they have ever had but the best in their lives.

Griffin pulls Sabrina to him, holds her head gently in his hands and plants a firm yet delicate kiss for their victory. But, in reality, the victory is that he finally had the courage to admit his love to her. And now, thanks to the last race, he achieved his dream to marry the love of his life and in an odd sense have the marriage he always dreamed and hoped.

Larry can't keep his head up he's so drunk. It took some serious effort and commitment to get to this point. Finishing off two bottles of Balvenie and starting on a third shows there's some experience there. But with the excitement in the air and his sincere support for Griffin to triumph is too much to let some liters of scotch steal his moment.

He plants his feet firmly on the ground, holds the arms of the chair and starts pushing up. He lifts up six inches then falls flat back into the chair. He can't lift his head so how on earth is he going to stand?

A hand gently lands on his shoulder from behind. Again, he is thankful for Tiffany's and Veronica's support but now he needs their help to stand up. He wobbles his head to his side to see the hand is not a girl's hand.

The hand from the ghost behind him holds out a cupped piece a paper with a nice long line of cocaine nestled in it and a cut off plastic straw. Jay instructs in a gentle but commanding tone, "Take the straw and sniff this powder with one nostril..."

"I know what'do." Larry interrupts. Jay pauses and is impressed he can understand or communicate let alone know how to snort a line of illegal substance. Larry somehow finds the straw and luckily Jay is holding everything otherwise his gesture of goodwill would have blown away, literally. Larry, now in full concentration, fully exhales, puts his index finger on his left nostril then executes the nose vacuum in one quick snort. The cocaine jolt hits hard forcing out an 'Oh God' that gives Jay a quick laugh.

With such amplification, he is able to lift his head to tilt back enough for the body to absorb the magic powder. He has obviously done this before, Jay sees. Jay pulls back his now powderless paper from Larry's face. Well, almost powderless, Jay takes care of the remaining dust with his own nose.

Larry is now blinking with an awaken look. His head is upright and has newfound strength. Well, newfound wheelchairs to his drunken obliteration. He turns to greet his new motivational coach.

Jay smiles feeling his own contribution, "Thought you might need some help to see the finale of the race. Especially since it's a good ending."

"Griffin alive?"

"Look," Jay says pointing over Larry's head. "He's right over there. Hear the crowd going wild?"

"With this race, you never know what this damn crowd cheer about. Help me up, my new friend. Can I have another one of those?"

Jay smiles and lets Larry grab his forearm to lift up into standing position. Although Larry's standing position is in debate of its definition. Jay reaches down and pulls out Jimmy's cocaine bottle from his backpack and starts preparing Larry his second course. Jay wasn't going to let all of that powder go to waste.

Larry is smiling as big as ever and able to stand and watch what he helped engineer for a happy ending to earth's little spot called Austin and its last race. He starts clapping as much as he is able while he intermittently looks down trying to find his drink.

CHAPTER 74

The Real Heroes

G RIFFIN IS IN FULL SPOTLIGHT and doesn't care. He and his new bride are waving to crowd smiling and walking robotically around trying to cool down from 26.2 miles.

A hand taps his shoulder as he looks at Sabrina's eyes go wide and smile even wider. He turns around to see Mom and Dad waiting there as they have done for dozens of races through the years. Sabrina immediately jumps into their arms crying in pure joy and exhaustion.

The new son-in-law joins in on the hugs thanking them for everything they have done through the years. Mom and Dad are little overwhelmed being in the middle of the frenzy. They usually stand on the sidelines patiently waiting for their turn.

"Come on Mom," Sabrina says. "You got to have a beer with us. I know it's not 5 o'clock but you can break the 5 o'clock rule for one day."

"We're actually have martinis dear," Mom responds. She looks to Dad holding up a stainless steel shaker.

"That's more like it. You're not as big of nerds as I thought."

"I'm having three olives with mine unlike your mother. She's only having one so she's the bigger nerd," Dad adds. Yet another

Mom look to Dad. He's on a roll. Time is on his side for his smart-ass comments.

Griffin turns around to Gilbert, Don, Raul, and Lori who have been silently walking behind them. "My team! My best friends and family. Thank you so much for everything you've done and what you mean to me. I am eternally grateful. Literally."

"Yeah, yeah," Raul responds smiling back. "You owe us big time for this one. Pay us back in our next lifetime." Raul tosses him a can of Lone Star then one to Sabrina. It's about time. Their after-race ritual has officially begun. The music is pumping, people are dancing and cheering as more racers cross the finish line.

Lori finishes a swig of a beer and looks to Griffin, "Guess what?" Griffin pauses waiting for the answer. "We beat you. You were last in the group. Ha! I knew one day we could do it." The whole gang starts laughing.

Now it's Gilbert's turn, "We kill people for you. That's how much you mean to us." The laughter stops. Gilbert looks around wondering if he said something wrong. Raul looks to Griffin, "I'll explain later. Gilbert is just saying that we helped. That's all."

Don looks to Lori, "We still have some time. You want to go back to the hotel room for some last minute humpty hump? I still have some energy." Lori is beyond annoyed. She shakes up her beer to shoot him a froth full of Lone Star while he's shielding his smiling face. He expected nothing less from her.

Lori in full exasperation responds to his relentless sex requests, "You are pathetic! And no! Go spank your monkey in the bushes somewhere if you're that horny." The group's laughter and kidding are now back in high gear.

They have some room now as the crowds are dispersing to their own mini celebrations. Griffin is getting his life back to his friends, family and celebration. This time, though, he has a whole new group of friends to join in the toasting.

Tank and gang are moving in their own circle alongside the Griffin train. They smile at all of the love and camaraderie happening. Marian stops the bike to let Tank slowly and carefully get off the motorcycle.

Once off, she lifts the motorcycle onto its kickstand to secure its parking. Now in park, Tank gets back on the motorcycle so he can sit safely while joining in the celebrations.

In the background, there is a loud annoying and obnoxious car horn beeping in morse code. And it's getting louder and more obnoxious. Marian rolls her eyes then grabs her phone and hits redial, "Hey girlfriend, is that y'all? Where are you? We're just beyond the finish line, 20 yards north with Griffin and company."

She listens to Melia's response then starts looking around waving her arms. "Look for my arms waving. You're obviously getting closer because your husband is getting even more annoying." Marian turns around and sees Martinez in his big white truck beeping away to disperse the crowd. Maria is in the lead on her motorcycle with little Melia holding on behind her mother.

Martinez looks like five-year old sitting in that truck that takes up two parking spaces and even makes 18 wheelers hesitate when changing lanes. Maria and Melia never understood why he got the truck in the first place. It's a waste of money and space but it makes him feel big and important. *Oh well.*

Martinez' got that grin on his face so Marian knows their appearance meets more than another couple of cases of beer. And then it dawns on her. *Lunch!*

"What up homies!" Martinez says as he jumps out of the truck. Tank stands up to give him as best of man-hug he can. The others surround him following suit with added high fives. Maria parks the bike while Melia jumps off to run and hug Marian then Tank. Melia and Marian have always had that special bond.

"There they are!" Ernie yells. "Central command! Give it up to Austin Homeland Security with their eyes in the net and ears on the ground telling us what to do and where to go!" Martinez smiles big at that comment. He's at 8½ beers so his light is burning a little brighter.

He's signaling the gang to come closer, "Dudes! Get your asses over here. I need your help." Martinez walks back to the truck bed, opens the tail gate and jumps up to look down at six large blue ice chests. And these ice chests carry their deer meat home from their annual hunting/drinking fests so are very big.

He opens each to reveal the eight briskets, smoked sausage, whole chicken and beef ribs. *Let the feast begin.* Martinez looks up to see the salivating dogs wagging their tails. "You think I was gonna leave all of that work Joe did for us go to waste? Hell no!"

"Hell yeah," Ernie says wasting no time reaching in to grab a few slices of brisket. Serving and protecting makes him hungry so now time to serve his belly.

"OK, there's paper plates for any non-Texans around. Paper towels galore. There's a butcher knife over there. The barbecue sauce is in those two big pitchers. In the ice chest over there, there's the potato salad and beans and those two other ice chests are beer." The ants begin the invasion. "Hey, where's Griffin? Want to make sure to save some for him and his homies."

"He's over there," Darren points. "Hugging family and cooling down. There will be plenty for him. And good job on bringing the feast. Almost forgot about it."

They all look at each other toasting a rib or chicken bone with pure victory and satisfaction. Griffin stops to view the police family stuffing what looks like some great Texas barbecue in their pieholes laughing it up.

They have no idea what they did and how much they mean to him for this moment. Add the fact to some great smelling barbecue. He looks at his running group still pacing around and waves them to his direction, "Come on, guys. We all need to properly thank our protectors and saviors."

Griffin walks up to Tank to offer the most appreciative shake as Tank's pain will allow. Tank's pain killers are helping just fine so Tank's handshake that makes almost anyone's hand hurt is returned.

Griffin walks to each of Tank's crew for an official and deeply sincere 'thank you' while Sabrina follows with a big hug. The crowd watches the moment and after Griffin shakes the last hand of little Melia.

Griffin turns back to Tank and points to him, "Come on everybody, let's give it up to the Austin Police." He starts clapping his hands that is followed in full applause of the group and then the surrounding crowd. It's a deafening applause which catches them off guard.

Tears start welling up in each of their eyes, even Tank's. They all return the applause with a wave and thank you back. Tank finishes his waving then looks to Griffin as he slowly but surely climbs off the motorcycle. He waves towards himself, "Come on guys and gals, thank you's are not done yet. Follow me."

Tank and Marian lead the group to approach Larry, Veronica, Tiffany and Jay all yakking it up. Larry just finished another line at the courtesy of Jay so Larry is back in action.

The girls are also enjoying some of Jay's hospitality helping regain their energy back. They look up to see the entourage walking directly at them. They finish powdering their noses and greet them with a big hug and smile.

Larry looks up to see the group and smiles, "Well hello. I'm Larry. These are my new friends and co-hosts." Larry says as he points to each introducing them.

"Don't worry," says Maria walking up to shake his hand. "We know who you are. We're the ones who talked to you from the bar when you sent us your Facebook message. And, come on, Larry, everyone knows who you are. You're famous to more than 100 million people but to us you're the newest member of the Austin Police force and family."

Larry smiles big at that comment. Maria turns to Griffin and the group and proclaims while pointing to Larry, "Here's the real hero. Griffin, you could have never finished without him so lets all give him a round of applause."

With the whole group surrounding him with full applause, their thanks, slap on the backs and bear hugs, Larry and his entourage are now in full glory. A spot that Larry always relishes and his thankful for. The last one to thank Larry is Griffin and Sabrina. They stand there silent for a moment just grinning at each other. Griffin looks at him, "Want to finish that interview?" Larry grins even wider.

But something they were never expecting happens. Behind them coasting up is Johnny. Marian and Darren look at each other in complete shock.

"What the?" Marian says.

"Hey guys. How's it going?" Johnny says in a painful but smart-ass manner.

They all approach Johnny wanting a hug, handshake, fist bump, anything. Johnny waves them off with a weakened smile.

He has a look of defeat losing his wife but also a look of peace helping others stay alive at the end of the world.

Marian approaches him and lifts up his makeshift bandage, "Here let me take a look at that. Martinez, hand me my bag please." Martinez runs over to get her medic kit. Martinez opens the bag and hands the alcohol to her. "No. The shot first. He needs to feel better." She looks to Johnny, "You did a good job on your bandage. Looks ugly but works well."

That nudges a small smile out of Johnny. Tank asks, "What the hell happened?"

Darren helps Johnny sit down on the concrete block holding up the park's streetlight. Marian pricks Johnny's arm as he winces with the feel-good, do-good shot. She then begins to clean his wound with the alcohol and dress it in a more secure manner.

"The first shot hit my shoulder then the second one knocked me on my ass to the pavement. I hit my head hard knocking me out for 15 minutes or so. The second shot hit my vest so nothing vital just a knock on the ass. But filled enough time for you two to escape, I see." He looks at Darren and Marian.

"Well now I feel like a complete dick," Darren confesses.

"Hey, you did what I asked and what had to be done. And, besides, look what we did." Johnny says nodding to Griffin and his team. Johnny looks up to see Griffin staring at him with a pleasant but confused look.

Marian nods to Darren while she continues to dress his wound. Darren gets the body language and begins the introduction, "Oh! Griffin and Sabrina, meet Johnny. He's one of the team and was here for you. Unfortunately, his wife…"

At that moment, Marian back kicks Darren right in the leg interrupting him from ending his sentence.

"Ow!" is the surprise ending to Darren's sentence.

Marian gives him the glare of infraction. She continues his sentence, "Unfortunately, his wifi wasn't working which is why he is a bit late trying to find us. His wound didn't help much either." She looks at Johnny who understands and agrees. It serves no purpose to let Griffin know his wife was killed in the mission.

Griffin looks to Johnny, "I can't tell you how thankful I and all of us are for what you did. I'm sorry you got hurt and it's my fault so I hope you can forgive me and cannot thank you enough. Can I get you a beer, water or..."

Griffin looks around to see Tiffany getting ready to snort down another line. Griffin turns back to Johnny, "a line of cocaine?"

Johnny smiles, "No thanks. I'm sure Darren can grab me a beer or two. He knows what I like. And thank you too for a great race. It's been an honor protecting you."

Johnny nods his head towards Darren who is still smarting over the kick. Darren's giving his best body language of an apology to Marian who is still berating him with her eyes.

"Uh. Yeah. I'll grab you a couple of Lites. I'll be right back."

CHAPTER 75

Unfinished Business

Y ES, MISSION ACCOMPLISHED. *Except for one,* thinks Marian. While real justice can't be handed down to Janine, there are many ways to skin a cat. And thanks to Melia, they've found a way.

Larry looks at Griffin and Sabrina readying them for the interview. "Janine, Janine, are you there?"

Janine, in pure form, barges in, "Shut up Larry. We're about to start an interview so the camera is on me. I'll let you know when I need you."

"Well, fuck you too."

Marian, Maria and Melia push their way into the pending interview. Griffin and Sabrina back up behind Larry as the girls are in full motion.

Marian walks up, "Larry, we need your help for one more unfinished business and I have a deep feeling you're gonna like this one."

Larry and entourage are at full attention with that statement until they see Marian take out her pistol and load the shell for fire. Jay is most unnerved since he was on the other side for the first part of the race.

Marian just smiles, "Don't worry. You'll see." She looks at Melia. "You getting everything ready?" They look over to Melia typing away.

"Yes, ma'am." She looks up at Larry and his entourage. "You have phones with juice?"

Jay looks at his, "Mine's at half."

"Mine's 39%," Tiffany answers.

Veronica, "Larry's at 73%. And Leslie has mine so I'm useless." Griffin and Sabrina are silent, wondering what's going on.

"Hand them to me please. And you can use Larry's. He'll be on the laptop cam," Melia politely instructs with eyes focused on the screen. Veronica walks up as Melia clicks one last button then grabs her phone and starts thumbing away.

Marian turns her attention to the scaffold and starts scanning around until her head stops and a slow smile comes to be. She closes one eye, aims and shoots.

On the scaffold, camera 3 flips off falling to the ground shattering to pieces. Marian keeps showing off her years of shooting range practice. Griffin is especially happy to watch another camera being turned off so to speak.

In the control room, Janine sees her third monitor turn blank. That gives her a pissed off look. She speaks out to Dr. Schuler and Orville while paying attention to the working monitors, "Yes. Dr. Schuler, would you please elaborate on your 'Too Much Technology, Not Enough Time' book."

"Uh, yes. As I was saying technology are merely tools so the real impetus is to focus on what the technology is being used for and why. The priorities that society, government, religion, commerce place upon those technologies. That's the key…"

Griffin and Sabrina turn to stare at Larry's monitor. And there they see Janine interviewing Orville and Dr. Schuler, the nerdy professor who showed up at Orville's house.

They're not sure if what they're seeing is real. The last two people they would ever expect on TV or ever see again nor want to are right there in front of them. Orville is in a full $20,000 suit along with Dr. Schuler with the perfectly made-up Janine. Orville obviously borrowed some make-up to help cover up where Griffin smashed his face.

Each of them have a tall crystal glass of champagne courtesy of Dr. Schuler. They can see Orville and Janine partaking at an aggressive pace.

Griffin turns to Sabrina with a face that has lost all color. "No wonder he was so paranoid. He was protecting Janine."

Sabrina just shakes her head. She's in the twilight's zone of the twilight zone, "And the irony that she was looking all over for us and we were just 50 feet away. Unbelievable."

They stand there silently trying to absorb the moment. They turn to each other and in unison say, "Coincidence doesn't exist."

"But, as we have learned from today, life is not what we have but what we do with it. So what do we do with this coincidence?" Sabrina asks. Her heightened marathon emotions are kicking in. "We now know where Janine is."

Ding, ding, ding goes Griffin's head as it hits him too.

CHAPTER 76

And Fuck You Too

JANINE TURNS AROUND and clicks her comm, "What happened to camera three?"

"Camera who?" Larry responds.

"The stationary camera affixed to the scaffolding. It's my go-to camera and now it's gone. If it's gone then all I have is you as my go-to and you're sloshing around like a liquor balloon. Go find someone to fix it so I don't have to waste camera time on a drunk idiot."

"For your information, sweetie-pie. Thanks to Jay over here, I'm a pretty, peppy, perky kind of guy who's doing just fine." Larry looks over at Jay, smiles and gives a quick nod. He wants another line. He looks at Marian, "She don't like me that much."

Marian cocks her gun again. "If she doesn't like you then that must mean you're pretty good guy. Everyone back away please. Just for a moment especially you Larry. You're too close. Melia, are you ready?"

The group starts backing away. Melia jumps up, grabs the Apple laptop and hurries to Larry and hands it to him.

"Here, hold this. This is yours for the rest of the race."

Melia scurries over to Marian who hands her the gun, "Like I promised, you can finally shoot a gun that your parents have been promising for years but never did."

Maria shifts on her right hip and gives the two that 'I know you didn't just say that' look. Melia smiles brightly.

"But, I am going to hold the gun with you because it has a kick to it that I don't want it busting your chin. So put your finger on the trigger. Hold the gun very tightly. Close one eye, aim by looking down the barrel and aligning that point on top of the gun to touch the target in the air then pull the trigger."

Melia closes one eye. Looks intently at the camera sitting on the tripod looking like its own high-tech weapon pointing at nothing. She waits for a moment because she sees some of the dumb asses in the background finally figuring out what's about to happen to get out of the line of sight.

She pulls. Camera smashes. Melia conquers. Janine is conducting her interview with Orville and Dr. Schuler when from the corner of her eye she can see camera two go static. She is pissed. She pushes the 'camera four' button so the screen only shows Orville and Dr. Schuler.

She pushes the comm button, "Goddammit, Larry! What the fuck is going on down there? Now camera two is gone!"

"Now, Janine I've been waiting a long time to say this to you."

Larry swaggers back and forth from both the scotch and the 'waiting for the dramatic pause' moment. All of sudden, Melia grabs the wireless lev, unhooks it from Larry's shirt then motions for his earpiece.

Larry confusedly takes it out and gives it to the precocious 11-year old. She lifts the mic up to her mouth, "Fuck you. That's what he says."

Larry smiles while Maria is a bit taken back at her little girl's foul language. *She must have learned it from her father.*

"Who is this?" Screams Janine. "What the hell are you doing down there? That is the property of KUTV so give that comm back to Larry NOW!"

Now it's Larry's turn. Melia nods then holds the lev up to his voice. With a big smile he winks at Melia then tells Janine, "And fuck you too."

They both laugh as Melia heaves the lev and earpiece as far as she can throw it. She grabs the laptop and sets it on the stool and points it directly at the chair. She pulls Larry over and sits him down.

Melia does a Vanna White hand gesture for Larry to look at the screen. He has to blink several times. Yes, he has newfound coke strength but still is drunk as Cooter Brown. He sees himself on a YouTube Channel titled 'The Great Larry Last Race Channel'.

"See. Made it just for you." She turns to Maria, "OK, Mom. Start sending and posting. I have it all set up just click away."

"I know. I know. I know. I'm not that bad with technology."

Melia just rolls her eyes and looks over at Larry admiring his new TV station. "Larry, it's not a mirror. Do your thing."

Larry looks up, blinks twice then it dawns on him that he's the on-air host again so a grin pops out, looks straight at the camera and starts his MC magic, "Good afternoon ladies and gents, it's a party down here. Y'all better be having one too out there with us."

He looks down at the bottom of the computer screen, "Hey, this number on the bottom is going crazy like a jackpot. What's going on?"

"Good," says Melia. "It's the viewer number. How many?"

"Looks like 10,000. Now it's 17,000. Whoa."

Melia smiles big. She looks at Marian who nods in satisfaction. Melia responds with a quiet whisper, "Just wait. That number will get even bigger, way bigger."

Melia is now executive producer. She turns back around and walks over to Larry's laptop and uses her index finger to move the mouse over to her phone's monitor window and clicks. She's now on screen.

"Hi everyone! It's Larry, Griffin, Tank, Marian and the whole Last Race gang here having our finishing party. I'm Melia and want to let you know we've switched all camera activity down here where all of the fun is going on. So stay tuned to us as we'll have cameras going all over the place showing you some crazy stuff. Okay. Here's Larry."

She pushes the mouse pad to switch the broadcast back to a smiling Larry. The number of viewers is now 780,000. The number of viewers for Melia's newly created channel is going up as fast as Janine's viewers are going down.

CHAPTER 77

Last Race Family

G RIFFIN AND SABRINA'S running high is kicking in. They think they have information that would settle a last day score. They head towards the group focusing on Marian and Tank. Marian has her wine and Tank his beer. They are very appreciative that Martinez was attentive and brought each of their special libations.

Both are happily feasting on a sausage wrap. They had to *borrow* some tortillas from J-Lo's parents fajita feast because Martinez forgot them as he was more interested in filling the ice chest with beer than added food necessities.

As Griffin and Sabrina approach their gang of runners, police force and family, they hear Lori and Raul playing verbal duel telling the updated shoelace story with a much more of an exciting ending. All laugh at Lori and Raul's antics while Gilbert happily listens to this version with much better appreciation.

The "Last Race" police force are paying close attention to the backstory of the shoelace taunt so they can finally understand how untied shoelaces got Tanner killed and saved Griffin's life. Griffin and Sabrina stop to listen when are blindsided by Mom and Dad with a plate of barbecue mandated upon them from both the cops and as good parents do. Sabrina and Griffin are most appreciative as the 20 minute cool down from the marathon has expired and their stomachs are now telling them they just ran 26.2 miles.

Lori and Raul finish the story to a round of hoorays and applause while Griffin and Sabrina finish one of many ribs to come. *It's now time.* Tank and Marian glance at each other noticing the two stars heading their way.

Griffin slows to a stop and with a wry grin begins, "I've been picking up on a few things. Seems like you don't like the news lady."

Tank answers with his booming voice, "No. We don't. We even sent a party to shut her down."

Marian lifts her wine glass to Darren and Johnny in toast to their failed effort while all the police lift their glasses in a silent toast to Dana. The running gang join their ears to the conversation. It's now the police's turn to fill them on their backstory.

"She's the reason Candyman wanted to kill you and she did everything she could to make sure he did. So, we sent Marian and some of our guys to the station to destroy her broadcast but found out she wasn't there.

Griffin and Sabrina turn to each other smiling widely. Now it's Sabrina's turn, "We know where Janine is FYI."

The 20-plus newly formed super friends who have smiles and laughter on their faces turn dead quiet. Each of the police force immediately look to Johnny.

"Where? And how do you know?"

"The guy being interviewed on the television right now, he owns the television station and tried to kill us. Now that I think about it, I understand why he was so paranoid.

We unknowingly ran into the owner of the TV station on our secret route here," Sabrina says turning to Griffin looking for confirmation. "What? About mile 6?" Griffin nods. "It was right before we saw Mom & Dad."

"And how do you know it was the owner and Janine is there?"

"He told us. We ran into him on our route and we just saw him on the TV being interviewed with another guy who showed up just when we were leaving. Apparently, he's some professor or something. They must have set up a studio upstairs," Griffin adds.

"We even saw him talk to the ceiling. Now we realize he was talking to Janine upstairs," continues Sabrina.

"This is getting weird," Darren says looking at them still wondering if this is a joke.

"And you're sure of this?" Tank asks.

"Yes," Griffin responds. "We both were there and we both just saw them on the TV right now."

"And what happened when you met him?"

"He tried to kill us. Griffin took his gun. Shot him in the leg. That's when the nerdy guy showed up. He looked scared. Griffin shot out all of the bullets then threw the gun across the street."

"Now we know why the nerdy guy showed up. It's because he was being interviewed," adds Sabrina.

Johnny enters the conversation, "It was you two. He and his gun. He attacked. You counter attacked then escaped. Correct?"

Griffin and Sabrina nod. Darren turns to Johnny then back to Griffin and Sabrina, "He's by himself and doesn't have the manpower otherwise you two would be dead."

Tank chimes in, "In the old world, we followed every lead. You have credible witnesses with credible stories. This is a lead you would follow immediately."

Marian presents their choice in a more succinct manner, "Are you going to spend your time with justice or forgiveness?"

Johnny responds immediately, "Both. I forgive her then kill her." Darren agrees except for the forgiveness part. For every action, there is an equal and opposite reaction.

Johnny walks up to Sabrina, "Where are they?"

Sabrina and Griffin relay the street corner to Johnny and Darren who embed the location into their minds. As Johnny turns to head for his motorcycle, Griffin shouts to him, "Hold on!"

Johnny and Darren quickly turn around wondering what surprise Griffin has now.

"He has a shotgun. We know that for sure. The other guy wasn't armed. And have no idea about Janine. Go through the sliding glass door on the right side of the house if you're facing it. It's closer to the stairs and easier to hide if they walk down. And would you do me one last favor?"

Johnny and Darren respond with a no-brainer 'yes' look.

"If you cut her head off, will you bring it to me?"

Sabrina pinches him hard in the side. The rest of the gang start laughing. Johnny is thinking about it. Griffin turns to Sabrina, "Ow! Would you quit doing that!" Sabrina returns his request with a 'you asked for it' look.

"Okay. If not her head then if you see any Orville Reddenbocker popcorn left, will you bring it back?" Sabrina pinches him hard in the side once again.

"Ow! I like Orville Reddenbecker, okay!" That leaves all with a bigger laugh.

"Will do," Johnny answers.

Johnny and Darren turn around and head towards their motorcycles. They all feel a relief that true justice will be served on this last day.

Griffin, Sabrina, Marian and Tank smile back then look at each other knowing the circle is complete. In the background, they hear Larry's voice, "Can we get this goddamned interview over with?!"

Epilogue

I WAS IN THE MIDDLE OF THE PACK of thousands of runners for the Amy's Ice Cream 10-miler in Austin, TX. We were running up the Mopac ramp next to Austin High School and the entire highway was void of any manmade machinery.

Mopac heading east into downtown is basically the highway traffic to hell so seeing it abandoned transformed my reality. No cars. No people besides runners. And all in their own running world heading into the same direction for the same purpose. And that's where it hit me that in the blankness and stream of runners, today was the last day of earth and we all decided to run.

And from that transformative experience lay the foundation to Last Race.

Thank you for joining our Last Race. If you liked the book and want to relay any comments, please email inquiries@LastRace.com.

Richard May
LastRaceNovel.com

CPSIA information can be obtained
at www.ICGtesting.com
Printed in the USA
LVHW011623260921
698753LV00016B/782

9 781736 316115